AWAKENING

Book 2 of the Keeping Shiloh Series

By Ashleigh Meyer

CHAPTER 1

Even over the heart-thumping reverberations of bass-heavy music pumping through the stereo speakers, Jude heard the satisfying *thunk* of three knives landing square in the center of the target behind her, and turned around to inspect her work. Glancing up at the clock, she realized it was nearly two. Time had a tendency to slip away from her whenever she got deep into a workout, and Shiloh needed to be picked up from school in thirty minutes. She grabbed her towel from the weapons rack, threw it over her sweat-dampened shoulders, and jogged up the stairs.

In the kitchen, she pulled a glass out of the cabinet, and turned the faucet on to get a drink. She splashed cold water on her face, then dabbed the back of her neck with her wet hands. Her heart rate was still elevated from the two hours she'd spent in the gym, and her muscles still twitched from the strain. She was in the best shape of her life, stronger, faster, and more agile than ever, but she was never satisfied. Every workout was about more cardio, more strength training, more weapons accuracy.

There had been no major upsets in nearly a year; just small things here and there, disrupting the community. Nothing got close to Shiloh. Jude was sure of it. In the midst of what seemed like a dry spell for demons and evil lurking creatures, it was more important than ever to stay sharp. Not only because Jude knew from experience that things could change in an instant, but also because idle hands were not good for her. Keeping busy meant having less time to sit and think, and nothing good ever came of long, quiet contemplation.

After cooling off, she held a glass under the stream and began to fill it up, but before she reached the halfway mark, the faucet began to gurgle and spit. She tapped it with her fingers, and when that didn't help, she went to turn off the flow. But just before her hand landed on the knob, she heard what sounded like clinking metal, and the unmistakable sound of rushing water. In seconds, the kitchen floor was sprayed with water pouring out from the pipe under the sink.

She dropped the glass into the sink and ripped the cabinet door open as water sprayed in her face.

"Everything okay?" Ezra called on her way down the stairs. "I heard something and— oh, no." She stood behind Jude, just out of reach of the water raining down in the kitchen. "What happened?"

"Who knows?" Jude snapped. "This damn house was built a century ago. Pipes have probably never been replaced." She had both hands wrapped around the leak when another sprung loose. Finally, she stood up, exasperated, with water still sprinkling out onto the kitchen floor. "What the hell do we do now?" She threw her hands up, dropped them down with a clap and let out a loud, dramatic groan.

Ezra shrugged regretfully. "At least now you don't have to shower?"

Jude rolled her eyes and sloshed out of the kitchen and into the living room.

"Call a plumber," Ezra advised, following behind her at a distance.

Jude pulled out her cell phone and rapidly dialed a familiar phone number.

"Hello?" Christopher picked up the phone after one ring.

"Hey, Chris," Jude said quickly. "Listen, I need a favor."

Ezra crossed her arms over her chest, cocked her head to one side, and watched with intrigue.

"Anything," Christopher answered.

"I have a leaky pipe situation I was wondering if you could help me with?"

"I'll bet you do," Ezra mumbled under her breath. When Jude shot her a murderous look, she turned quickly around and pretended to be busy stacking magazines on the coffee table.

"A pipe?"

Jude cleared her throat. "Yeah, under the kitchen sink. It's a mess."

"Well, I don't have a whole lot of experience

with...uh, plumbing, but I can come take a look, sure."

Jude ran her hand through her soaked hair and rested it on the back of her neck. "Great, thank you so much."

"Sure," said Christopher. "Be there in twenty", and they hung up.

Jude turned to Ezra, who was still shifting things around on the coffee table. "Can you get Shiloh from school today?"

Ezra glanced back at Jude and nodded. "Sure," she said, turning fully around and crossing her arms. "So, how'd the pipe break?"

"I'm not sure," Jude answered, jogging upstairs to change out of her wet clothes. "I just turned on the water and it went everywhere. Those pipes are barely holding together. Probably need to get all the plumbing done."

"You mean you didn't whack it with a hammer?" Ezra chased after her, taking two stairs at a time.

"I'm sorry, what?" Jude stepped into her room peeling off the damp tank-top.

Ezra looked at her with a coy smile.

"Oh, Ezra, grow up," Jude shot back. "The pipe is broken. I need *someone* to fix it."

"A preacher?" Ezra asked as she sat down on the edge of Jude's bed.

"Okay, he's *not* a preacher," Jude corrected, as she dug through her dresser for a new shirt.

"He's not a plumber, either."

Jude exhaled sharply and pulled her Blink 182 t-shirt over her head. She'd cut the sleeves off years ago, leaving big, loose holes around her arms.

"Come on, don't be mad," Ezra pleaded.

Jude shrugged, whirling around from her dresser to her closet. "I'm not," she answered, her voice too high. "I just think you're looking for something that isn't there. Your imagination is getting the better of you."

"Jude," Ezra leveled. "I don't think *my* imagination is the one in question."

"What is that supposed to mean?

"Just that this guy comes over at least twice a week for some vague reason or another." Ezra stood up and walked toward where her best friend was pulling her damp hair back in the mirror. "I've spent the whole winter watching you mentally rip off his sweater vests."

"Oh, you have not," said Jude defensively.

"Jude," Ezra interrupted. She placed both hands on Jude's shoulders, forcing eye contact. "There's nothing wrong with you wanting to spend time with him. He's a nice guy. You deserve a nice guy! But why not do it over dinner, and maybe a movie, away from home and your eight-year-old daughter?"

Jude shook her head dismissively. "No, that sounds like a date."

Ezra shrugged. "Well, that's because it would be a date."

Jude pulled away and let her hair back down,

inspecting it again in the mirror, dissatisfied. "For the millionth time, Ezra, I can't date him," she said decidedly. "It would be a disaster."

"He's already involved," Ezra reasoned. "What's the worst that could happen?"

"He could die," Jude retorted quickly, pulling on a pair of worn denim shorts.

After a small laugh, Ezra regained her focus. "Come on, he is crazy about you. Why are you being so obstinate?"

"Ezra, love is a dangerous enough game without the monsters in my closet. Literally. Best to keep things simple." She knew she was talking more to herself than Ezra. "Get intimate with someone and your priorities shift. Guards get dropped. Plus, he's my friend. We would date, we would break up, it would be messy, and I'd lose that. Then I'm down to one. And you're a good one, don't get me wrong. But one friend is not a great stat."

Truthfully, her relationship with Christopher was already complicated, ever since a particularly awkward encounter left them questioning the direction of their friendship. For four years, it was pretty stagnant and clear- cut. They were friends. Partners, in the professional sense of the word.

Then there was the Thanksgiving incident. After dinner had been cleaned up and Ezra and Shiloh were laying on the living room floor listening to old records and playing games, Jude stepped out onto the porch for some fresh air and to quiet her ever-buzzing mind. Christopher came out behind her a few minutes later with an unopened bottle of wine. He sat down beside her on the porch swing and popped the cork, taking a swig right from the bottle. He handed it to Jude, and draped his coat over her shoulders as she took a long sip. It was a nice gesture. She offered him a faint smile and the conversation turned to Shiloh, as it often did. The holidays were always difficult for Jude, and Christopher knew that. He'd fought alongside of her for four years. He had been instrumental in taking down Molech when they first met. He'd helped her eliminate countless threats since then, big and small, and he never asked questions or ran away. They had gotten to know each other and spent a lot of time together, professionally and personally. Like Ezra, he knew what she was thinking much of the time. He witnessed Jude as she juggled her frequently overlapping roles as mother, warrior, and twenty-something girl, and he knew that she was more fragile and scared than she would ever let on.

But on Thanksgiving night, with cheap merlot warming the back of her throat and blurring her senses, and Christopher's olive green sport coat wrapping her in the scent of his cologne, she felt vulnerable. Lonely. Her eyes welled with tears, and between sips she tried to sort out the mingled emotions: festive holiday joy that came with seeing Shiloh happy, and the unforgiving chill of reality that always hung over the whole scene like a death shroud. As she was about to lose it, she caught herself and pulled back, laughing out loud at her own girlish behavior.

"I must be drunk," she said with a tight exhale, as she swirled the deep red wine in the now half-empty bottle. "I'm sorry."

She went to stand up and hurry back into the house, but Christopher grabbed her hand. Without a word, he leaned in and kissed her.

At first, it was awkward. She did not see it coming, though on reflection she probably should have, and she froze a little, her lips taking some time to react to the sensation of his. Finally, when her awareness reached them, she kissed him back, leaning in just a little before snapping out of it.

She pulled her head away and looked at him, open mouthed and speechless for a second, and then stood up wringing her hands, her bottom lip still tingling from the encounter. "That was probably a bad idea," she said breathlessly.

He stood up, too, and went to touch her but she backed away. "See, I told you I'm drunk." She let out another nervous laugh, then ran back into the house, knowing too well that she wasn't drunk at all.

That was six months ago, and it hadn't been mentioned since. Though she never told Ezra about what happened, Jude assumed that Ezra had suspicions and had picked up on the details, as Ezra always does.

"You're already convinced it would end?" Ezra questioned.

Jude gave Ezra her patented *duh* expression, and continued pulling on her socks.

Ezra backed down, though she remained unconvinced. "Well, I'm going to go get Shiloh," she said, giving Jude a quick pat on the back before heading out of the room.

Jude inspected herself in the mirror once more. Twenty-seven years old, and still she felt she didn't look like an adult. Something about the way she carried herself, kind of haphazardly, moving too quickly most of the time. Paired with her careless, dated grunge aesthetic, she projected a youthful, devil-may-care appearance. She was ungraceful in all circumstances except for battle, when her body somehow managed to come into itself. Her facial features were soft, and her lower lip was always cracked just a little from biting it every time she was nervous. Despite her strength and muscular body, she was naturally small framed, with deep-set hips and sharp elbows; not like the curvy, filled-out women at Shiloh's school, and like a child, she was always covered in little cuts and scrapes. Sometimes it didn't bother her, but when it came to things like interacting with other parents, or imagining herself as someone who could actually pursue a man romantically, she felt inadequate.

Her hair was still wet and tangled and once again she threw it back into a loose knot tied up at the back of her head. She ran her hands over her shirt, smoothing it out over her sharp edges, exhaled deeply, then made her way downstairs.

Christopher arrived just a few minutes after Ezra left. Jude had the door open before he could knock, and found him standing on the porch in blue jeans and a green button-up shirt, toolbox in hand. She grabbed him by the arm and ushered him quickly into the kitchen.

"Wow," he said, standing in a shallow puddle of water.

Jude stood next to him, arms across her chest, inspecting the mayhem. "Yup," she answered lightly.

"Well," he placed his toolbox on the table and opened it up. "I guess I'll see what I can find."

He stuck his whole upper body under the sink and began inspecting things with a flashlight. Eventually, he rolled over onto his back to look up at the bottom of the cabinet.

"See anything?" Jude asked, trying not to notice as his shirt peeked up over his waist, revealing just a sliver of somewhat pale, but shapely, abs.

"Yeah," he answered. "I see some rust. Quite a bit of rust actually." There were the sounds of tinkering and dripping water. "And there's a huge spider under here. You may consider just burning the place down and collecting the insurance." She heard something smack the inside of the cabinet. "He's dead now."

"Thanks," Jude squeaked, shuddering at the thought.

He pulled himself out, wet and dusty. Brushing the grime off of his shirt, he asked, "So you can fight demons, but not spiders?"

"Totally different," Jude stated, crossing her arms defensively.

"Well," he went on. "Looks like you're going to need to replace a lot of the plumbing under there. But for now, I think I can get the leak to stop." He walked over to his toolbox and pulled out duct tape and a wrench, then climbed back under the cabinet. Jude heard the wrench clink and the duct tape unwrap from the roll as she stood leaning against the counter next to him.

"Turn the water on," he asked after several minutes of tinkering.

"You may want to take cover," she answered, reaching over to turn the faucet. It gurgled at first, then came out in a nice, steady stream, no spray or leaks. "You fixed it!" She turned the water off and he emerged from under the sink, noticeably proud of himself.

"Oh, no problem," he shrugged. "Just patched the cracks and tightened the connectors. Really though, you are gonna want to get a plumber in here to replace those old pipes. Until then, you should probably avoid using the kitchen sink too much. Use the one in the bathroom when you can."

Jude nodded. "Well, thanks again, we really appreciate it." She got two mugs out of the cabinet and poured two cups of coffee. "It's from earlier, but it's still hot," she said, handing him a cup.

He thanked her, even though he never drank

coffee after noon, and helped her lay towels out over the floor to sop up the mess.

"So, do you have any weekend plans?" he asked casually, as he dragged a towel over the floor.

Jude hesitated. "Um, no, not really."

The back door swung open and Shiloh and Ezra could be heard coming inside.

"Well, that Spring Fling is this weekend. I think the weather is finally going to hold." He was squirming, staring at his feet. "I was thinking, ya know, maybe we could all go."

Just then, Shiloh bounced into the room with her backpack slung over her shoulder. "Oh, that sounds like so much fun!" she cheered, diving into the conversation. "Mom, remember, we talked about going?"

Jude nodded and gave Shiloh a hug. "Yeah, I remember. How was school?"

Shiloh spun around and gave Christopher a hug, an always-in-motion blur. Next, she was at the pantry, unwrapping a package of Pop-Tarts. "So can we go?" she asked eagerly.

Jude looked at Christopher, who was also awaiting an answer. "Sure," she said finally. "Why not? Could be fun."

Truthfully, she wasn't sure that the Bedford Spring Fling sounded fun at all, but she *had* been promising Shiloh that they would go for a while.

"Yes!" Shiloh rejoiced. "School was great! I'm gonna go find Jack!" Then she was gone, taking two steps at a time to her room, where her hound was always waiting.

Jude laughed, shaking her head at Shiloh's energy.

"Well, tomorrow morning at ten?" asked Christopher. "We can meet there, or I can pick you up?"

"Oh, meeting there is fine," Jude answered quickly.

"Okay, we'll meet there then. By the Ferris wheel? That should be an easy place to find."

She gave a quick nod. "Absolutely. Ten by the Ferris wheel."

He took a few small sips from his coffee cup just to be polite, and placed it in the sink. "Well, I'll let you get back to your afternoon then."

"Oh, sure, alright," Jude replied, surprised that he was hurrying off so quickly. "Thanks."

"Call that plumber," he said again, packing up his toolbox.

"Oh, I will."

He smiled and touched her briefly on the shoulder. "Alright then," he stated, then hurried out the kitchen door.

Jude finished mopping up and went into the living room to relax. Ezra was on the couch, already deep into one of her paperback mysteries.

"So, is the Spring Fling—" she said teasingly, glancing at Jude through the top of her reading glasses.

"It's not a date," Jude interrupted, collapsing beside her.

She gave a slow nod, looking up at Jude without lifting her head. "Alright." She turned the page. "Does he know that?"

"Yeah," Jude said confidently. Then she thought about it. "Well, I think he does." She put both of her hands over her eyes and rubbed slowly. "I hope he knows. You're coming. That'll clear things up."

Ezra shook her head. "Sorry, I'm working."

"Call in sick!" Jude pleaded. "No one goes to the library on a Saturday anyway."

Ezra rolled her eyes. "Shiloh will make a fine wingman."

Jude groaned. "I don't need a wingman because it's—"

"Not a date. I heard."

Jude looked at her anxiously and she laughed.

"It will be fine," Ezra promised, as Jude shifted in her seat. "You hang out with him all the time. Jeez, don't be so squirrelly."

Jude sighed deeply, pulled her feet up under herself on the couch and clicked on the television as Shiloh bounced back down the stairs with the book she was reading, and the afternoon slipped into another quiet evening.

CHAPTER 2

The next morning, Main Street was flooded with Spring Flingers swerving between craft vendors and food trucks below brightly colored banners. The enticing scent of kettle corn and carnival food wafted on the almost undetectable breeze, and the sounds of a delightfully off-key a capella group rose above the sounds of indistinct chatter. It had been a long winter of unpredictable snowstorms and lingering gray clouds. It seemed that all of April had been erased by rain. Everyone in town was going a little stir crazy, including Shiloh, who had been pressing her face against frosted glass windows since November.

After having been postponed three times, the Spring Fling drew quite a crowd. Mercifully, the day was perfect: seventy degrees and sunny. Just what was needed to coax the sleepy community out of a long hibernation.

Shiloh was up and dressed three hours before the festival even began. Much to her mother's obvious frustration, she was demanding more independence every day. She had grown taller than most of her classmates and slender, with long, bright blonde hair twisting between her shoulder blades, just like Jude. Shiloh was developing a style of her own, taking pages here and there from her mother's dress code, blended with a softer, uniquely Shiloh aesthetic. She liked to borrow Jude's old band shirts and flannels and tie them around her waist and she often kept her hair tied back in a red bandanna like Rosie the Riveter, if Rosie had been a florist rather than a wartime munitions worker. She loved bright colors and overalls and flower-printed anything. Though she had grown, she was still very much a child. She still had the full, rosy face of childhood. She was clumsy and uncoordinated, and her pants always had grass stains at the knees.

As Shiloh dragged a reluctant Jude this way and that, and Jude scanned the horizon looking for the Ferris wheel, a loud and familiar voice called out to them. "Miss Doris!" Shiloh called out just before bolting off in the direction of the St. Mary's Church fund-raiser booth.   "Well good morning young ladies!" Doris squealed. "Are you enjoying the festival?"

"Yes!" answered Shiloh, wrapping her arms around Doris's plump waist.

As Shiloh was being squeezed to the point of coughing, which she didn't mind, Miss Doris looked across the table at Jude. "It looks to me like you both need to put some meat on your bones." She released Shiloh and began boxing up two slices of cherry pie. "Honey, no man likes a woman with all them sharp edges. Gotta give 'em somethin' they can grab hold to."

Shiloh giggled and grabbed a plastic spoon from a cup on the table. Immediately, she dove into her pie. It was deliciously cool and sweet and her love for Miss Doris only grew.

"Right," Jude said, with her cheeks reddening. "I'll keep that in mind."

"Well have some pie, darlin', do you want to be single forever?" Doris handed Jude a spoon and poured Shiloh a cup of lemonade.

Jude reached for the small purse she carried across her body, pulled out five dollars and dropped it into the donation bucket.. "What's the fundraiser for?" she asked, handing over the cash.

"Well you know the roof in the sanctuary is leakin'. Right over the choir loft. Rain drips on the hymnals and suddenly an *a flat* looks like a *c sharp* and the whole choir is off key. Linda, is that you?" She yelled suddenly and Shiloh nearly dropped her pie as Miss Doris waved ferociously at someone on the other side of the street. "Oh, Linda! How is the new grandbaby?" Linda, who looked surprisingly like Miss Doris, made her way toward the table. "I'll see you two girls later. Enjoy that pie!" said Doris, giving Shiloh a quick poke in the ribs before gabbing away with the other woman. The next thing she knew, Shiloh's arm was gripped in Jude's hand and she was being pulled quickly in the opposite direction.

"Crazy woman," she heard Jude mumble

under her breath.

Shiloh shrugged. "Idunno what's not to like," she commented, as she struggled to get another bite of pie from the spoon to her mouth.

She spotted the Ferris wheel spinning above and behind the bank building, and sure enough, by the time they made it there, Christopher was already leaning up against the temporary metal fence that encircled the base. Shiloh started to run toward him, but halfway there, she caught sight of the pony corral just to the left, and made a sharp turn for it.

As kids climbed down from their saddles and made their way out of the corral, Shiloh reached over the gate to pet the long nose of a little brown pony. She wore a little blanket that read "Sadie" in yellow thread, and as she stroked her head, the pony pushed back gently against Shiloh's palm.

Finally, Jude and Christopher showed up behind her and Jude, reading her mind like she usually did, handed her two dollars. Shiloh threw her arms around her mother's waist, said thank-you, and hurried to the pony line.

While standing and waiting for her turn, she kept a close eye on Jude and Christopher. She couldn't say for sure, but Jude had been acting a little strange around him for the past few months, and Shiloh suspected that maybe there was something going on there. Christopher was always around, always the first one in line to help her mother with projects around the house, or pick up a forgotten item from the store. Sometimes he gave Shiloh a ride home from school if Jude had gotten caught up in something. It wasn't new, he'd always been that way. And Shiloh could tell by the way he looked at Jude that he thought she was the most beautiful, interesting woman alive. She always wondered why Jude didn't see it. But recently, there had been a shift in their relationship, which Shiloh found to be very interesting.

Finally, she stepped up to the ticket booth, handed her two dollars to a teen-aged girl with a ratty magazine on her lap, and skipped into the pony corral, right up to Sadie. "Remember me?" she asked the pony, while the attendant helped her climb into the saddle. Of course, the pony didn't *actually* answer. That would be nonsense. But sometimes, Shiloh felt like non-human things could communicate with her. In their own way. And when the pony turned its head all the way around to give Shiloh a good nudge on the arm, she knew they were best friends.

Sadie let out a warm snort through her nose and the ponies started walking around the coral all together.

It seemed to be over so quickly, and when the girl blew a whistle, all of the ponies came to a stop, like robots. All of the ponies, except for Sadie. She just kept on trotting around, casually strolling in circles inside of the fence. Shiloh wasn't exactly sure what to do, but finally, the ride attendant came and grabbed on to Sadie's reins, and pulled her to a reluctant stop.

"Well, Sadie doesn't want you to leave," said the girl, smiling as she helped Shiloh down.

Shiloh gave the pony a kiss on the side of her head, and wandered through the crowd of kids back to Jude.

As she got closer, she noticed that the two of them were still leaning on the fence where they'd been watching her, and their hands were so close on the railing that they were practically touching. She didn't know what the conversation had been about, but Jude had clearly been laughing.

"How was the pony?" Jude asked, quickly letting go of the fence rail and stepping away from Christopher.

Shiloh reported that she'd enjoyed it, and that a pony would be a nice pet to have. Before Jude had time to reject the idea, Christopher offered to build a barn in the back field of their house and Jude shot him a disapproving look. The three made their way through the festival, led primarily by Shiloh. They all took a ride on the Ferris wheel, and Shiloh tried to locate their house from the top, but the landscape was too hilly, and the house was tucked too far back to be found. They played ring toss and balloon darts, and when Shiloh couldn't manage to pop any balloons, Jude tried her hand and hit every time. She won Shiloh a giant stuffed monkey, which Shiloh gleefully carted around town for the remainder of the afternoon.

On her final game of the day, she won a goldfish. It was handed to her in a plastic drinking cup by an unenthusiastic old woman, and the fish just hovered motionless in the artificially blue water, but Shiloh felt like she'd won a million dollars. Jude seemed happy, because the goldfish meant that they had to head home.

As they began to make their way toward the parking lot, Shiloh noticed a man sitting on the curb, half hunched over, drifting in and out of sleep with his scrawny dog laying on the pavement next to him. Really, she noticed his dog first and started casually toward it, all but ignoring Jude's quiet demands that she stay put. She had already reached the dog and was leaning down to pet it by the time Jude caught up with her. She placed her hand on the dogs head and scratched behind its ears, and it perked up. "Hello," she whispered to it, and it licked her right in the mouth. The dog and the girl made eye contact, then the dog laid its head back down, closer to Shiloh's bended knee, and continued to nap in the sun.

"What's her name?" Shiloh asked the man.

It took a second for him to respond, but finally, he did. He looked at Shiloh and she noticed his bloodshot eyes and his trembling hands. His clothes were sort of stained and he smelled like sweat and something she didn't recognize, but that she knew she didn't really like. Still, she offered him a tender smile. "Name's Daisy," he answered quietly.

Shiloh scooted closer to him. "What's your name?"

"Moby," said the man. They were nearly at eye level with each other, and Shiloh could see in his expression that something was wrong.

"I'm Shiloh. Do you not feel good?" she asked innocently. "You seem sick."

Moby took a long breath. "Got the mornin' shakes, girl."

"Oh," said Shiloh sweetly, even though she had no idea what he meant. Suddenly, she felt overwhelmed by a tremendous feeling that she couldn't quite identify. It was like sadness, mixed with a tingling in her heart and in her fingers and it buzzed inside of her until she couldn't resist.

She knew it was against the rules. She knew her mother wouldn't like it.

Still, she leaned forward with both of her hands extended, and placed them on Moby's left shoulder. At first, the man retracted, looking at her in confusion, but after a few seconds, he began to relax, and almost lean in toward her. He took a deep, cleansing breath as his color began to improve. She had done this before, to Jude, and once to Ezra. She felt the urge to do it way more often than she actually did. But it was getting harder to bottle up. She didn't understand it. Not at all. But she knew she could do something special. Something good.

CHAPTER 3

It took Jude a moment to realize what was happening. When she did, she rushed toward Shiloh, and grabbed her by the arm.

Moby looked up at Jude, then back at Shiloh. "That's a nifty trick, little girl, how'd you–"

"Maybe you should have some water, Mr. Thacker," Jude interrupted. "Get some rest."

Chris stepped in. "I can get Mike to come get you, take you home," he added.

Moby leaned back and nodded. "I suppose that's not a bad idea," he answered, wavering again. But he couldn't keep from staring at Shiloh with a look of bewilderment.

"I think that little girl is magic," he said, moving to stand. "There's somethin' strange about her. She's special."

People nearby started to notice the fiasco, but most of them knew of Moby's habit and did their best to look the other way. Jude pulled Shiloh off of the street and into a small alley while Chris called Moby a ride home.

"Shiloh, what were you thinking?" Jude scolded as soon as she confirmed that there was no one else in the alley. "We've talked about this!"

"I know mom, but that man was sick. I only did a little."

"You can't do *anything*, Shiloh, not in public like this." She let go of her daughter's arm.

Shiloh stepped back and crossed her arms over her chest; a defiant posture that Jude rarely saw from her even tempered child. "I don't understand that," Shiloh challenged. "I'm just helping people."

Jude exhaled loudly and tried to level with Shiloh. "I know you just want to help, and that's a great thing. But if people saw you, or found out you had these…abilities, you could get hurt."

Shiloh uncrossed her arms. "Well, I don't understand that either," she said, this time less defiantly, but more innocently. "How could helping people ever be a bad thing?"

And Jude was backed into a corner that she was all too familiar with. The one where the only real way out was to tell Shiloh the truth. In the past, she offered vague and flimsy reasons for why Shiloh had to keep her gifts a secret, but she was beginning to see through them. She was old enough to know that something wasn't adding up, but young enough, Jude thought, to be shielded from the heavy weight of her destiny. All the while, it was becoming more and more dangerous for Shiloh not to know. Jude pulled Shiloh toward her and took her hands. "I'll explain everything later," she said solemnly. "I promise."

As they stepped out of the alley, Christopher offered a concerned look to Jude, who took a slow, deep breath and rubbed the tips of her fingers over her forehead where she could feel the familiar twinge of stress. Christopher placed his hand between her shoulder blades and they continued toward the cars.

"It'll all work out," he said quietly, as Shiloh climbed into the Jeep, already over the incident with Moby.

Jude nodded doubtfully, and crossed her arms over her chest. "I hope so," she answered in a whisper.

As soon as they were home, Shiloh ran up the two flights of stairs to her room, carefully holding the fish so its cup didn't spill. The attic, which had once been a makeshift library, was converted into Shiloh's bedroom when she was six. She wanted her own space, and Jude wondered what it would be like to not share a bedroom with a kindergartener. She had her anxieties and reservations, but the only access to the attic was through Jude's room, making it the safest place in an already safe house.

Jude trailed in, dragging her feet and obsessing about how she was going to address the Moby incident. She was irritated that it happened in the first place. It was adding up to a perfectly pleasant afternoon, and Shiloh should've known better. Deep down, she knew that wasn't fair. How could she expect Shiloh to understand the limitations and dangers of her own abilities if she didn't even know who she was? Jude had been holding back for a long time, making excuses, redirecting questions, creating diversions and distractions.

She seriously considered going on with her day as normal, and completely forgetting about the morning's encounter with Moby. Shiloh obviously wasn't fixated on it, and it wasn't like she ran around performing miracles all over town. It would be easy to keep putting it off. But Jude knew it was inevitable. Protecting Shiloh as a baby meant protecting her from the truth as much as anything else because she didn't have the tools to handle it, or the capacity to understand. Protecting Shiloh as an observant, intelligent, and growing child was a different matter, and knowing the truth was becoming critical. Unconfidently, she made her way up the stairs and toward Shiloh.

She entered through the closet door in her bedroom, which was always left open, and climbed the attic stairs that were tucked away behind the wall. The old wooden stairs creaked underfoot and Shiloh's light glowed up above. It was late in the afternoon, and there was not a lot of natural light in the attic. The only window was a small, round port-hole just below the peak of the sloped ceiling, which Shiloh had covered in colored crepe paper to make it look like stained glass. The ceiling was pitched somewhat steeply, and met at a peak in the center, where Shiloh had strung Christmas lights. The bookshelves had been vacated of all of Jude's books on demonology and religion and paranormal history. Instead, they were full of Shiloh's picture books, stuffed animals and figurines. Most importantly, no one unwelcome would be able to go in or out. The room had been cleansed, blessed and protected by just about every ritual that the Synedrion had access to. Not to mention, accessing it meant getting past Jude. No easy task.

Jude stepped into the room and found Shiloh coloring in her sketchbook with Jack lazing beside her on the giant, round throw rug that covered most of the wooden floor.

"Hi, Mom," Shiloh said happily without looking up from her coloring picture.

"Hi, Shiloh," answered Jude. "Can we talk for a minute?"

"Sure, what do you wanna talk about?"

"Well, could you come sit with me?"

Shiloh looked up, somewhat concerned. "Okay," she answered, letting her crayons roll off the sketchbook and onto the rug.

Jude sat down on the edge of Shiloh's bed and motioned for Shiloh to join her. She climbed up and sat cross-legged with her purple flowered quilt and stuffed animals bunched around her. Chief among them was her beloved Herschel the Alligator, propped up like a king on her pillow. Herschel was five years old now and had seen better days. He was mud-stained where Shiloh insisted that he join her for a walk in the rain, and crudely stitched back together at his tail where Jack decided to give him a taste. But he was still, without question, her favorite. Jude could see the corner of a book poking out from under her pillow; the book that Shiloh always read after bedtime thinking Jude had no idea, though of course she knew. Most nights, after Shiloh went to bed, Jude would lay and listen to the turning of pages from her own bed below, and rest easier knowing that her daughter was still safe in her room. Now, she looked at Jude with big, expectant eyes and Jude felt small under their gaze.

"I've been thinking for a long time about how to talk to you about this," Jude began. "It's sort of confusing, and I've worried sometimes that it wasn't the right time to tell you."

"Is this about that guy from the festival? Mom, I promise I won't do it again, okay?" Shiloh began absently arranging her stuffed animals along her headboard.

"Well, it is kind of about that, but it's more complicated." Jude reached for Shiloh's hands and pulled them toward her, regaining the little girl's attention. "I guess you've known for a while now that in some ways, you're a little different from other kids?"

Shiloh shrugged. "Yeah, sure," she answered. "I can read better than almost everyone in my class."

"Well, that's true," Jude answered. "But there are other things. You know that you can do things other people can't."

Shiloh cast her eyes downward. "Yeah," she mumbled.

"It's nothing to be ashamed of," said Jude. "You are special. The things you do can help people."

"Like healing people when they don't feel good?" Shiloh asked.

"Exactly," answered Jude. "And other things, too."

"Like what?"

"Well, you are really good at talking to people, and people really like talking to you. People sometimes feel happier when you're around. Not just because you're a great, loving kid, but because you have an energy. It's hard to explain, but you are more sensitive to things than others. And as you grow, more things will probably start to happen. More things that make you special."

Shiloh paused. "Why?" she asked.

This was the question that Jude didn't want to answer. That she had no idea how to answer. "Well–" she stammered, but stopped. She racked her brain for an answer as her eyes wandered around the room. Then, as she noticed Shiloh's bookshelf, an idea struck her. An idea so obvious she wondered why she didn't think of it before.

"You know what, I have something to show you," she told Shiloh, standing up from the bed. "Wait right here." Then she jogged down the stairs to her room.

When the attic became Shiloh's bedroom instead of the library, all of the books and materials had to be moved to the basement. Most of them contained dangerous information that didn't belong in the hands of a child. There were very few books on the Chosen and the bloodline, and most of what did exist was kept hidden away by the most powerful Synedrion leaders. They lived in complete isolation, having taken vows of poverty and prayer. The Codex was really the only book in Jude's possession that detailed the circumstances of the lives of Shiloh's predecessors. It had been hand-written and passed down through her family for hundreds of years. It was lost in the Dark Ages, thought to have been destroyed, but it was later recovered from a vault that contained several other sacred texts, and returned to the rightful hands of the Synedrion.

This particular book Jude did not keep in the basement, but instead tucked away in her dresser, in the bottom drawer, under a collection of Shiloh's baby clothes. Inside of it were fragile pages detailing the creation and purpose of the Chosen, the history of the sacred bloodline, and an explanation of their destiny and sacrifice, and through it the restoration of balance between good and evil. Most intriguing, it was written by those Chosen before.

Jude lifted the soft baby clothes that covered the book. She held one yellow jumper like a relic in her hand for a moment, tracing the seams with her fingers and breathing deep what was left of the sweet scent of baby Shiloh. This information would change things. Finally, she set them aside, lifted the heavy, hand-stitched book, and returned the clothes to the drawer.

Back upstairs, she sat down again on Shiloh's bed and laid the Codex in Shiloh's lap.

"Wow," Shiloh whispered, as she leaned down to study the gold stitched letters on the cover, spelling out the word *Restitutio*, or "Restoration". "It looks old."

"It is very old," answered Jude.

"What is this book about?" Shiloh asked, opening to the first brittle page.

"You," answered Jude.

The book was written in a number of languages, based on wherever the bloodline existed at the time. Being maternal, the lineage was easily disguised by marriage and name changes, but it moved to America in the 1740s. Before that, they had lived in Scotland, Hungary, Bulgaria, and everywhere else, running from, or towards, whatever evil pursued them at the time. The first entry in the Codex was written, according to Gideon, in Aramaic sometime around 600 AD. Luckily, much of it had been translated into English in the 1800s.

Jude had read the whole thing carefully, many times. The first few chapters did not explicitly mention death. Her plan was to allow Shiloh to read it, and monitor her as she did, that way she could explain anything Shiloh didn't understand, and keep her from information she didn't yet need to know. Besides, it was a challenging read even with the aid of the English translation, but it would be a good way for Jude to bring Shiloh into the light of her own destiny.

Shiloh pulled the book close to her face and began reading the very first page. "Introduction. The earth is full of fickle creatures. Darkness and wickedness spreads like a plague upon humanity," she read, pausing to sound out the more archaic words, "until the best are rendered incapable of righteousness and the worst are vile, manipulative, and full of corruption." She stumbled over the text, repeating sounds until they formed words with which she was vaguely familiar. "But there is one light illuminating still the darkness, sent to restore balance so that virtue and goodness may prevail, until that day when forces beyond our realm take to the field of final battle, annihilating evil once and for all."

She glanced briefly at Jude, and silently re-read the first few sentences. "I don't get it," she said, exasperated. "This all makes it sound like the world is a really bad place."

Jude restrained herself. What she wanted to say was: *it is a really bad place. Humanity is worthless. They don't deserve you and everything about this is wrong.* What she said was, "sometimes bad things happen, but there are forces of good in the world too, and you're one of them."

"The light in the darkness is me?" Shiloh asked, surprised and skeptical.

Jude nodded and forced a smile.

"Wow," answered Shiloh. "But why? How'd that happen?" But her mind was moving too quickly for answers, and Jude's was moving too slowly to offer them.

She read on. "The child comes not to save the world, but to make even the scales that would otherwise tip toward chaos and vulgarity. She comes to offer the hope that all is not lost, to re-assure the weary that promise and plenty still await those who seek goodness while their feet tirelessly tramp the barren earth. That these men and women of conviction and discernment may live reasonably happy in this life, and exceptionally happy in the next."

A cold chill ran up Jude's spine and clawed at the base of her neck, and she unconsciously squeezed tighter on the edge of Shiloh's bed. Shiloh looked up at her with a bright glint in her eye. Through it, Jude could see the wheels turning in Shiloh's head.

For the next hour or so, they laid together on her bed, shoulder to shoulder, flipping through the Codex, reading about the lives and histories of those who were chosen before, and talking about the steps that Shiloh would take to bring her into her own destiny. Training, studying, exploring the limitations of her abilities. Never was death men-tioned. Jude couldn't utter the words if her own life depended on it. Besides, there was time. For now, Shiloh deserved the chance to celebrate what mea-ger joy her destiny afforded. And if there was any-thing Jude could do about it, the day would never come when Shiloh was offered as a sacrifice to restore some supernatural balance. There was time to figure out another way.

Finally, when it was time to go downstairs for dinner, Jude closed the book.

"Listen," she said slowly, sure to hold Shiloh's attention. "I need you to promise me that you'll never look at this book without me."

Shiloh wrinkled her brow. "Why not?"

Jude should've known it wouldn't be that easy. "Well," she started. "Some of the stuff in here could be really confusing, and I want to make sure you understand what you're reading."

"Oh," answered Shiloh. "Okay, I promise."

Shiloh moved to hop off the bed, and Jude stopped her, throwing her arm around Shiloh's waist. "Promise?" She repeated, locking eyes with her daughter.

Shiloh looked back deeply. "I promise."

Jude kissed the top of her head and then let her go. She sat on Shiloh's bed for a moment more, looking down at the Codex but seeing something far beyond it. Movies playing out in her head of the day she would have to bring Shiloh into the full light of her destiny. Somewhere deep down, she knew that she should be coming up with a plan to handle it. She knew she should stop shoving it out of her mind, because the last thing she wanted was for it to sneak up on her, and catch her off guard. God forbid Shiloh overheard a conversation, or somehow found out on her own. But the movies that she saw in her head were enough to make her want to shut her eyes and run from the events transpiring on the screen. It was too easy to shut it off. Too easy to convince herself that they had made progress with the Codex and that was enough. So that's exactly what she did.

She went back down to her room, opened her dresser drawer, and returned the book back to its place beneath Shiloh's baby clothes.

CHAPTER 4

Jude spoke to Gideon and told him what they were doing. She was hesitant to tell him, because it meant that, eventually, the Synedrion would get involved. They would start to etch micro-cracks into Jude's relationship with Shiloh, and they would treat her like a tool, not a human child. But she hoped that telling Gideon would stave off the interest of the Synedrion. Gideon trusted Jude to handle the delivery of the basics, and she could drag that out forever.

In the three weeks leading to Shiloh's last day of third grade, she and Jude slowly read through the Codex and Jude monitored Shiloh's progress in the book to be sure she didn't read anything she wasn't ready for. Shiloh was fascinated by the other girls' stories and the powers that they had. They could channel their emotions to affect their physical environment, they could manipulate the thoughts and feelings of others, some had prophetic visions, and one girl from the 1500s could read people's minds. They were clairvoyants, sensitives, seers and healers. Every day, she bugged Jude about starting her training. When's Gideon coming? When's the last day of school? When could she practice turning off the lights without touching the switch?

Jude's answer was always "soon," but really, she was in no hurry at all. All of the things Shiloh was excited about were smoke and mirrors designed to distract from the truth of her destiny. The only reason any Chosen could do those things was because her energy was different. It had to be, because it was formulated to change the course of corruption on earth. Those other things were side effects that came with the real sickness of that energy; restoration through certain death.

On the last Friday in May, Jude sat sweating in the Jeep, waiting in line to pick Shiloh up from school. St. Mary's was a small Catholic school, and had fewer than 200 students from preschool to middle school. Still, the car rider line was long and slow, wrapping around the church to the school entrance where a few teachers sat outside ushering students into vehicles. There was no A/C in the old Jeep, and so the vinyl windows were unzipped and Jude's elbow rested on the door. Behind her, minivans and bubbly SUVs sat bumper-to-bumper, and at the front of the line PTA moms stood around chatting, holding up traffic.

Despite how hard she tried, Jude never could find patience for the other parents at St. Mary's. They were always stopping her in the hall whenever she had to go in for something, asking her to volunteer for bake sales or canned food drives, or help coach the cheerleading team. She was bombarded with emails about joining the PTA and attending carnival night, or whatever else was going on. All of these things were reasons for not having children that Jude would have quickly cited at the age of seventeen or eighteen. She'd never been one for social functions or community involvement. And now, community involvement could lead to exposure, which could lead to tragedy.

Nonetheless, she waved politely to Cathy Smithson, president of the fundraising committee, and made small talk with Erin Sweeny, pee-wee soccer coach, as she sweated out the window of the slow-moving Jeep. Finally, she arrived at the front of the building, where Shiloh stood hand-in-hand with the school librarian, her purple backpack slung over her shoulder. Jude got out of the car as she always did to greet her daughter and help her climb into the vehicle. Even from this distance, she could see that Shiloh had spilled some kind of red liquid down the front of her yellow shirt, one strap of her overalls was twisted, and her shoelaces were untied.

Shiloh spotted the Jeep and took off, only to be gently reprimanded by the crossing guard for running, before throwing her arms around Jude's waist. Jude glanced at the crossing guard and offered an apologetic nod. She then tossed Shiloh's backpack into the car as Shiloh climbed in. As soon as Shiloh was seated and began buckling her seatbelt, she caught sight of a boy that Jude had never seen before, but Shiloh exclaimed that he was her friend and jumped back out of the car.

"Shiloh, no, there's a whole line of people waiting–" Jude pleaded, but Shiloh was already standing in front of the boy, pointing to Jude from the sidewalk.

Jude glanced back at the row of cars behind her, full of parents shooting her dirty looks. She glanced at them quickly and grudgingly made her way to Shiloh.

"Hey, there's a long line of people waiting to pick up their kids. We have to go."

"Mom, this is my friend Elliott. We were wondering if he could come over to play this weekend?"

Jude looked down at Shiloh's new friend and smiled faintly, distracted by the invisible daggers being thrown at her from car windows. He was cute. A little shorter than Shiloh, and scrawny like little boys are, with long, curly reddish hair.

"Hi, Elliott," she answered, then looked back at Shiloh. "I don't know, I'd have to talk to his parents first, okay? Let's work it out on the phone later."

Shiloh pulled a marker out of the front pocket of her overalls. "What's your phone number?" she asked him, poised to write the digits on the back of her hand.

Elliott rattled off his phone number in the voice of a child who was proud to have it memorized, and Shiloh dramatically returned the cap to her marker with a snap. "Excellent," she said. "We'll talk tonight."

Shiloh was in the house and on the phone before Jude was even out of the Jeep. The screen door clattered behind her where she had flown inside. Jude got her backpack out of the back, slung it over her shoulder, and followed her inside. The Blue Ridge Mountains in the distance breathed the earliest inklings of the coming summer, slowly shedding the damp, shimmering green of spring and embracing the full-bodied, deep-sea color of the warmer months, the bold, teal blue for which they were named. The field that separated the Mikhale house from the mountains began at a hard line maybe fifty yards away, where Christopher stopped mowing and the land was left to grow wild. It was lush and green, about knee-deep, and spotted with the fluffy white caps of Queen Anne's Lace and the occasional sprig of Golden Alexander. Blackberry vines tangled through the brush, and one in particular had taken to climbing the shed at the edge of the field. At Jude's request, Christopher mowed around this particular bush rather than over it, and in a few short weeks, it would yield ripe blackberries the size of your thumb. Shiloh loved to pick them by the basketful on the days that she went to pluck tomatoes and carrots from the small garden that she and Ezra had planted years before.

This was certainly not the life Jude would've ever imagined for herself when she was young. Of course, she never could have predicted that she would someday be the mother and protector of a child destined to save the world. But even the rural, pastoral setting that she had found herself in surprised her. What surprised her even more was how much she liked it.

As she stepped up to the porch, she gave a satisfied glance to the window shutters that she had given a fresh coat of candy apple red paint a few weeks before. The old metal glider on the porch she had acquired from a yard sale last fall was made new with cushions and pillows that she and Ezra stitched together themselves late one night during an Andy Griffith marathon. The back door, which once hung crooked on a broken hinge, now hung straight and opened smoothly, with a new porcelain door-knob that Christopher installed. They had been in the house for four years, and for most of that time referred to it as "The Old Wesley Estate" like everyone in town. But it was finally turning into a place that Jude thought of as her own. A place in which she could imagine a future. Sometimes, when she thought no one was paying attention, she indulged in those fantasies, momentarily forgetting the insurmountable obstacles that would present themselves down the road.

When Jude stepped into the kitchen, Shiloh flagged her down and called her over to where she sat at the table, phone pressed to her ear.

"Uh huh," she said, nodding. "Okay, great.

Here's my mom."

"Hello?" Jude asked. It was quiet for a second. She looked skeptically at Shiloh. Finally, there was some shuffling on the other end, and a male voice picked up.

"Uh, hello?" His voice sounded deep and rough, like he'd just woken up from a nap.

"Hi," Jude said again. "This is Jude Mikhale, Shiloh's mom." She hated making phone conversation with people she didn't know. Every time she had to do it, she remembered her mother, and how personable she was to everyone she encountered. She could've been calling to dispute some billing mistake, or order a pizza, but she always asked the voice on the other end how they were doing, genuinely interested in the answer, and she insisted that it set the tone for the rest of the phone call. So, automatically, Jude asked the man how he was.

"Uh, fine," he grumbled. Then said nothing.

"Oh, well...good," Jude answered, looking again at Shiloh. She pulled the phone away from her face and covered the receiver with her hand. "Who am I talking to?"

"Elliott's dad," Shiloh whispered, pushing the phone back to Jude's face.

Jude rolled her eyes, but kept talking. "So, I think that Shiloh would like Elliott to come over for a little while tomorrow. Would that be okay with you?"

"Sure," the man answered with no inflection.

"Terrific," Jude said, not trying very hard to

disguise the annoyance in her voice. "Well, want to bring him by around ten or eleven?"

"Ten's fine," the voice answered.

Jude gave him the address and hung up the phone. "I hope Elliott has more personality than his dad," she told Shiloh, who was dancing around the kitchen excitedly.

"Oh, he does," she assured her. "Maybe we can go do something fun? Like go see a movie or get ice cream or something!"

Jude nodded and stood up from her seat at the kitchen table, promising to think about it.

Later that night after dinner, Shiloh and Jude put on *The Lion King* and laid on opposite ends of the couch with their legs entwined. They spent a lazy evening singing along to the soundtrack and trying to catch airborne popcorn kernels. When the movie ended, Shiloh decided to go upstairs and work on her puzzle. Jude was contemplating going to bed even though it was only nine. A solid night's sleep would do her good. Of course, it was as Jude was making her way upstairs that the phone rang. Ezra answered, and Jude paused half-way to her bed, hoping the call wasn't for her. Then, Ezra called for her to come to the kitchen.

"It's Christopher," said Ezra. "He said someone reported seeing something strange in town."

Jude took the phone and said hello.

"Hey Jude, sorry to bother you." Much like Jude's rehearsed *how are you* for phone conversations with strangers, Christopher always opened with this line. "I just wanted to let you know, I just saw Charlie at the filling station and he said he heard some kind of animal attack behind his dumpster. Said it was kind of loud and he thought he saw something big run off toward the country club."

"Huh," Jude said, half interested. "Did *you* see anything?" She sat down at the kitchen table and rested her elbows on top.

"No," he answered, almost disappointed. "It happened just before I got there,"

Jude glanced out the window. The glow that lingered where the sun had set was almost gone. Soon, Shiloh would be in bed and Ezra would be dissolved into her latest mystery novel. Friday evening, and the rest of her plans involved falling asleep to Andy Griffith reruns. But it was beautiful outside, a breezy sixty-five degrees, and if nothing else, a nice evening stroll sounded like a good way to end an otherwise uneventful day. It was unlikely that they would find anything of the demon variety lurking around in town, but it provided a sufficient excuse to go out for a while.

"Well, let me throw my shoes on and meet you at the country club," she said, already standing from the table.

Christopher sounded much too delighted. "Really?" he answered. "Great, I'll meet you there in ten minutes."

They hung up the phone and Jude laced up her sneakers, then went into the living room to tell

Ezra she was going out.

"I'm going on patrol. Won't be gone long I don't think."

Ezra nodded, looking up from her book. "Do you think there's something out there?"

Jude shrugged. "Better safe than sorry, right?"

"Is Christopher going too?"

"Mhm." Jude dodged eye contact by fixating on the zipper of her hoodie.

Ezra gave a slow nod of the head. "Alright. Well have fun."

Jude looked narrowly at Ezra. "It's not a party, Ez. Just going to follow up on a possible incident, that's all."

"Right, sure," Ezra answered, quickly returning her eyes to her book.

Jude wanted to respond, but honestly couldn't think of anything to say, so she settled for shooting her a look and moving for the stairs to tell Shiloh she was going out. She jogged up the steps, then through her room and closet door, up the attic stairs to Shiloh's room.

As usual, Jack was stretched out on her bed. The Christmas lights that she kept taped around the edges of the ceiling were plugged in, sending long beams of colored light down the walls. Shiloh was laying on her stomach on the floor using Herschel the Alligator as a pillow, working diligently on her puzzle.

"Wow, you're making a lot of progress," said Jude, stepping into the room.

Shiloh started the puzzle about three days before, and for a while there was nothing but pieces scattered all around. She had placed the box standing upward on its side in front of her and began meticulously sorting by color into piles. She had then separated out all of the edge pieces and finished the frame the day before. Now, little patches of incomplete images started to form in the center; a blob of navy sky, a patch of sea, the wet, shimmering back of an orca whale cresting in moonlight.

"Thanks," answered Shiloh, staring intently at a puzzle piece in her palm. "Wanna help?"

Jude knelt down beside her to get a better look. She picked up a piece and popped it into place. "I can't right now, I have to go out for a while."

Shiloh looked up, concerned.

"Everything's fine," Jude assured her. "Just making my rounds."

"Okay," Shiloh said, nodding and returning to her puzzle.

"We'll work on it some tomorrow, okay?"

"Sure," Shiloh answered. "What about the Codex?"

Jude only patrolled once a week. Twice, if some strange happening was making its rounds on the gossip mill, or if she just desperately needed some fresh air. It had become a standing appointment since the Moby incident to read a little from the Codex before bed on the nights that Jude stayed home. It was the only time they could both sit down and read together, uninterrupted. Plus,

Shiloh loved being read to before bedtime. Jude preferred the tradition when they were reading children's poetry and *Harry Potter*, but a deal was a deal.

Jude ran her hand through her daughter's tangled hair. "We'll read double tomorrow, okay?"

"Okay," Shiloh answered. "After Elliott leaves."

"After Elliott leaves," Jude confirmed. "You decide tonight what you want to do tomorrow, and we will do it. Ice cream, movie, you name it."

Shiloh smiled wide and nodded her head. Jude gave her a goodnight kiss and stood for the door. "Be good for Ezra."

"I will," Shiloh answered. "Be careful."

Jude smiled. "Love you."

"Love you, too." Shiloh answered.

Jude made her way back downstairs, said goodbye to Ezra, and drove to the country club to meet Christopher.

When she pulled up to the clubhouse the sky was dark and clear. Christopher was already there, leaning against his car under a street light, cleaning his glasses on his shirt.

He stood up when he saw her walking towards him.

"Sorry, it took me awhile to get out of the house." Jude started speaking a few feet before she reached him, then stopped beside him and looked out over the golf course. The filling station where Christopher had been tipped off about suspicious activity was just across the road. She looked out over the rolling green hills illuminated by light posts and spiked here and there with red flags and sand traps. It was a wide open space, so any movement would've stood out, but she saw nothing. Even the air was still.

"I haven't been here long," he answered. "So, shall we walk?"

She nodded and pulled a wooden stake out from her pocket, fairly certain she wouldn't be needing it, and the two of them set out over the green.

"So, did he describe this beast?" Jude asked skeptically.

"Oh, not really. Just that it sounded bigger than a cat or something."

She gave a slow nod and bit her lower lip. Lately, she'd responded to a lot of calls involving what turned out to be cats or dogs or raccoons. She felt more like an animal control officer than a demon hunter. They walked along the edge of the course, which was lined by trees where something could reasonably be hiding out.

"So, how's Shiloh?" Christopher asked, even though he'd seen her just that afternoon at school. "I saw that she made friends with Elliott Todesco."

"Oh, yeah," Jude answered, spinning the stake between her fingers. "He's actually coming over to play tomorrow."

"Great," said Chris. "He's a sweet kid. He and his brother just got placed with their uncle."

"Oh, really?" Jude asked, furrowing her brow. "I spoke with his dad on the phone."

He shook his head. "Nah, must've been his uncle. Their dad isn't in the picture. They live with their mom's brother."

Jude's footsteps slowed as she thought back to her brief phone conversation with *someone* associated with Elliott.

Christopher noticed her lagging and paused. "I'm sure he just said he was their dad so he didn't have to get into their life story. Things are pretty complicated. From what I understand, they're finally in a good place."

Jude nodded. "Yeah, you're probably right." She let it go, chalking it up to her usual paranoia and picked up the pace again. "Do you happen to know his name?"

"Walter, I think. Walter Murdoch. Anyway," Chris continued. "It's good she's got a friend. It's good for both of them."

"Yeah, it is."

"I actually just applied for a new job at the school. There's a spot open for a history teacher. Father Mitchell is running out of reasons to keep me on as his assistant, but I'd like to stay put. It's good that one of us can be there with her to make sure nothing goes awry."

"That's great," answered Jude genuinely. "If you weren't there, honestly I'd probably pull her out and homeschool her. I just want her to have the chance at a social life."

"Well, my chances are pretty good for the job," he told her. "I'm already well-liked by the staff, and I'm not totally unqualified."

"You'd be a great fit," she said, absently looking at the night sky and having completely abandoned the hope of finding anything lurking.

"Well, it seems like this might be a bust," he finally admitted, after they'd meandered across the entire grounds. "It probably *was* just a cat."

She laughed weakly. "I guess that's a good thing, right?"

He shrugged. "You seemed to be hoping for more."

They slowly turned and began the long walk back to the clubhouse and their respective vehicles. "Well, I've felt a little useless lately," she said laughing. "But believe me, I don't want or need any trouble. Shiloh is doing really great. Making friends, being a normal, happy kid. And she's reading the Codex and understanding a little more. Which is good for me in a way, because I've always felt horrible guilt for lying to her."

"Does she know about..." his voice trailed off, and Jude was already shaking her head.

"No, not yet."

"You don't think she's ready?"

Jude took a deep breath and tucked a loose strand of hair behind her ear. "I don't know if she's ready. I know I'm not."

"I don't blame you."

"And she's finally sleeping through the night. No more nightmares."

"And you?" he asked.

"Well," she paused. "I've always been an insomniac."

"The ten gallons of coffee you drink a day probably doesn't help."

She laughed and playfully smacked his arm with the back of her hand. "Believe me, it helps. It keeps me alive." She took a deep breath and her voice dropped. "I dunno, I just keep making excuses. I don't even know how I could tell her. It's not even something that I can think about without totally melting down."

He offered a comforting touch on her shoulder. "You'll both get there. Don't question your decisions. You're an awesome mom, and she knows that."

Jude tried to relax and gave him a half smile as they reached the parking lot.

"Sorry to drag you out here for nothing," Christopher lamented as they stood between their cars.

"Oh, it was fine. I wanted to get out anyway," she admitted.

There was a moment of pause. Christopher looked down at his shoes where he was digging his toe into the gravel.

"Chris?" she asked, dropping her head to meet his eyes. "What's up?"

He looked back up at her slowly, seemingly

nervous. "So, I have to go to this thing tomorrow night," he said finally.

She waited in confusion for more and noted a distinct tension that had suddenly pricked the inside of her chest.

"And," he continued. "I was wondering if you wanted to maybe go with me." His hands were so far in his pockets that if it weren't for his belt, his pants would've been on the ground.

Her eyes widened and she stiffened, surprised by his invitation. "Are you asking me out on a date?" she clarified.

He cleared his throat. "Yeah, actually. Is that, uh…"

She could see that he was suffering. "What is this thing you have to go to?"

"It's a gala for the historical society. They want me to present Father Mitchell with an award."

"Fancy."

"Yeah, I don't know why they chose me," he said, shaking his head.

"Well, you are well liked around here, Mr. Alighieri."

"I dunno, it's stupid. You can say no, I won't be hurt by it. I don't know why I asked. I don't even want to go to this thing. It's just that they gave me two seats, and I kind of got the impression that I was expected to fill both of them."

"Misery loves company," she said, laughing at the quick pace of his voice.

He looked at her hopefully, even though he'd

just let her off the hook.

She thought about it. Crossed her arms over her chest and narrowed her gaze at him. She knew that she should be saying no, although she couldn't really identify the reason. She had been fighting this possibility for so long that it just came as second nature, and she couldn't remember the long list of excuses that she had convinced herself were reasons to remain uninvolved. Truthfully, she wanted to say yes. Ezra had called yet another play. That girl really was always right.

"A gala, huh?" she said, uncrossing her arms. The surrender was clear in her voice and he perked up a little bit.

"Yeah, now I know it sounds a little stiff, but I think it could be fun. There will be music and dinner." He looked hard at her and smiled. "What do you say?"

She inhaled slowly and let it out in a quick breath. "Sure, I'll go with you."

His smile was unconcealable and he nodded in satisfaction. "Great, can I pick you up at six?"

"Yeah," she answered, pretending to have just lost a battle and trying to disguise the fact that even she was blushing just a little. "Six is fine."

They said goodnight and turned for their cars, but just as Jude was about to climb in, she stopped and turned back to him.

"Christopher," she called over the hood of his sedan.

He looked back at her expectantly.

"Did you even go to the filling station to-night?"

For a moment, he held her gaze and the corners of his mouth perked up into a boyish grin. "Goodnight, Jude," he answered and climbed into his car.

CHAPTER 5

At 9:30 the next morning, Shiloh was up, dressed, and waiting by the door for Elliott to arrive. She had already pulled out a pile of games and all of her stuffed animals were seated on the couch. Jude was halfway through her second cup of coffee and Ezra, who had the day off, was in the kitchen making breakfast.

"So, how was patrol last night?" she asked, flipping a peanut butter chocolate chip pancake, Shiloh's favorite, at the stove.

Jude glanced at Ezra without turning her head, then looked quickly back at her coffee cup. "Oh, it was fine. Uneventful."

"Huh," Ezra chirped. "You were gone for awhile. I thought maybe you found something."

"Nope," Jude said as casually as possible.

Ezra turned around and leaned back on the edge of the counter, spatula in hand. "Jude?"

She sighed and dropped her head into the crook of her arm on the table. "Christopher asked me out," she grumbled into her sleeve.

"What's that?" Ezra asked, and Jude could

hear the smile on her face.

She lifted her head slightly. "He asked me out."

"On a date?"

"Mhm," Jude groaned.

It wasn't necessarily that she was regretting saying yes. But she'd had a night to sleep on it and the bullet points on that list, the ones she had forgotten the night before, were all starting to come back to her.

Ezra had been standing quietly at the counter for a minute, and Jude turned her head slowly to look at her. She shot her a tired, irritated look that meant she didn't want to hear it, and Ezra laughed.

"I'm not saying a word," Ezra promised, turning back to her pancakes.

Jude put her head back down and let out a whimper. "I have to figure out what I'm going to wear."

"You're going?" Ezra responded with so much enthusiasm that she almost flung a pancake across the kitchen.

"Mom, Mom!" Shiloh yelled from the living room. "He's pulling into the driveway!"

Jude, eager to be elsewhere, threw back the rest of her coffee like a shot of hot whiskey and hurried to the living room. A station wagon was half way down their long driveway, and Shiloh was moving for the porch. A smile crept across Jude's face when she saw Shiloh's excitement. She had so few friends, and the numbers were only likely to drop as her life became more and more complicated. She laughed when Shiloh bounded out the front door.

"Don't attack the boy," Jude said laughing, standing in the doorway.

The car stopped and Jude was about to make her way toward it to say hello to Elliott's uncle, but before she even made it across the porch, Elliott was out of the car and the driver was backing down the driveway.

"What a strange family," Jude mumbled quietly as she watched the car back all the way out to the road and speed off. Her attention quickly moved to Elliott, who climbed the porch stairs with both hands on his backpack straps, already talking to Shiloh about plans for the day.

"Hi, Elliott," said Jude, taking his backpack and ushering both kids into the house.

"Hi, Ms. Mikhale. Thanks for letting me come over today," he answered sweetly.

She smiled and brushed off the *Ms. Mikhale* accusation. "Well, we're glad to have you."

Shiloh led him into the kitchen where Ezra had breakfast laid out on the table. She stacked two plates high with pancakes and slathered them in syrup, and poured them both glasses of orange juice. Shiloh dug in, and after some coaxing, Elliott warmed up and started in on his pancakes.

Once he started eating, Jude realized for the first time how small he was. It was normal, she thought, for boys to be smaller than girls. They hit their growth spurts a little later, usually. But he was very skinny, with his pants too big around the waist and tiny wrists that even Shiloh's little hands could have easily wrapped around. When he cleared his plate, Jude quickly refilled it with pancakes and he thanked her, telling Ezra that he had never had something so delicious.

Jude sat down at the table. "So, Elliott, are you in Shiloh's class?"

He nodded, swallowing a big bite. "Yes, we sit next to each other."

"Oh, that's nice," Jude answered. Ezra poured herself a cup of coffee and joined them. "When did you start at St. Mary's?"

"Last month, when we moved here."

"Where did you move from?"

"The Eastern Shore," the boy answered. "My Uncle Walt lives here. We live with him."

"Oh," Jude answered, trying to weigh how many questions were too many. He didn't seem to notice.

"What does your uncle do?" Jude asked, refilling his glass with orange juice.

Elliott looked down at his plate and shifted in his seat. "Um, I don't really know. He's busy a lot," he answered.

Shiloh finished the last few bites of pancake left on her plate and poked Elliott on the shoulder. "Wanna go play?" she asked eagerly.

He ate another bite and put his fork down onto the plate. "Sure," he said, hopping down from the chair. "Thanks for breakfast!" He and Shiloh ran into the living room and Jude listened for a minute as they giggled and talked and dumped a box of Lego bricks onto the living room floor.

"He's really cute," said Ezra, clearing the plates.

Jude smiled. "Yeah, he is. And sweet." She picked the glasses up from the table. "Do you think he's like, freakishly skinny?"

Ezra leaned to the side and peeked into the living room where the kids were playing. "Nah," she said, shaking her head and scrubbing the plates down in the sink. "He's probably just an active little boy. A lot of kids are scrawny around that age."

"Yeah, you're probably right," Jude agreed.

* * *

After lunch, Shiloh and Elliott wanted to play outside. Shiloh called for Jack, who came bounding down from her room, eager to get out the door. Jude followed them out as far as the porch, and sat on the swing to read while they ran out into the yard.

Shiloh pulled her bicycle and scooter out of the old wooden shed by the garden, and asked Elliot which one he'd like to ride. Elliott chose the scooter, and Shiloh led him toward the back field.

Christopher had carved a long, winding path through the tall field grass so that Shiloh could walk and bike and wander. When she was back there, only the top of her head stuck out above the grass, and she felt like she was in a jungle, or some faraway place. They pulled the bike and scooter to the start of the path, and took a spin around so Elliot could learn the trails, with Jack galloping behind them. All the while, they talked about school and movies and the things they liked to do.

Shiloh had never really had a friend before. She liked Elliott. They liked a lot of the same things, and he didn't make her feel nervous or weird like some kids did. He was kind of quiet, and he had a lot of good ideas, like building castles out of sticks and leaves, and pretending they were explorers dis-covering the New World, and having a race, which is precisely what they decided to do once they reached the end of the trail.

"Whoever makes it to the yard first is the winner," said Shiloh with one foot on the pedal.

Elliott agreed, and counted down from three. When he yelled out, "Go!" Shiloh lifted her other foot onto the pedal, and skidded off the starting line.

Elliott was trailing behind Shiloh as they neared a sharp bend on the path. Shiloh made it just fine, having done it before, but when she glanced back to check on Elliott, she didn't see him. She pulled the handlebar breaks hard and stopped. After leaping off of her bike, she ran back to check on him.

She found him sitting in the bend, scooter dumped over to the side, holding his leg.

"Are you okay?" She asked, reaching him and kneeling beside him.

He nodded, catching his breath and wincing

a little from pain. "I think so, I skinned my knee a little."

Shiloh pulled his hand away and saw the gash where his knee had driven into the rough cut grass and dirt. "It's bleeding," she told him. "It looks kinda bad." She swept little bits of dirt away from the cut and noticed that he was holding back tears. "You're gonna be fine," she promised him. "Hold on just a sec." She glanced back toward the house, and realized that she couldn't see it at all. They were below the grass, hidden away. She knew she didn't have long before her mom came looking for her. Quickly and without really thinking about it, she laid both of her hands on his leg, on either side of the wound. She closed her eyes tightly and tried to focus. The energy washed over her and quiet whispers began to fall from her lips. In a few seconds, she looked back at his knee, and the cut was healed, leaving only the faint hint of dried blood where it had been.

She caught her breath and steadied her spinning head, leaning back on her hands while Elliott just sat there, wide- eyed and staring. He inspected his injury, but it was as if it never happened.

"So it really is true," he said finally in a whisper.

Shiloh looked up at him.

"You healed me. You have super powers," said Elliott.

Shiloh felt her face go cold. She shook her head rapidly, already fearing the trouble she would be in if her mom found out. "No, no, they're not superpowers, I just-"

"My brother said you have super powers," El-liott interrupted. "I didn't believe him, but it's true. That was so cool!" He was still looking at his leg, running his hand over the place where the scrape had been.

Shiloh looked behind her toward the house again and didn't hear Jude coming, then whipped her head back around to Elliott. "Listen," she said, her voice rising. "You can't tell anyone. If my mom finds out I'll be in so much trouble. I'm not supposed to show people."

He nodded. "I know. Don't worry, I'll never tell."

He pinky-promised as Shiloh heard the back door clatter and Jude calling her name.

"Are you guys okay?" She yelled, as Shiloh stood up. She could see Jude walking rather quickly toward the field, with her book open in her hand.

"Yeah," Elliott answered first, standing to his feet. "I fell off the scooter, that's all," he told Jude, as she reached them.

"You're not hurt?"

He shook his head. "No, I'm fine."

Shiloh tried not to look guilty as her mom looked her over.

"Shi, you alright?" she asked.

"Yeah, I'm fine," Shiloh answered, noticing that her voice sounded too high.

"Okay, very good," Jude replied. "You guys have to be careful on these trails, the ground is uneven."

"Yes, ma'am," Elliott answered.

"I think we'll do something else now," Shiloh said, her voice still shaking slightly. "Come on Elliott, let's play on the swing."

He agreed and they returned the bike and scooter to the shed and ran to Shiloh's tire swing.

Elliot, once Jude had gone back to the porch, was not interested in playing on the tire swing, but instead had a million questions.

"What other things can you do?"

"Can you bring someone back to life?"

"Can you make things levitate or move on their own?"

"Do you use your powers for good or evil?"

"Can you teach me?"

Shiloh tried to deflect them all, attempting to steer the conversation toward other things. Finally, Elliott got the message that she did not want to talk about it, and he gave up. They played outside for a little while longer, then Jude took them to see an early movie. Shiloh felt strange and uneasy, and couldn't relax or enjoy the story at all. Her belly felt too fluttery for popcorn. She sat right between her mom and her friend, and didn't want to look either of them in the eye. She didn't dare ask Elliott, but she burned with the desire to know how he knew about her. Why did she heal him? He wasn't hurt badly, a band-aid would've been all he needed. It was such a stupid idea. Now, she had to deal with feeling guilty, and weird about her one and only friend.

Elliott went home after the movie. He left in pretty much the same way he arrived. A car pulled up the driveway, but didn't come all the way to the house. Elliott ran out the door and jumped in, and the car backed out. Shiloh was relieved to see him go.

CHAPTER 6

Christopher was coming to pick her up for the gala at six o'clock, and Jude had spent most of her day trying not to think about it. Entertaining Shiloh and Elliott had been an effective distraction, but now Shiloh was sitting on the couch watching television and the clock was ticking down quickly. She made Shiloh a grilled cheese for dinner, then went upstairs to face what was quite possibly the aspect of dating that she hated most: dressing for the occasion.

There was a point in her life where she thought of herself as having some kind of style. Certainly not one that kept apprised of the latest magazine trends, but a style that was uniquely her own and not altogether unfashionable. For the last eight years, however, her wardrobe was almost exclusively functional; yoga pants and soft, worn in blue jeans, band t-shirts and flannel and maybe three tops that she felt were reasonable options for formal occasions like a job interview or professional outing. Fortunately, her profession did not require such professional attire, and they mostly stayed hanging in the back corner of her closet.

She dug through the half-dozen hooded sweatshirts that she owned in search of anything that would pass for a historical society gala, knowing all the while that she wouldn't find anything. There were a few articles of clothing that she wished she could get back from her college apartment. One in particular was a red cocktail dress that she wore to dance recitals and events in the short time that she attended NYU. Out of luck and suddenly tingling with anxiety, she sat down on the floor of her closet, in front of the full-length mirror that hung on the inside of the door, and mourned the loss of her red dress.

"Hey Jude, do you have any idea where I put my book?" Ezra asked, speaking before she fully stepped into the room. "I swear, I left it on the coffee table, but it's…" her voice trailed when she saw Jude's foot sticking out of the closet door. "Jude?" she asked, laughing slightly. "What are you doing?"

By this point, Jude was simply laying on the closet floor. "I think I'm going to cancel," she said flatly, with both hands resting on her abdomen and her eyes staring upward at the ceiling.

"No," Ezra said emphatically. "No, you are not. What's the problem?"

Jude sat up slowly, tossed her messy hair back behind her and pulled her knees up to her chest. "I remembered something about myself. I'm not especially good at this."

Usually her self-confidence hinged on brazen, and she never let on to any kind of weakness. But she knew Ezra knew the truth. She was a spaz.

Ezra stuck out her hand and Jude reluctantly let herself be yanked up off the floor. "I really don't think there's anything you have to be *good* at," Ezra reasoned. "He knows who you are, and he likes it. This is just a formality."

"I don't like formalities."

"Oh, now you're just being difficult. You have less than an hour, what are you going to wear?"

Jude looked at her with one eyebrow raised and released a notable sigh.

"Let's go," she said, tugging on Jude's arm. Ezra pulled her into her room across the hall. "Here," she said, opening her closet. Ezra always managed to look good, even when engaged in physical combat. They were about the same size, though Ezra was a little taller. She rifled through a bunch of hangers until she pulled out something from the back, and held it up in front of Jude. "Perfect," she said with a brisk nod.

"Oh, I don't know, that looks expensive."

"Yeah, it's a fancy event, right? Featuring Bedford's social elite? The last remaining vestiges of the Old South. I picture... tall champagne flutes and crystal chandeliers." She was already pulling the dress off the hangar and ushering Jude back to her room.

"I guess. Are you sure? What if I spill wine or... blood on it or something?"

Ezra looked at her skeptically. "I'll tell ya

what," she said finally. "I don't think you'll encounter yours or anyone else's blood at the historical society gala, but if you do, I will not be mad." She laughed slightly. "Where am I going to wear this? I don't even know why I still have it. I just always thought it might come in handy, and now it has." The next thing she knew, Jude was being shoved into Ezra's closet to change, while Ezra sat on the edge of her bed, waiting.

When Jude emerged, Ezra smiled, satisfied. "I knew it," she said standing up to help zip up the back.

Jude inspected herself in the mirror. It really was a beautiful dress; an elegant navy blue, with wide shoulder straps, a reasonable v-shaped neckline and fitted to the waist, where it made a gentle and thin A-line to the floor. Though she didn't quite fill out the top, it hung nicely off of her narrow hips and the fabric had a graceful sway when she walked. She thanked Ezra, and dug out the one pair of heels that she owned, but kept buried deep behind boxes and junk in her closet.

She left her hair down, wore just enough makeup to indicate that she was wearing any at all, unearthed her only pair of dangly gold earrings from the bottom of her jewelry box, and decided that it would have to work. On her way out of her bedroom, she spotted the small box that she kept on her mantelpiece. It was full of knick-knacks and sentimental things she'd managed to hold on to, and one of those sacred items was a mostly empty bottle of her mother's perfume. It smelled like sunflowers, and Jude never used it. Sometimes she took the bottle out of the box to admire the etching and glass work, and to catch a whiff of her mother, but she almost never put her finger on the spritzer.

Trying not to over think it, she sprayed the aged liquid twice into the air in front of her, and stepped through.

At 5:45, she made her way downstairs to wait for Christopher to show up. It had been a lifetime since she'd worn anything other than tennis shoes and sandals on her feet, and as she stepped down from the final step, the slender heel landed slightly sideways, and Jude stumbled, grabbing the banister for stabilization.

Of course, the racket of her imbalance caught the attention of Shiloh, who had been watching television on the couch.

"Whoa," she said, in a shocked, low voice. She clicked off the television and straightened up. "What are you all dressed up for? You look like a movie star."

"Doesn't she look awesome?" Ezra called from the kitchen.

"Uh," Jude stammered. "I just have a thing to go to." She bit her lip, knowing Shiloh would not be satisfied with that answer.

"A *thing* with Christopher?" she asked, the corner of her mouth popping into a grin.

Jude went expressionless and wide-eyed.

Shiloh giggled. "I pay more attention than

you seem to think."

"Well, look, it's just a dinner thing. Not a big deal."

She could hear Ezra snickering from the other room as she awkwardly smoothed the dress over her hips.

"Right," Shiloh answered, rolling her eyes just slightly.

Jude exhaled and ran her hand through her hair as she nervously waited for Christopher to show up. It had been a very, very long time since she'd been in this position. Really, she didn't know if she'd ever been on a *date* in the traditional sense. In college, she became well acquainted with one particular fraternity. She had what she called a boyfriend in high school, but all they ever did was go to the movies, sit in the back and make out. She didn't even like the word "date". She didn't like the connotations, or the way it felt stiff on her tongue, and she definitely didn't like the pressure.

Finally, Christopher pulled up to the driveway. When she saw the car coming, she said goodbye to Shiloh and Ezra and made her way to meet him. As she was walking carefully down the front steps, desperate not to wipe out in front of him, he was coming up the walk. They met awkwardly between the house and the driveway.

Christopher was clearly impressed, which gave Jude a small sense of satisfaction. "Wow, you look great."

She smiled. "Thanks," she answered. "You do too."

He was dressed in a nicely fitted black suit, with a whimsical yellow tie and yellow handkerchief sticking out of his breast pocket. His black shoes looked new and caught the glint of the evening sunlight, and he had apparently combed his usually messy, curly hair. It looked fairly effortless for him, which Jude found to be just a little annoying. He smiled wide, trying to conceal his excitement as she let him walk her to the car, open her door, and close it behind her.

The sky was dark orange over the mountains as they drove into town with the windows down. When they pulled up, a teenage boy in an ill-fitted suit opened Jude's door, and then took the keys and parked Christopher's car. The gala was being held in an old plantation home called Tanglewood, owned by the historical society. At one time it housed a very wealthy tobacco farmer and served briefly as a Civil War hospital. Now, it was used for weddings and social functions.

It was a stunning federal style brick mansion with a double porch and stately pillars in the front. A long sidewalk led up the steps and to the heavy, polished wooden doors, where a greeter stood and ushered guests inside. Christopher handed him his tickets and the man welcomed them inside to reveal a sight that Jude had only seen replicated in movies.

The great room was beautiful on its own,

with high vaulted ceilings and big chandeliers, and a grand staircase that curved up to a landing above. At the far side of the room, a three-piece brass band stood and played in front of a deep stone fireplace. The fireplace was unlit, and instead had been filled with red and orange flowers. Jude couldn't help but laugh and think of Ezra when she noticed the dangling chandeliers and the long, polished bar topped with glistening champagne flutes. A podium was set up on a small platform near the bar, and the whole room was lit with white string lights.

Christopher offered his arm and, feeling as though it was the proper thing to do at an event such as this, Jude placed her hand around it, laughing a little as they moved further inside.

"Well, Christopher, it's such a delight to see you here. And with such a beautiful young woman." The voice was heard before it was seen, but Jude knew immediately who it was coming from. "Gracious, don't you two clean up nice." Doris Overstreet grabbed both of them by the hands and leaned in too close. "And you make a handsome couple."

She winked at Jude, who just stood there, searching for a response. She started to speak, but decided quickly just to close it and keep quiet when she inhaled a powerful breath of Doris's perfume, strong enough to make her eyes water.

Christopher laughed and patted her on the shoulder, trying to wriggle his arm free of her grip. "Well, you look very nice yourself, Mrs. Doris."

"Oh, you're too sweet. Now, you kids have a good time." As she walked away, Jude shot Christopher an exasperated look. Just when they thought they were in the clear, Doris turned back around, forcing them to look alive once more. "I'm just delighted that you two are getting on so nicely." She clapped her hands in front of her face to emphasize the over-the-top gushing. "I like to think I have something to do with it." She gave them both a wink, laughed a little too hard, then turned for good, forcing her way back through the crowd and jabbering with people as she went.

Jude let out a sharp exhale. "She's exhausting," she whispered to Christopher as they recovered and continued moving.

CHAPTER 7

Shiloh and Ezra were playing a card game when the phone rang. Ezra went to answer it but called Shiloh into the kitchen moments later.

"It's for you," she said, handing over the phone.

Shiloh took it and sat down at the kitchen table, holding the phone with both hands. "Hello?"

"Hi," answered Elliott on the other line. "It's Elliott. Are you busy?"

"No," she answered. At the sound of his voice, all the anxiety that she'd managed to overcome from the afternoon's events came swelling back.

"Are you alone?"

It seemed like a strange question for him to be asking, but she looked across the room at Ezra, who was putting dishes in the sink. "No, I'm not," she answered slowly.

"Can you go someplace and be alone?" He asked. "There's something I need to tell you."

"Uh, sure." She stood from the chair with a weird gurgling sensation in her stomach. "I'll be in my room," she told Ezra, then hurried up the stairs.

Once in Jude's room, she closed the closet/her bedroom door behind her and climbed the last flight to her own bedroom. "Okay, I'm alone now," she told Elliott. "What's up?"

"My brother Caleb is here," he said in a low voice. "There's something important that you need to know."

She waited silently, sitting on her bed and leaning into the phone.

There was some static on the line. "Listen, you're not safe," said a grumbly and unfamiliar voice on the other line.

Shiloh recoiled. "What? What do you mean?"

"I mean, you're not safe at home. You know who you are, right?"

She wondered how Elliott's brother knew about her, but had not gotten the chance, or had been too afraid, to ask. "Yeah," she answered. "Of course I do. How do you?" Nervously, she got up and checked that the door below was still closed, and that she didn't hear anyone coming up the stairs.

"I can't explain all of that right now," said Caleb. "But you need to know the truth."

"What truth?" She was pacing.

"The truth that you're going to die."

She inhaled sharply and the tiny hairs on her arms and neck stood up stiff. "What are you talking about?" she asked, as it felt like the heat drained from her body.

Caleb paused. "You're not going to make it past eighteen," he said, his voice quickening. "I know you think your mom, if that's what you call her, is watching out for you, but she's counting on your death. Everyone is."

Shiloh shook her head. She couldn't even process what he was saying. "That's not true," she said with quiet anger in her voice. "My mom would never let anything hurt me."

"She's lying to you, Shiloh. She's not telling you the truth."

"No, it's not possible," she insisted. "You don't know what you're talking about."

"It's true," said Elliott. "Just let him prove it."

Caleb came back on the line. "There's a book, right? That you read with her?"

Shiloh swallowed a lump in her throat. "How do you know about—"

"Do you know where it is?" Caleb interrupted.

Shiloh hesitated. "No, my mom keeps it in a safe place."

"Do you think you can find it?"

"Y-yeah. I'm not supposed to, but—"

"Find it, and meet us outside your house tomorrow night. At midnight."

Shiloh agreed numbly and hung up the phone.

* * *

At the gala, Christopher and Jude walked around and mingled with the crowd. Jude was terrible at small talk and had no interest in it, but there was no escape. She was in a room loaded with people who were all looking for mindless chatter and an easy, good time. Christopher, for all of his awkward nervousness, was remarkably good at crowd-pleasing and pleasantries. He was charming and light on his feet, and he stood in a casual posture, jabbering about sports games and laughing with ease at bad jokes made by stuffy town councilmen and board members. The whole time, Jude stood awkwardly at his side, her laugh too stiff and her input too unnatural. She was obsessively preoccupied with the state of her arms and couldn't shake the feeling that no matter what she did with them, they were gangly and strange, so she kept moving them from front to back, clasping and unclasping her hands. Aware of her discomfort, Christopher occasionally grinned in her direction or put his hand on her back. But, eventually the inevitable that Jude had been fearing all night happened, and Christopher stepped away for a moment to get them both a glass of champagne, leaving her vulnerable to face tipsy small-talkers alone.

"Jude!" Dr. Hubbard from the Acadia Museum called out. "What a pleasure to see you! How's Shiloh?"

"Oh, she's fine," Jude answered. "Doing well at school and looking forward to summer. Only one week left."

"Perfect," he responded, as Becky Pittman, head librarian, stepped up to join the conversation.

"It's nice to see you out and about, Jude,"

said Becky. "You know, we don't see enough of you. What do you keep so busy with?"

Jude's palms began to sweat as she glanced around looking for Christopher, who had gotten trapped in a conversation with someone from the school by the bar. He shot her an apologetic look and she turned back to her company with a tight lipped smile.

"Oh, ya know," she answered. "Shiloh keeps me pretty busy."

"But she's in school during the day, right?" asked Becky.

"Do you work out of town?" asked Becky's husband, with a half-masticated mushroom cap in his mouth.

She shook her head. "Well, no-"

"She's quite mysterious," chimed Dr. Hubbard, taking a step closer. She always got a strange vibe from him.

"I've seen you walking in the graveyard," said Becky. "That's an interesting pastime. Strange, but interesting."

Jude could barely breathe and suddenly her dress felt way too tight and her heels felt way too high and she felt completely out of place. "Yeah, I uh..." she stammered as they awaited her answer. Just as she was about to pass out or run away, Christopher stepped up to the group with a snap.

"Evening," he said politely, but loudly, diverting all of the attention to himself. He handed her one of the two glasses of champagne that he carried and did that move that Jude always loved in movies, where he swiped the right side of his suit coat aside and slipped his hand into his pants pocket. "Sorry to interrupt, but," he looked at Jude's red face and darty eyes, "do you want to dance?"

She would've done anything to get away from them so she eagerly agreed. As he led her toward the dance floor, she swallowed her entire glass of champagne in one gulp, and set it on an empty tray as it passed by in the arms of a caterer.

"Want to finish mine too?" Christopher whispered, laughing.

"Oh, no. That's okay," she answered.

"Sorry I got caught up," he told her as they stepped onto the wood floor in front of the band. The music was elegant, classical, played by a string ensemble. He took her right hand in his and she placed her left on his shoulder, noticing the shape of it under the stiff coat. This was much closer than they typically were, outside of the context of brief hugs and the few occasions where one of them had to pick the other up in a fight. She liked him in this context. He was warm, and smelled good, like the forest after it rains, and he was oddly confident and casual as he swayed along the dance floor.

"I forget sometimes that you're a dancer," he said smiling, with his face only a few inches from her ear. "I should warn you that I am not so good myself."

"*Was* a dancer," she corrected.

"Well, it must be something like riding a

bike, right? You don't ever forget."

He wasn't wrong. It felt nice to move and flow, with her whole body aware of itself without the pressure of some kind of battle. It felt nice, too, to have someone moving and flowing with her; to feel the crisp fold of a suit lapel under her hand, and to have an arm above her waist and warm eyes looking back. She was fighting the urge to fall naturally closer to him, resting her head on his shoulder, and it was a losing fight, until someone announced that dinner was being served.

As Jude pulled away, Christopher cleared his throat anxiously and looked down at his shoes, stuffing his hands into his pockets. "Let's find our seats, shall we?" he asked, looking up again.

They made their way to their little folded name tags at Table Six, and Christopher made a big show of pulling out her chair. They shared a laugh and settled in for dinner. Everything was going surprisingly well. So well, in fact, that Jude barely noticed when someone shrieked from across the room.

It was the rising volume in the room that finally drew her attention toward the commotion, and when she looked behind her to see what was up, she noticed a crowd gathered around a window. They were all pointing and gaping at something they saw outside. They sounded shocked and horrified as more and more people ran to the window. Jude looked regretfully at Chris, then stood from her seat to see for herself.

She had to crane her neck to see over the throngs of socialites who were now all at the window, clutching half empty champagne flutes. Barely over their heads, she could make out the disfigured body of what appeared to be a sleeper skulking around in the yard.

Christopher, who stood behind her, instantly began damage control. "Looks like an animal," he said, drawing the attention of only a few spectators. Jude looked at him with skepticism and he shrugged, improvising the best he could. Luckily, the sky had almost completely surrendered to night, and the darkness and bushes outside obscured the details of the creature.

She waited until it was almost out of sight around the corner of the building, and people were talking about calling the police and animal control, before she slipped quietly out the back door to find it. In her purse, she carried a stake and a few other essentials on the same theme, but had forgotten to grab it before she ran out of the gala. She would have to make do without it, and crept up behind the thing as it lumbered towards the center of town. After sinking three inches into the soft grass with each step. She unbuckled her high-heeled shoes, and left them behind. She knew people had gathered on the front porch of Tanglewood. She could hear their rising concerns, but she did her best to keep to the shadows, and the sleeper made it easy enough. She was hoping to follow it a little farther, where there was no chance of being seen, but she didn't get the opportunity. As she did her best to stay quiet and close behind, something—a twig—snapped beneath her foot. The sound was unmistakable and the creature turned toward it, showing its gnarled teeth in the pale moonlight.

While she stood, knees bent and ready to engage on the grass, she prayed silently that Christopher had convinced the crowd to go back inside and continue dancing and milling around as they had been before. She didn't have any time to glance behind and check though. The creature lunged at her while she was still scanning the ground for a suitable weapon.

It lurched in the typical sloppy, unskilled manner of newly risen sleepers, throwing both arms out toward her head and clawing aimlessly. She ducked below them and pushed it over from behind, allowing its own forward leaning weight to do most of the work. The sleeper hit the grass face first and Jude pounced on it while it was down, grabbing its wrists and yanking its arms backwards. It bucked and snarled, hacking thick mucusy saliva onto the ground. As always, it smelled horrible, like decaying flesh, and it's skin was papery and mangled. She did her best to pin it down and ran her hand over the turf around her in search of a rock or a stick, but found nothing. It was fighting back hard, and she could feel that she was losing ground. Unable to dig her knees in because of her dress, she was slipping and the creature was wriggling free.

Finally, it managed to thrust her off of its

back, and she landed hard on her hip about a foot away. It leapt up onto its feet with renewed ferocity, and as it leaned over to dig its claws into her exposed shoulders, she kicked as hard as she could at its abdomen, sending it flying. Once again, she was standing and it was squirming, trying to regain balance.

"Ezra is going to kill me," she mumbled. She grabbed the fabric of the evening gown at the knee, and in one swift yank, she ripped a long slit into the dress, allowing her legs to bend more freely. Still without a weapon, she roundhouse kicked the sleeper in the head and it stumbled for a second. She took the opportunity to throw a few punches, but it was not enough. She approached the sleeper and locked arms with it, grappling in the cool evening, in a much-too-public place. She wrestled it back against a tree and slammed its body against the trunk three times, hoping to weaken it as it snapped at her neck and sunk it's nails deeper into the flesh of her forearm.

Out of the corner of her eye, she saw Christopher running toward her, carrying her purse.

"Here," he said, out of breath as he offered her the stake and grabbed the sleeper from behind, pulling back it's shoulders and exposing his chest, giving Jude a wide open target. She gripped the stake and pulled her arm back like she was going to throw a punch. She thrust forward and plunged the sharpened wood directly into the creature's heart. It gasped. Its eyes widened, and then shut, and it fell to the ground, turning to dust on impact.

Jude clapped her hands together in finality and looked down at herself; dress torn and covered in dirt and grass stains.

Christopher pulled a leaf from her hair, then rested his hand on her back. "You're okay?" he asked.

"Fine," she answered. "He was surprisingly spry, I'll admit that much." Looking back toward Tanglewood, it appeared that no one had followed them out of the building. She looked at him apologetically. "This wasn't exactly part of the plan."

He shrugged. "Don't worry about it. It's your job, and it's more important than some stupid gala."

"Yeah, well," she mumbled. "Still, now I'm a mess and our date is all screwed up-"

"So it is a date?" A big smile spread across his face.

She shuffled her feet and stammered and he laughed. "Let me take you home," he said sympathetically as she examined a minor scratch on her arm. "You can get cleaned up and we can go grab a nice dinner and maybe a movie someplace else. You haven't had anything to eat, you must be starving. The night is still young."

She was starving. She was always ravenous after a fight. He began to lead her away, but she stopped. "Wait, aren't you supposed to give a speech?"

"Yeah, but it's fine, they'll get on without me."

"You're presenting an award."

He waved his hand through the air. "Really, it's fine."

"No," she answered, suddenly very self-conscious about her ripped dress and frazzled hair and generally disheveled appearance. "You should stay. Make your presentation. I'll call Ezra, she can come pick me up."

Christopher cocked his head and gave her a reluctant look and she knew he was going to protest.

"Please," she said quietly, taking a step toward him and putting her hand on his upper arm. "They're expecting you. Ezra can be here in ten minutes. Besides, I'm actually pretty sore, so I'm probably just going to crash when I get home. There's no reason for your Saturday night to end so early. Please."

She wasn't really sore at all, but she *was* frustrated and no longer in the mood to be out and charming.

He sighed. "Are you sure? It's really no problem, I can just take you home and we can reschedule."

She offered him a soft smile. "I'm positive." Jude pulled her phone from her purse and started dialing Ezra. "I'll be fine. Please, go enjoy your dinner. Tell everyone that I had to leave because Shiloh got sick. That way they don't think I stood you up."

He laughed a little and nodded in agreement and defeat. "Fine, but I'm going to wait with you until Ezra gets here," he said, stuffing his hands back into his pockets as Jude pressed the phone to her ear.

Ezra answered and Jude briefly explained the situation. "She's on her way," she told Christopher as she put her phone away and they both sat down on a bench by the street.

Sitting down, Jude realized she actually was a little tired. Her shoulders were tight and the cuts and scrapes she had collected were stinging a little. He put his arm around her and they sat quietly and awkwardly under a flickering street lamp until Ezra pulled up in her car.

Ezra let out a weak sigh when she saw Jude in the tattered dress.

"I'm sorry," Jude said through the window. She turned back to Christopher who was standing behind her.

"So, we'll try again?" He asked, hopeful.

She nodded, half-heartedly. "Yeah, of course."

He squeezed her wrist, waved to Ezra, then turned back toward Tanglewood. Jude climbed into the car and they headed for home.

As soon as she was seated and the car started to pull away from the curb, Jude groaned loudly and threw her head back onto the seat. "Ezra, this was a ridiculous idea."

"How?" She asked, defensively. "This was a freak accident. You've hardly seen anything in weeks. How could you ever have predicted this? It is not some omen, predicting your entire romantic future, Jude. It was just an unfortunate coincidence."

Jude laughed sharply, the short sound dripping with disbelief. "There are no coincidences."

"There are."

Jude turned around to the back seat where Shiloh sat, looking confused and distressed. "Everything's okay," she told her. "I just fell and ripped my dress." Jude continued, obviously lying and hardly trying to conceal it.

Ezra made a face at the terrible explanation, but Jude ignored it.

"You fell?" Shiloh asked. "Outside?"

"Mhm," Jude answered after a brief hesitation. "Anyway, Ezra, I'm so sorry about the dress."

"Don't worry about it," she answered genuinely. "You can make it up to me by promising you'll try again."

Jude rolled her eyes and sat quietly for the rest of the drive. It didn't take long for her to notice that Shiloh was sitting quietly, too. Not quietly, silently.

CHAPTER 8

At home, Jude went straight for the kitchen and started pulling things out of cabinets.

"I'm exhausted, but I'm starving," she said to anyone who was listening. "Food, then sleep."

She offered to make Shiloh a snack, but she turned it down, which was unusual, and ran up to her room. Shiloh was not a child to lock herself away.

"Is she okay?" Jude asked Ezra, as she dumped a pack of microwave noodles into a bowl and filled it with water. "Did something happen while I was gone? Was she upset that I was out with Christopher?"

Ezra shook her head. "No, nothing. I don't know what's got her acting strange. She's probably working on a puzzle or something and doesn't want to be pulled away."

"Maybe," answered Jude. She put the noodles in the microwave and sat down at the table with a bag of potato chips.

Ezra sat down across from her. "So, how was your night before the whole vampire incident?"

"Eh," Jude replied. "I mean, the place was beautiful." She popped a small handful of chips into her mouth. "And Christopher was totally in his element."

"Really?" Ezra asked, surprised.

"Oh, yeah. I mean he's awkward, but he's so likeable and polite, and everyone eats that up."

"Everyone, including you," Ezra commented.

"Yeah, well, I tend to make social gatherings more awkward for everyone, even the most confident and aloof."

"What happened?"

"Questions," she stated, as the microwave beeped and she retrieved her dinner. "Everyone's got questions. And I don't have answers." She looked at Ezra. "Have you ever had the feeling that everything is a lie?"

Ezra looked a little startled. "I mean, I suppose. Sometimes I feel like I'm playing a part."

"Yes, that's exactly it. Playing a part. Tonight, I felt like I was acting."

"Well, I don't think you have to do that for Christopher. He knows you and he likes you. The real version."

She shrugged. "I wasn't really doing it for him, but sometimes I just get overwhelmed by this feeling. That my whole life is some charade, and it works okay when I can fool myself too, but when I can't, it just starts to crumble and I can feel cracks forming."

Ezra nodded, trying to understand. "You

have to keep a lot of secrets. It isn't easy."

Jude twirled the noodles around with a fork. "I felt this way before the secrets."

After she had satisfied her hunger, Jude went upstairs to go to bed. First, she went up to Shiloh's room.

"Whatcha reading?" she asked, peeking over the stairs at her daughter, who was laying in bed with a book.

Shiloh looked up at her and Jude could see it in her eyes that she was processing something. Usually, whenever Jude popped into Shiloh's room unexpectedly, or sat down next to her on the couch, or picked her up from school, she was met with a wide smile. Neither of them liked being apart from the other, and their relationship was a source of strength for both. Concerned with this palpable shift in demeanor, Jude continued into Shiloh's room and sat down on the edge of her bed.

She brushed a long strand of hair away from Shiloh's face and caught a glimpse of the book she was reading, *A Wrinkle in Time.*

"Good choice," Jude said, gesturing to the novel. Shiloh nodded and kept her eyes on the pages, though Jude could tell that she wasn't actually reading anything. "Hey," she said, gently pulling the book away from Shiloh's face and nudging her shoulder. "What's up?"

Shiloh avoided eye contact. "Nothing," she said, unconvincingly.

"Nothing?" Jude asked. "You're hardly talking to me. You said no to ice cream." Jokingly, she put her hand across Shiloh's forehead. "Are you feeling okay? Should I call a doctor?"

Shiloh didn't laugh. She didn't even smile.

"Buddy, are you mad at me?" Jude asked, decidedly concerned.

Shiloh shook her head "no".

"Are you sure?"

"Mhm."

Jude nodded. "Alright, well what's wrong then?"

Finally, Shiloh looked up at Jude. "Nothing," she said again. "I guess I'm just tired."

Jude looked back at her quietly for a minute, sensing that there was something Shiloh was holding back, but she didn't press. "Okay," she said, running her hand down Shiloh's skinny arm before standing up. "Well, I'm pretty tired, too. Let's get some sleep, and tomorrow we will go to the park or something?"

Shiloh nodded, picking her book up again and turning the page.

"I love you," Jude told her.

"Love you, too," answered Shiloh. But there was no spark in her voice.

Jude lingered by the bed for a minute longer before taking the stairs back down to her room. She wriggled out of the shredded party dress, collapsed onto her bed and took a deep breath, sinking into the soft mattress below her back. She stared up at the ceiling. On the other side of it was Shiloh's bed. Something was up with her, but she was an eight year old girl. There was no telling what was troubling her. This is what Jude told herself so she could get some sleep. Tomorrow, she would dig deeper and get to the bottom of it.

Just as she was falling asleep, her cell phone rang on the table next to her. Blurry eyed, she picked it up and studied the caller ID Screen. It was Gideon, which usually meant trouble. Reluctantly, she pressed the green call button and pressed the phone to her ear.

"Hello?" She asked, disoriented.

"Jude?" Gideon asked. "Are you sleeping? It's not even eleven."

She rolled her eyes. "I'm not sleeping anymore. What's up?"

"Well, there are some things going on not too far from you that I thought you might want to investigate."

Jude sat up and rubbed her eyes. "What things?"

"A small town by the coast. I suppose you haven't heard any of the news?"

"Gideon, the coast if four hours from here. What's going on?" She was growing frustrated, and had been awoken from much needed rest.

"I got a tip from the Synedrion to keep an eye on the place. About two weeks ago, some unusual things started happening that may suggest a malignant supernatural presence. I'll send you some articles. Read over them and see what you think. Whatever is going on there, it seems to be escalating. It could indicate that something looking for Shiloh is getting closer."

"Okay," Jude answered. "I'll check it out."

They hung up and Jude's phone started beeping with email notifications. Her inbox was quickly flooded with news articles and Gideon's own research on the small town of Tidewater, on the Rappahannock River. Chucking her phone onto the bed, Jude stood up lethargically, grabbed her laptop from her nightstand, and headed downstairs to brew a pot of coffee.

CHAPTER 9

The next thing she knew, Jude was blinking her eyes open to weak sunlight and Ezra standing over her. She was laying on the couch with a blanket draped over her and her laptop on the floor with about a dozen tabs open. She didn't remember falling asleep, but assumed it happened around two or three in the morning.

She sat up slowly, rubbing the sore lump in the back of her neck.

"Why are you down here?" Ezra asked, handing her a hot cup of coffee. Jude didn't know what time it was, but Ezra was still wearing her glasses so it couldn't have been after eight.

She graciously took a sip. "Must've passed out in the middle of research." She had a dull headache behind her eyes and felt like she hadn't gotten any rest at all.

Ezra sat down next to Jude and picked up the laptop. "Researching what?" She began to flip through the tabs. "*Rabid dogs in Tidewater, Tidewater Hospital Overrun, Jogger Goes Missing in Tidewater,* what is all of this?"

Jude clutched the warm mug in both of her hands and leaned forward with her elbows on her knees, coaxing her body from sleep. "Gideon called last night and said that the Synedrion was watching some activity in the Tidewater area. It's out on the coast, a few hours away. He's concerned that whatever is out there is looking for Shiloh."

"And you?" asked Ezra, scrolling through articles.

Jude shrugged. "It's definitely alarming. Apparently this is a fairly quiet town, but in the last four days they have had over a dozen people come through the ER disoriented and suffering severe blood loss. Something is going on out there."

"Are you going to go?"

"I don't think so. Not yet, anyway." Jude finished her coffee in four big gulps and stood to get more. She groaned and rubbed her back where it grabbed from sleeping on the couch and not her bed. Then, she returned to her research. The deeper she dug, the more she found. Strange things had been happening in the area for months. A few obscure bloggers were making fringe suggestions about what they thought might be going on: devil worship, gang activity, government conspiracies. One suggested that the water had been contaminated with radioactive substances. One blogger even mentioned vampires. But it all seemed very disorganized and random. Whatever was happening, there didn't seem to be one centralized source. But there had to be. Evil beings generally didn't set up camp in random towns unless something bigger was present there, drawing them in.

* * *

When Shiloh woke up, she didn't come out of her room right away. Already, she was obsessing about the coming evening, when Caleb and Elliott would come to her house and try to convince her of something that couldn't possibly be true. But if it couldn't be true, why did it feel like she had swallowed a ball of lead? Why should she be so nervous?

She laid in bed for a short while, trying to think about anything else. She picked up her book from her bedside table and flipped through it, but she couldn't seem to take in any of the words. There was a half-completed puzzle on the table across the room, but she just stared at it. Jack was still curled up at her feet sound asleep, and she knew that if she got up, he would have to go outside and she would have to go downstairs to take him. She couldn't face her mother. Not until she knew that Caleb was wrong. She couldn't look Jude in the eye and lie to her when she asked if everything was okay, which was a question she would definitely ask because it was written all over Shiloh's face that everything was not okay at all. Shiloh couldn't lie about anything, it was completely against her nature and the whole thing made her queasy. She just wanted it to be over. Once she could prove that the boys were wrong, and that her mother would never hide something like this from her, then everything would be okay.

* * *

Jude waited for Shiloh to come downstairs, but by the time ten thirty rolled around, she still hadn't heard footsteps above her and went upstairs to check. She found Shiloh laying in bed, rolled over on her side and wrapped in her blankets.

"Kiddo, what are you doing?" she asked, as Shiloh produced a cough from the back of her throat.

"I don't feel too good," Shiloh said weakly.

"Maybe you really *are* sick," said Jude, feeling Shiloh's head just like she had the night before. She felt normal, but was sniffling and looked flushed. "Okay," she said after her quick examination. "Well, stay in bed and get some rest then, okay? We can go to the park when you're feeling better. I'll bring you some juice. Do you want anything to eat?"

Shiloh shook her head "no" and rolled back over. Jude rubbed her back for a few minutes and then went downstairs to get her a drink.

For the rest of the afternoon, Jude was in and out of Shiloh's room delivering snacks and drinks, even though Shiloh had no interest. She set up her computer by Shiloh's feet so she could watch Netflix, and together they watched three old episodes of I Love Lucy because it was Shiloh's favorite, but she didn't laugh like she usually did. She didn't turn to her mother and imitate Lucy's voice, or rest her head on her shoulder. All day, Shiloh was mostly silent, seemingly somewhere else entirely.

At around two o'clock, after Shiloh had fallen back to sleep and Jude was sitting in the kitchen checking to see if any new tragedies had befallen Tidewater, there was a knock at the door. Christopher stood on the porch, still in his church clothes. He smiled boyishly as she opened the door and he stepped into the kitchen. Discreetly, she tried to adjust her messy hair and straighten out her baggy sweatpants, but she didn't have time to do anything more.

"How's it goin'?" he asked, as Jude filled the coffee pot with water and poured it into the machine. She dumped the rest of a nearly empty bag of grounds into the filter and flipped the "on" switch, then sat back down.

"Not too bad. Just looking into some incidents near the beach. Gideon called last night."

Christopher looked over her shoulder at the computer screen. "Wow, rabid dogs?"

"Oh, that's only the beginning," she said, closing her eyes tightly and rubbing behind her eyes where the dull pain still lingered. "Anyway, what's up?"

He took a step to the side so that he was standing in front of her, and pulled a folded and creased paperback book from his pocket. "Well, I was thinking about something."

She watched him and waited as he shuffled around anxiously, a completely different guy than the one she was with the night before.

"Maybe I've gone about this the wrong way."

"Gone about what the wrong way?"

He took a deep breath and tapped his fingers on the back of the book. "Well, I've been trying to spend time with you lately. And honestly, I've been trying to impress you."

He blushed and she tried not to smile as his eyes struggled to hold hers.

"Christopher," she started. "Really, it's okay."

"No, I know. But I have been trying to take you out someplace nice, or do something fun, and I realized that maybe that's not what you want to do."

She wasn't exactly sure what to say.

"So I thought maybe I could try again. Start with something much simpler."

Too tired to argue, she gave in. "Okay, what did you have in mind?" she asked.

"Do you read?"

"Uh," she said, hesitantly. "Not much."

He lifted the book higher. "I was thinking maybe I could read you something." When she looked at him puzzled, he added, "it's my favorite book."

She gave a slow, confused nod. "Yeah, okay sure."

"Can we go sit in the living room?"

She stood up and grabbed her mug off the table. "Yeah, just let me fill this up."

"Do that after," he said, suddenly more confident and taking a step toward her. "It won't be long, come on." He grabbed her hand and pulled her toward the couch.

Jude trailed reluctantly behind him, one arm connected to his at the other end, and sat down after him on the living room couch. Playing it off as completely normal, he threw his arm around her and she couldn't help but let go if a quiet laugh. He ignored it entirely and opened his wrinkled, pocket-stuffed book.

"Have you ever read Proust?"

Jude looked at him and studied his expression. He had to have some kind of plan but so far, he had done a good job of keeping it completely under wraps and she had no idea where this was all heading. Finally, she answered. "No, I have not."

He gave a curt nod. "Well, this was my go-to in college when I needed a break from all the studying. I think you'll see why. The language is mesmerizing."

"It's mesmerizing?" she repeated, mocking him just a little.

"Well, yeah," he said laughing defensively. "Just give it a chance. Here, listen."

And he started reading.

"*When a man is asleep, he has in a circle around him the chain of the hours, the sequence of the years, the order of the heavenly bodies. Instinctively, he consults them when he awakes, and in an instant reads off his own position on the earth's surface and the time that has elapsed during his slumbers; but this order of procession is apt to grow confused-*"

"Christopher?" Jude interrupted, her voice unusually high-pitched and suspicious.

He looked at her, blinking.

"What is this?"

"I don't know what you-"

"Is this how you win all the girls?" she asked laughing. "Stun them with some sprawling literature?"

He laughed quietly. "All the girls? Jude, how many girls do you think I've been with?"

She thought about it and chose not to respond. Christopher squeezed the round top of her shoulder and leaned in a little closer.

"Just trust me, okay? It's about to get interesting."

She nodded, very much doubting it, and rested her head on his shoulder, surprising even herself. For a second, he took in the simple pleasure of that moment, and so did she. It was warm. Comfortable. Then, he continued on.

"*...this order of procession is apt to grow confused, and to break its ranks. Suppose that, towards morning, after a night of insomnia, sleep descends upon him while he is reading, in quite a different position from that in which he normally goes to sleep...*"

When Jude woke up, she was laying almost completely over on Christopher, pressed up against his side and draped in a blanket. He was leaning back on the back of the couch, one hand still dutifully around her, and the other in his lap, head back, sound asleep. She sat up quickly.

"Oh my god," she muttered, still tingly and out of sorts.

Christopher slowly blinked his eyes open and sat up. "Morning," he said happily. "How was your nap?"

Jude looked at her wrist and found that she was not wearing her watch. She didn't even own a watch. She grabbed his cell phone off of the coffee table. It was 3:30. She pulled the arm she'd been laying on across her chest to stretch out the tight muscles of her shoulder and back. "Fine, I guess," she answered. "I didn't mean to fall asleep. I'm really sorry, I must've- it wasn't you, or your book I swear, I must be getting even less sleep than I thought."

He was grinning in a very suspicious and mis-chievous way.

"What?" she asked. "Oh no, was I drooling or something?"

He laughed. "No, you are a very elegant sleeper."

"Then what is with your face?"

"It's nothing," he answered, fidgeting with the book in his hands and still smiling from ear to ear.

"Christopher?"

He looked at her sideways.

"Did you... *plan* this? Was I supposed to fall asleep?"

He shrugged, but it was written all over his face that she'd uncovered his master plan.

"You intentionally chose the most boring book in history and took my coffee away from me so that I would take a nap? That was your big idea?"

By now, he was laughing pretty hard and she feigned anger while trying not to laugh herself.

"I'm sorry," he said, trying to control himself. He paused, took a breath, and tried again calmer. "I'm sorry. I know, it was pretty sneaky but you are always so busy." His face took on a more serious appearance and he covered the top of her hand with his. "You do so much. Worry so much. I have been trying to figure out what you want, but I think first, I should try to give you what you need. A break. Someplace safe, and quiet. Boring, even, couldn't hurt. Even if it's just for an hour."

It was a brilliant and touching, if not a little annoying, thought. She looked down at the book, then back up at him and slowly, as if her hand had taken on a mind of its own, reached toward his scruffy cheek. Then, to the back of his neck. She wasn't entirely sure what she was doing, but she had no plans to stop, and she leaned in towards him. They were an inch, maybe two, apart from each other when her cell phone rang.

She jumped and backed off instantly. As he blinked in confusion and disappointment, she picked her phone up off the floor where it had fallen during her slumber, and heard Gideon's sobering and entirely un-sexy voice on the other line.

"Hello?"

"Gideon, what's up?" Jude responded, a little

too punchy.

"Jude, have you seen the latest news out of Tidewater?" There was a solemnity in his voice, a kind of hushed urgency that made Jude nervous, and she felt the flutter of bad news in the pit of her stomach.

She shook her head like he could see her, and stood up from the couch after placing a hand momentarily on Christopher's leg. She made her way into the kitchen. "No, I haven't checked in a few hours. What is it?"

"There was a murder. A body... turned up. It looked like some kind of ritual sacrifice. All of the blood was drained. It was really bad. Gruesome, honestly. I think you should go out there. You may be the only one who can help."

"Whose body was it?" Jude asked, leaning up against the kitchen wall. "Not that missing runner?"

Gideon hesitated. "Jude..." he said, trailing.

"Whose body, Gideon?"

"A six year old boy. Marco Sanchez."

"Oh my god." Jude brought her free arm up to her chest and gripped her opposite shoulder to ease the sudden tightness that swelled around her heart and lungs. She wanted to say more but the words caught in her throat.

"You should go," he whispered again after a moment of silence. "This thing could be after Shiloh. Go and gather any information you can."

"Right," Jude answered. "Of course. I'll leave tonight."

They hung up and Jude stood in the kitchen supported by the wall, holding the phone to her chest until Christopher appeared in the doorway. "What's wrong?" he asked.

Jude knew that her emotions were plastered all over her face, and she stood up straight, stiffening her back and quickly pressing her fingers against the bottoms of her damp eyes. "I have to go to Tidewater," she resolved. "A little boy was... his body was found today. Some kind of sacrifice."

"Oh no," he said mournfully, stepping in closer to touch Jude's arm. "Do you think there's a connection to Shiloh?"

Jude shrugged through his grip. "I don't know. I don't think it matters. Some parents are living out their worst nightmare and a little boy is dead. I have to go before someone else gets hurt. It's kind of my job."

"Sure, I get it," Christopher answered, pulling her off of his chest to look at her face. "But you shouldn't go alone. I'll come with you."

"Don't you have work? I don't know what I'm getting into, Chris. You don't need to commit to that right now, I know you're busy."

He was shaking his head, rejecting her idea before it was fully stated. "I have not taken a vacation day in the entire time I've been here. I'm overdue. I'm going to go home and get some stuff together and I'll be back here to pick you up. What do you say, an hour?"

She nodded without arguing.

CHAPTER 10

Upstairs, Shiloh was laying with her back to the door, playing games on Jude's laptop. Jude came in, sat down beside her, and reached around to feel her forehead. She still didn't feel like she was running a fever.

"Listen kiddo," Jude started. "I have to go out of town tonight. Maybe for a few nights."

Shiloh turned her head and looked up at her wide eyed for the first time all day. "Why?"

Jude searched for excuses. "There's just something I have to take care of. Some people need my help."

Shiloh nodded solemnly, and her eyes fell back on the laptop screen, but she wasn't thinking about her game.

Jude laid back and put her head on Shiloh's pillow and tickled her back with the tips of her fingers. Shiloh had loved that since she was a baby. "Still not feeling good?" Jude asked, even though she doubted very much that it was true.

Shiloh lifted her shoulders, then dropped them back down.

"Shiloh, come on." Jude closed the laptop and took Shiloh's hands. "I know you. I know when there's something spinning around in your busy little head. What's going on? I need you to talk to me."

Finally, Shiloh rolled over and locked her eyes on her mothers. Her expression was so serious, and Jude suddenly was overwhelmed with concern.

Shiloh laid there, staring, holding words that she was hesitant to speak on her tongue.

"What is it baby?" Jude pleaded.

"Do you love me?" Shiloh finally asked, her voice breaking. Her eyes were welling with tears.

Jude was taken aback by this question. For a second, she didn't even know how to respond. *Yes* seemed weak and pathetic, and not at all sufficient to explain what she felt for Shiloh. Her heart sank into her stomach. She tried to take a deep breath.

"Shiloh, I love you more than anything I've ever loved in my entire life."

When that didn't seem to be enough, Jude scooted closer and pulled Shiloh into her arms. "I can't even tell you how much I love you. There aren't even words, do you understand? Shiloh, without you I don't even know who I am."

"Do you just love me because I'm special?" The question came so quick that Jude could tell Shiloh had been bothered by this for some time.

A tear escaped the girls eye and Jude quickly wiped it away. "Because you're special?"

"Because I can do special things?"

Alarmed by this line of questioning, Jude

doubled down. "What? Absolutely not," she said adamantly. "I love you because you are my little girl. Where is this coming from?" As she spoke, she was fighting back tears of her own.

"Idunno," Shiloh answered. "It was just something I was thinking about."

Jude shook her head and squeezed Shiloh against her body. "Do you know what happened to me the first time I saw you?" she asked. Against her chest she could feel Shiloh shaking her head. "When I found out about you I was scared to death. But the first time I actually saw you, I couldn't look away. Shiloh, it was like electricity. I swear, I got dizzy. The little hairs on my arm stood straight up. I could feel every blood cell flowing through my veins. Suddenly everything made sense. Everything in my messy life became clear and I knew there was a reason I was around. You were beautiful. And you had those big blue eyes and you looked at me and I couldn't even think straight. You still do it, every day. It was like you had cast a spell on me. I didn't even *like* babies." She laughed a little, and Shiloh suppressed a grin. "But you were something completely different. From that moment on, I knew that everything I was ever going to do for the rest of my life was going to be for you. Because you're mine. The best thing that's ever happened to me, and I love you. Unconditionally."

"Okay," answered Shiloh, in a slobbery, congested voice into Jude's armpit.

Jude exhaled. Maybe she dodged the bullet,

but for some reason she felt that more were coming. "Okay," she answered. "Listen, I don't think I'm gonna go on that trip after all, okay?"

"Why not?"

"I can go later. Maybe in a few days. I think I wanna stay home and hang out with you."

Shiloh sat up and furrowed her brow. "Are there people who need your help because they're not safe?"

Though she was hesitant to answer, Jude knew that she wasn't fooling anyone. Shiloh was aware of what Jude did. She didn't know, exactly, that Jude was protecting her from evil things that very specifically wanted her dead, but she knew that evil things existed, and she knew that Jude protected people from them. Jude gave a slow nod. "Yeah. That's why."

"Then you should go. Tonight." Shiloh threw her arms unexpectedly around Jude and hugged her tightly. Jude let out a deep exhale of relief that Shiloh was Shiloh again, at least for now. "They need you. I don't want anyone to get hurt."

After their talk, Shiloh seemed to pick up. She got out of bed and went to work on a puzzle. She let Jude make her a snack and sat on the couch with Ezra watching television. Everything appeared to be returning to normal, and Jude felt that Shiloh was going to be okay. She still didn't understand where Shiloh had gotten those questions; why she doubted even for a second that Jude loved her, and she wanted to get to the bottom of it. But every time she looked at Shiloh, she thought of Marco Sanchez and his parents, who were definitely not alright, and she felt a sense of responsibility to them. If there was any way she could help, or prevent more tragedy from happening, she had to do it. So, when Christopher came to pick her up, she kissed Shiloh goodbye, triple, quadruple-checked with Ezra that she could keep a close eye on her, and promised to be back within a few days. Then, she threw her bag into the back seat of Christopher's Explorer, and they headed to Tidewater.

* * *

Shiloh breathed a sigh of relief when Jude pulled away from the house on her way to the coast. After the conversation they'd had in her room, she wanted even more for the whole night to be over, and to prove to Elliott and Caleb that they were wrong. Of course her mother loved her. She was ashamed for ever doubting it, but they had gotten to her somehow. She was sure to not let that happen again. Now, Jude was out of the way and Shiloh could find the book, show them that Jude would never lie to her like that, that her mother was a hero, and put it away before she ever found out it was missing.

There was, of course, still Ezra to contend with, and while she was thorough and cautious, she was not nearly as obsessive and aware as Jude, who tracked Shiloh's every move like a bloodhound.

At eight-thirty, Shiloh saw her opportunity

to go and look for the book. She knew it was someplace in her mom's room, and Ezra was situated on the couch, deeply interested in some old movie. As casually as possible, Shiloh stood up from her seat next to Ezra and stretched her arms way over her head.

"I'm gonna go put my pajamas on," she stated. It wasn't that unusual on a Sunday night for Shiloh to be in bed early. She had school in the morning.

"Okay sweetie," Ezra answered. "I was thinking, do you want to sleep in my room tonight?"

Shiloh said no maybe a little too quickly, then backtracked. "No, I think I'll be okay in my room. Jack will sleep with me. But thanks."

In truth, she did not want to sleep all the way up in her own room alone without Jude sleeping just below. But sleeping with Ezra would disrupt the entire plan and there was no way she'd be able to sneak out of the house. She decided that she could go into Ezra's room later, after she met with Elliott and Caleb, and say that she had changed her mind. Ezra would think nothing of it.

"Alright," answered Ezra, a little surprised. "Well, go get comfy I'll make us some popcorn."

Shiloh jogged up the stairs and into Jude's room. She continued walking, especially aware of her footsteps, to the closet door, then up her bedroom steps. Once at the top she moved around a little to really sell the idea that she was up there. Then, once she felt that she had satisfied Ezra's expectations, she crept back down the stairs as silently as possible.

The staircase was old and constructed of raw pine boards which squeaked and sagged under every step. She had never been so aware of how noisy it was. Nonetheless, she made her way down, trying to spread out her weight between the stairs and the handrail. Finally, she made it to the bottom. She still had to make a conscious effort to monitor her steps, but the solid floor was much more stable than the staircase and she could breathe a little easier. The challenge now was going to be locating the book quickly and silently.

Standing in her mother's room, next to her unmade bed, and the little pile of dirty laundry that always accumulated by the closet door, Shiloh felt incredibly guilty. The room smelled like her; like lavender lotion and the earthy, nutty scent of her hair that clung to everything and brought Jude to the front and center of the room. It made it hard to focus. Shiloh felt the wrongness of her actions in her stomach, and the palms of her sweaty hands.

But the plan was already in motion and she couldn't call it off. She kept reminding herself that if she took care of it now, she wouldn't have to deal with it later. She could clear her mother's name and go back to feeling normal in her own home and skin.

The first place she checked was under the bed. Before she even looked, she assumed she wouldn't find it. Her mom was more careful than that. Next, she checked her bedside table. On top of it was a picture that had been there for years. Shiloh was probably three in the photo. It was taken when they still lived in Indiana with Gideon; a time that Shiloh couldn't really remember clearly, like there was a hazy film over the images in her mind. But this picture helped her to remember. Gideon had a big front porch that she and Jude spent a lot of time on. On that particular autumn afternoon, they had been blowing bubbles and watching them get carried away by the wind. Tall, golden grass willowed in the fields surrounding the house. The light wooden boards of the porch were darker where Shiloh had accidentally knocked over the bubble jar. Her hands were sticky. Gideon must've snapped the picture half-unexpectedly because Jude, in her baggy brown sweater, was holding Shiloh in her lap and looking down at her, laughing as Shiloh shook the bubble wand and flung soap everywhere. A drop landed on the camera lens and at the top left corner of the picture was a liquidy blur that made the colors thin and distorted.

She picked up the purple frame and studied the expression on her mother's face. It was a moment of pure affection caught on film. There was no way that wasn't real. She touched the image with the tip of her index finger and placed it quietly back on the nightstand. Then she opened the drawer.

Once she opened it, she realized it was too small to contain the Codex. Jude had all kinds of junk stuffed in there: a collection of pens, a couple of notepads, a bottle of Tylenol, almost empty, a wooden cross, and about a hundred little odds and ends that had been tossed in there for the sake of having a place to put them. But no Codex.

She stepped into the middle of the room and crossed her arms over her chest. If she were Jude, where would she hide it? It had to be big enough to fit the book and disguise it well. Someplace no one else would need to get to. Then her eyes fell over Jude's dresser.

Quietly, she crossed the floor towards it. Starting at the top, she had to stand on her tippy toes to see into the drawer, and even then her eyes barely made it over and she had to run her hand around inside of it, feeling for the hard edges. All she found was socks and underwear. The second drawer down was full of black and gray tank-tops and Shiloh had to fight to keep from laughing when the image of her mother as a cartoon character came into her mind. If SpongeBob's closet is nothing but box-shaped khakis hanging from the rod, Jude's would be nothing but dark-colored tank tops and sweatpants, like it was her uniform. But, there was no book in the drawer.

The third drawer was just t-shirts and by the fourth, after having felt underneath the pairs of jeans folded and stuffed inside, Shiloh was losing faith and starting to think maybe she could just tell the boys that she couldn't find the book and that would settle it. But as she opened the bottom drawer, she noticed something different. Amid the scarves and random articles of clothing inside, there was a yellow baby jumper. Shiloh knew it had to have been hers, and picked it up. It was soft and small and again the guilt flowered in her stomach. Beneath it were a few more of her baby clothes, and a tiny, knit blanket, and it was clear that Jude was holding on to these things as a way of holding on to baby Shiloh, as parents do. They weren't things anyone would make the effort to keep if they didn't care; if they were just marking time.

She had a feeling that she was about to find it before she did, and when her hand fell on the worn leather, she regretted looking at all. Before she pulled it out, she weighed the choices. It wasn't too late, she could still say she never found it. Put it back in the drawer, go downstairs and cuddle with Ezra until she fell asleep and Jude came back home. Then she would tell her mother everything; about Elliott and his older brother, and the horrible things they told her, and Jude would reassure her that they were making it all up.

Just as she was about to slide the drawer back into the dresser, Ezra called for her.

"Shiloh, you alright?"

She almost jumped out of her skin at the sound of Ezra's voice. "Yeah, I'm fine," she yelled back, pulling out the Codex and sliding the drawer shut. As quickly as she could, she slid open the third drawer and pulled out one of her mom's t-shirts. She shed her clothes and pulled the shirt over her head, then crept back to the closet that concealed the stairs to her own room above. She tucked the book under the first step, and made her way down to the living room to Ezra.

Ezra smiled when she saw Shiloh coming down the stairs in Jude's NYU shirt, and pulled her onto the couch. "She'll be home soon," she promised, and the two of them sat snuggled together eating popcorn and watching *The Lord of the Rings*; one of Shiloh's favorites. But all she could think about was the Codex waiting for her under the stairs.

CHAPTER 11

Jude and Christopher reached Tidewater around 10:00. The town looked relatively quiet, with nothing but bluish glows from televisions and flickering yellow porch lights emanating from most houses. But moving closer to town, there began to appear the suggestion that something was off. Several shop doors were boarded or barred, with signs reading, "Temporarily Closed" taped to the front. A few windows looked to have been broken into, with shards of glass littering the street in front of them and police tape tacked up to the walls and wrapping corners. No one was walking the streets, and nothing was open. Street lights all blinked yellow.

"This is a little eerie," said Christopher, as he turned the car onto Main Street and continued slowly through town.

"Very," Jude agreed. She rolled the window down and was on high alert for movement or noise, but there was nothing; just the warm, salty breeze blowing through her hair. She felt a little guilty, but couldn't help taking a deep breath and embracing the saturated night air which carried with it the sticky scent of coastal waterways and coming summer.

Through the windshield, Jude noticed a dull glow coming from what appeared to be a town square or pavilion, and asked Christopher to stop the car as they got closer. When he pulled over and parked along the street, she realized that the glow was coming from several dozen candles that had been scattered among a flower-crowded and deserted memorial. She got out of the car, her heart already dead weight in her chest, and walked to the memorial. A wreath in the center held a photograph of the little boy, Marco Sanchez, smiling wide and missing his two front teeth for a school picture. Scattered around were other photographs of him being a kid. Riding his bike with a big fluffy dog running behind him. Jumping from a diving board in a Superman swimsuit. Blowing out the candles on his sixth birthday cake. Suddenly Jude's grief was transposed into a hot rush of anger, as it often did.

"Heartbreaking," said Christopher as he walked up with his hands in his pockets.

"Something like this should never happen," answered Jude through gritted teeth.

As she moved to turn away, wiping her eyes on the sleeve of her zip-up hoodie, the wind kicked up a flyer announcing the time and location of the funeral service.

"Tomorrow at eleven," he said, reading the crumpled paper.

"We should go," she answered, crossing her

arms over her chest.

"Come on," he told her. "Let's check into a hotel room and drop off our stuff, then we will go out and find some answers."

"Right," she said as a surge of righteous energy elevated her blood pressure and flushed her neck with heat.

As they drove through town looking for a hotel, Jude's fingers twitched and her knees bounced. She wanted to be out there, tracking whatever was wreaking havoc on this town. The first place they found was a one-story, L-shaped motel with a flickering pink "vacancy" sign.

"Looks a little desolate," said Christopher as they pulled into the cracked parking lot.

"Yeah, well I imagine that recent events have put a damper on tourism in the area," Jude remarked, opening her door and stepping out into the night. She grabbed her backpack- the only bag she'd brought- from the back seat and slung it over her shoulder. It was loaded down with weapons, mostly, and the few things she needed for an overnight trip. Christopher pulled his duffle bag from the trunk and they headed into the dated old motel.

Behind the front desk stood an old woman, half-asleep with a water-stained magazine open on the countertop She was startled when they walked in.

"Oh," she said, looking up and closing the magazine. "Didn't see your car pull in." She peered around behind them to check the parking lot, as if she thought they could be just a mirage. "You need a room?"

"Please," said Christopher.

Jude pulled out her bank card and laid it on the counter while the woman punched information into an old computer.

"One bed?" she more stated than asked.

"Uh, no," Jude interjected. "Two, please." She glanced quickly at Christopher and darted her eyes away again, tapping on the veneer.

"Okay," said the woman. "You're all set for room 16. Just go out of the office here and take a right. It's about five doors down."

"Thanks," Jude answered, accepting the little plastic door key and turning to go outside.

"Oh, and," the woman spoke up as they were leaving. "Just be sure to lock your door. Can never be too careful, right?"

"Yeah," Jude answered slowly. "Of course."

The room was old and smelled like wet carpet and burnt popcorn but nonetheless Jude tossed her backpack onto one of the beds and sat down on the edge of it before falling back to lay on the springy mattress.

"Where do you think we should start?" Christopher asked, sitting down next to her.

Jude rubbed her forehead with both of her hands then sat back up again. "I'm not sure," she admitted. "There were no signs of life at all in town. Even Acadia is more lively than this at this hour."

She stood up and pulled back the heavy curtains over the hotel window and looked into the parking lot. A plastic bag skidded across the pavement under a street lamp.

"Tomorrow we'll go to the memorial service. Tonight, maybe we should just drive around? I mean, we can sort of get a feel for the place. Maybe take downtown on foot. See if we see anything."

This was the weakest plan, and she knew it. They'd just come from town and there was nothing. Whatever was out here had taken to hiding, and reasonably so, considering the community was on high alert after the boy was found. But Jude was anxious, itching to find and kill whatever was terrorizing Tidewater.

Christopher turned the television on and flipped through until he found a news station. Of course, they were talking about Marco. A flustered-looking news anchor in a navy blue blazer sat stiff behind a counter and held a pen over a short stack of papers. She talked about the family and the memorial service, and she mentioned a police investigation, but said that no progress had been made in determining who was responsible, or why someone would do such a thing. He flipped off the screen.

"I wonder if they know more than they're sharing," Christopher suggested.

"Don't they always?"

As Jude spoke, a shrill, mechanical screech came from outside and they both ran to the window. Moments later, three police cars with blue lights flashing flew by, heading out of town.

Jude looked at Christopher wide eyed.

"Let's go?" he asked, already grabbing the keys.

Jude grabbed her backpack and they rushed out the door and to the car.

The squad cars were out of sight by the time they got to the highway, but their sirens could still be heard in the distance and every now and then, they would catch the glow of blue lights and knew they were moving in the right direction.

"What do you think is happening?" asked Christopher.

"No idea," Jude answered, digging through a small weapons bag and taking inventory. "Right now, it's all we've got. And whatever it is, it must be serious or they wouldn't be sending three cops to the same place, right?"

As they drove closer and closer to the river, the ground began to loosen as tall marsh grasses and dark, shimmering waterways wandered past both sides of the road. Old wooden docks were tied to weathered posts and tree stumps with fraying rope, bobbing on the water's surface.

"This could be a nice place to live," Christopher mused, as the speedometer reached 65 mph on the winding back road.

Jude shot him a look of skepticism and he chuckled. "Well, not right now of course."

Finally, they turned a corner and caught sight

of the police cars, pulled over on the side of the road next to an old factory.

"Stop here," said Jude. "Let's not draw attention to ourselves."

Christopher pulled over and turned off the headlights. Jude rolled her window down and craned her neck to see what was happening. Just barely, she could make out the shapes of several people gathered by the squad cars. They appeared to be talking, but she was too far to hear any of the conversation.

She pulled a stake from her bag and slid it into the waste of her jeans. "I'm gonna get out," she said, already whispering. "I have to get closer."

"Are you sure that's a good idea?" Christopher asked, but Jude was already outside of the car, shutting the door quietly. He exhaled in defeat, grabbed another stake from the bag and decided to follow her.

They crept up the road, doing their best to stay in the brush until they were close enough to make out faces and hear voices. Four cops stood around three teenage boys who were lined up against the crumbling brick wall in handcuffs.

Christopher pulled out his cell phone which lit up the tree line where they were hiding, and just as Jude was about to scold him for it, he crouched down, lowered the brightness of the display, and turned on his camera to record.

One of the officers was over to the side, speaking into a pager attached to his jacket near his shoulder. "We've got three males," he said to the dispatcher. The radio made a lot of crackling white noise but Jude could just barely make out the words. "Eighteen-year-old Charles Anthony, sixteen-year-old Rick Thomas, and twenty-year-old Sean Webster." The officer crossed his arms and looked at the boys. "Do you want to tell me what you guys were doing out here?"

The youngest boy glanced at the others, then back up at the cop. "We were just out for a walk. We were bored. That's all."

"Out for a walk, huh?" He looked at them skeptically and placed both of his hands on his hips, tucking his thumbs into his belt at either side. "Got a call from a concerned resident that you guys were out here breaking into the building."

"No sir," one of the older boys answered weakly.

"Hmm," the officer hummed. "You boys got anything on ya that you wouldn't want me to find?"

"No, no we don't," answered the third.

The officer stood the youngest boy up and was about to pat him down when the other officer called from inside the factory.

"Hey, I've got something," he yelled, as he came through the doorway with several wooden crates.

"What's in the boxes?" The first cop asked the boys.

They squirmed. "We've never seen them before," one of them answered.

The officers gathered in front of them and pried the wooden lid off of the crate. Jude couldn't see what was inside, but the cops looked up at each other in confusion.

"What is this?" they asked, pulling out a dirty milk jug full of some clear liquid.

The boys said nothing and the female officer popped the top off of the jug and sniffed the contents. They were talking quietly now and Jude couldn't hear what was being said.

One of the officers loaded the crates into the trunk of the squad car while the other ushered the boys into the back seat. "We'll sort it out at the station," he told them as he closed the door. A few moments later, the police cars pulled away.

Once they were out of sight, Jude and Christopher emerged from the woods. "Let's go check it out," Jude said, already heading for the factory. Once again, Christopher reluctantly followed.

The police had done a poor job of securing the building and all Jude had to do to get inside was push aside a flimsy piece of plywood that was propped up against the doorway. Inside was cool, damp, and completely dark. They used the flashlights on their phones again to navigate, and still knocked into things as they moved their way through the industrial structure.

"Do you see anything?"

"No not yet," Jude answered, kicking an empty beer can across the cement floor. "Maybe they really were just here drinking or something. I definitely did my share of breaking and entering in my teens."

"That doesn't surprise me." Christopher took a step and kicked something with the toe of his shoe. He cast his flashlight beam down at it and called Jude over.

"Looks like they missed a couple of those crates," he said, kneeling down to open it up.

Just like the ones that the cops had found, this crate was stacked on top of another and was full of jugs of some liquid. Jude pulled one out and opened it up. Like the cop, she took a quick and cautious sniff.

"It doesn't really smell like anything," she said, dipping her finger into the jug. "I think it's just water.

She touched her tongue to her wet finger even as Christopher protested. "Yeah," she confirmed. "I think it's just water. Maybe sea water? It's a little salty."

"Jude, what if it had been acid or something?" Christopher asked, frustrated.

She rolled her eyes. "It wasn't. Come on, let's get this stuff into the car."

They each lifted one of the crates and were headed for the door when a startling sound crashed behind them.

"What was that?" Christopher asked, freezing in his path.

Jude didn't answer, but turned toward the sound to listen for more. She could hear rustling.

"We're not in here alone," she whispered.

"Maybe it's just an animal."

"Maybe," she answered, putting down the box and heading deeper into the building. Christopher stayed beside her, both flashlights illuminating only a small area.

All at once, Jude heard the thudding of heavy, hurried footsteps and felt something wrap its hand around the base of her neck. She dropped her cell phone as she fell back toward her attacker.

Instinctively, she drove her elbow backwards but didn't hit, and Christopher shined his phone in her direction. "Sleeper," he yelled frantically, as he rushed toward her and the creature.

Again, Jude swung but this time she reached farther and her first landed on the soft, bloated flesh of some undead thing, which grunted against the force of the strike and let go of her neck. She turned around to face it and pulled the stake out of her belt.

The monster circled around them both, keeping its knees bent and it's claws extended, waiting to pounce. Jude waited for her opportunity and drove her shoulder into its chest, knocking it to the ground. It carried her with it in the fall, and she sat on top of it, pinning it to the cement floor at the waist. It slashed at her as she landed several hard blows against its face, cracking it's skull above the eye. As quickly as she could, Jude drove the stake into its chest and it turned to dust.

She caught her breath as she stood to her feet. "Dead now."

She went to pick up her phone and get out of there as quickly as possible, but when she did, she heard Christopher gasp behind her.

"What is it?" she asked, turning to face him. But he didn't have to answer. In the glow of his flashlight beam, she could see several other sleepers, maybe six, gathering around them. They had been hiding in the shadows, presumably hoping she would just drop the crates and leave. But she didn't, and they had chosen to fight.

"Dammit," she mumbled. "We should've brought more weapons."

CHAPTER 12

Shiloh had gone upstairs to her room at ten forty-five, claiming to be ready for bed. She got dressed again, leaving Jude's shirt on over her clothes, and lay in bed listening. She heard Ezra follow only a few minutes later. On most nights, Ezra read one of her mystery novels for about an hour before falling asleep, and by the time midnight rolled around, Shiloh could only hope that Ezra had put her book away and turned in.

She sat by her tiny window, looking out over the field for Elliott and Caleb. They were supposed to shine a flashlight from the woods on the other side of the field, but only for a second, so as not to wake anyone in the house. Finally, at eight minutes past midnight, she saw the blink of a pale yellow light in the trees, and took a deep and steadying breath. She hugged the Codex to her chest, and tip-toed down the stairs to Jude's room.

Ezra's door was open across the hall, but all of the lights were off, and her bed was around the corner so she wouldn't be able to see Shiloh as she inched out of Jude's room and to the stairs. She could feel her heart racing in her chest, and even her pulse punching against the cover of the codex from her middle finger. She was so nervous she could practically hear her body's anxious energy, and it was loud inside of her head, flushing her cheeks and ears with humid heat.

With each step down, Shiloh paused and waited for the floor to settle under her foot. She dared not touch the railing, which was a little loose and sometimes rattled. About half-way down, she thought she heard movement upstairs and cringed, hesitating for an extra-long time before taking another step. After a long minute, she decided that she'd imagined it and continued on.

At the bottom of the stairs, she took a breath for the first time in several minutes. The rest would be easy.

The front door was right in front of her coming down the stairs, but she chose not to use it. Ezra's bedroom was just above and she would definitely hear Shiloh turning the finicky antique knob and pulling open the creaky door. Instead, she went to the back door, off of the kitchen. That door opened quietly because Christopher had fixed the knob and leveled out the jamb a while back. She slid her feet into the sandals that waited for her by the kitchen table, then silently slipped out the backdoor and into the warm evening.

Again, she took a deep breath. She hated the dark and now had to cross a very large field alone with it pressing down on her. Glancing back at the house, she was almost disappointed with how easy it had been to sneak out. Once she came to the edge of the field where the mowed part of the yard ended and it was just tangled weeds and rye, she kept her eyes focused on the spot where Elliott's light had been, and took off running.

* * *

Jude and Christopher were surrounded on all sides by vampires of varied strengths and ages. Jude was unprepared for something like this and felt like an idiot. She should've been prepared. She knew that she would find trouble in this town. She was counting on it, even. But she had been too anxious to get out, and now she was paying the price. Two wooden stakes were really insufficient to take on this many and she couldn't help but think of all of the supplies she had in her bag back in the car.

The creatures closed in on them and, deciding not to wait for them to make the first move, Jude closed the distance between herself and one of the larger ones and swung her leg to roundhouse kick it in the face. It staggered back and the other monsters automatically turned their heads to watch as it stumbled and fell. They took it as a declaration of war, and piled on top of Jude and Christopher all at once.

Jude could feel sharp claws slashing her skin and cold, decaying bodies pressing up against her own, shoving her this way and that. Christopher was pressed up against her, his back to hers, and they fought to maintain their standing positions.

It was impossible to make sense of the chaos in the pitch darkness, and so they both did their best, throwing punches and plunging stakes at whatever targets they could feel out. Some of their efforts were certainly rewarded, as one of the monsters would take a hit and stumble backwards, leaving an opening for Jude and Christopher to regain their balance or move in to attack again, but they were outnumbered, and had yet to get the upper hand. Christopher was losing strength and Jude could feel his knees weakening as he would lean against her under the weight of some attacker. Still, they continued to fight, with Jude turning toward him every few minutes to help lighten his load.

Jude's knuckles stung and though she couldn't see anything, she could feel a warm, thick trickle running down her fingers and knew that her fists were shredded. She didn't have time to catalogue the injuries she had sustained, but powered through. Even as a child, she was kind of an adrenaline junkie. Now, as a trained fighter with her supernatural bloodline fully activated, she was at ease in combat. She had become fairly skilled at evaluating each attacker in a multiple threat situation, quickly learning their individual strengths and weaknesses, and tracking each one as they moved about the group. She could rapidly calculate and manage the distance between her and them, developing a strategy that evolved and shifted with the circumstances. She took out the closest first, unless two or more attacked at the same time, and then she took out the weakest, using their own weight and balance against them. She was breathing heavily, and each gasp burned in her heaving chest, but she was holding her own. After a few minutes of intense battle, they had knocked the group down to just three vampires shifting around over the dust of their fallen comrades.

With only three remaining, it was easier to move around and maintain distance when necessary. Jude reached out for Christopher. He was still standing and she didn't feel any major injuries. "Are you okay?" she asked, keeping a close eye on the shadows that lurked around them.

"Mhm," he answered unconvincingly. "Yeah, let's finish them." He was doing his best to speak strongly, but he couldn't catch his breath. He was a skilled fighter, and experienced after four years of following her around. But he was a regular guy. When put to the test, she would outlast him every time because she had strength and stamina that came from a calling, sourced by the supernatural. She would fight harder and longer, and when it was all said and done, she would heal faster.

She grabbed him by the shoulders and pulled him to the side of the room. "No," she insisted, as he tried unsuccessfully to resist. "Sit right here. I can handle the rest."

He protested, but once he was down, he found himself struggling to stand back up. Once she felt that he'd given up, Jude rushed back into the swarm. They were huddled together which may have seemed like a good strategy, but it made it easier for her to take on multiple at once. She shoved one aside and grabbed the other two by the backs of their necks. The smaller of the two lurched backwards, leaving it's chest exposed and Jude plunged her stake through the cavity. It made that familiar popping sound as it pierced the skin and clavicle, and he turned to dust in her hand. She was about to stake the other when the third got up from the floor and rushed her, shoving her to the ground. It leapt on top of her but before it landed, she lifted her leg and plunged her heel into its lower abdomen and then launched it behind her. It went flying head first through the air and landed against the wall, crumpling in on itself.

Christopher, who was sitting nearby, crawled over to it and staked it through the heart as it struggled to regain control.

There was one more vampire remaining, and it slinked in the shadows, suddenly lacking in confidence now that all its friends were gone. Jude waited patiently, eyes closed because it was too dark to see anyway, and honed in on the sounds it made. Mucusy, belabored breathing, feet shuffling across the cement floor, teeth gnashing and grinding. It was animal-like. All of them had been. Most had to be young vampires, sleepers only raised a month or so ago. Mature vampires were able to reason. They were more cunning and deductive, not to mention stronger. Sleepers were little more than feral coyotes, able to follow basic orders from their leaders and desperate for blood, desiring only to kill and consume, completely unaware of their own mortality.

It seemed to be staying farther back, moving around her in circles, hoping to lure her in. But Jude was much, much smarter. Eyes still closed, she took a deep breath and gripped the wooden stake tight in her hand. She heard every flinch and flutter, and steadied herself. She regulated her breathing. In through the nose and out through the mouth. Her fingers twitched, but she calmed them. She listened, intently focused, as the sleeper moved back around in front of her, maybe four or five feet away. Slowly and with incredible control, she lifted her arm. All noises ceased and she knew that the vampire had stopped moving. With every ounce of strength she had, she flung her arm forward and released the stake, sending it end over end through the air until she heard it land with a muted thud in the chest of the monster.

She waited. It gasped. She heard it sputter and cough, and then the rain of dust that followed. The stake clattered on the factory floor.

She released a sound that was almost laughter and began to breathe more heavily again as her target had been neutralized and her focus melted back down to a normal level. She turned for Christopher.

"That's all of them, right?"

"Yeah," she answered confidently. She found

his arm and pulled him up. They felt around on the floor for their cell phones. When they found them, Jude's was cracked but was still working, and she re-opened the flashlight. They grabbed the crates and made their way back to the car, exhausted.

* * *

When Shiloh arrived at the tree line, Elliott and Caleb were there to meet her.

"You made it," said Elliott, smiling as she came closer.

"Do you have the book?" the older boy asked.

"This is Caleb," said Elliott.

Shiloh nodded at him but kept the book tight against her chest. Caleb was taller than her, and much taller than Elliott, but she could see that they were brothers. They had similar curly, reddish hair and the same face shape. But Caleb didn't smile. He was kind of lurky, with slumped shoulders and baggy clothes. In the moonlight, she could tell that he was kind of dirty, and he kept wringing his hands and looking around like he was nervous.

"The book?" he repeated. "You said you wanted proof."

He stuck his hands out toward Shiloh and the Codex, and she breathed sharply in through her nose. She looked at Elliott, who was standing patiently beside her, and who put his hand on her shoulder.

"It'll be okay," he told her gently. "We can keep you safe."

She shook her head. "You won't need to. You're wrong."

"I hope so," answered Elliott. He gave her a soft smile and finally, reluctantly, she placed the Codex in Caleb's grimy hands.

"It's very old," she cautioned him. "And important. I shouldn't even have it outside like this."

"We will be quick," Caleb answered without looking up. Already he was flipping rapidly through the pages like a dog after table scraps. His eyes seemed a little wild and something about him made her chest tighten with anxiety. She didn't trust him, but he was Elliot's older brother. Elliott trusted him and she trusted Elliott, so she waited.

Without warning, Caleb stopped flipping and began scanning one page in particular. "Here," he said, tapping his finger on the book a little too hard. "Read right there."

Shiloh couldn't do it. She couldn't make her hands reach for the book. It was all she could do to keep standing upright. Caleb groaned, irritated, and began to read aloud.

"There was never a time that I did not know I was destined for death," he read from an entry made by a Chosen before her. "Even before I was told, I could feel it following me. It reached for me every day, falling just short of snatching me up in its talons. I knew, however, that one day it would latch on. It would sink its sharp claws into me and carry me away."

Shiloh looked at Caleb doubtfully. "See, you

are wrong. That has nothing to do with me," she said with confidence.

Caleb shook his head. "Fine, maybe another Chosen will convince you." He flipped some more until he came to a page that Shiloh was sure she hadn't seen, covered in small sketches and words written at funny angles among them. He moved his face closer to the book to read the small, faded writing beside a particularly frightening picture of what appeared to be some kind of hole in the ground, with monstrous looking creatures clawing out of it. "I believe tomorrow will be my final battle," he read. "Today I found the place where I believe the sacrifice will be made. A scorched crevasse in the earth, and below it, demons of unimaginable numbers. This is where I shall die, my blood satiating the hungry vipers, to lull them into sleep for some centuries until the next of my lineage comes along to retrieve my extinguished torch. I am unsure that I will even see the dawn. I can feel the universe quaking. My time has come."

Shiloh swallowed a lump that had crept into her throat at the thought of the girls horrific description. She could feel her thoughts being jumbled. "No," she said quietly. "No, that won't happen to me. You're just looking for stories of people who died. My mom protects me."

Caleb exhaled. "Shiloh, didn't you hear what I said? *Until the next one.* The next one is you. Every one of the girls before you died. Every one of them. Think about it. Have you ever finished a single one of their stories?"

Shiloh racked her brain. As a matter of fact, she had not. Jude always stopped her before she got to the end. Sometimes way before. And when they picked up to read more the next time, they would start with a new chapter. A new Chosen.

No, she still refused to believe it. There was no way that her mother would keep something like that from her. Her mother, who taped all of her school papers to the refrigerator. Her mother, who read her bedtime stories and gave her extra dessert. Who kept Shiloh's picture pinned to the sun visor in the Jeep, and tucked her baby clothes away in a special place. She wouldn't lie to her. She kept her safe.

This is exactly what she related to Caleb, crossing her arms over her chest.

He let out an exasperated breath. "Are you really this stupid? Of course she keeps you safe," he said, becoming more visible in Elliott's flashlight beam. "It's her job. She was *hired.* She keeps you safe because she needs to keep you alive until you're eighteen. So you can be sacrificed. You're going to die."

Shiloh was shaking her head so hard that her neck hurt. "No!" She said, almost shouting in the quiet night. "You've got it all wrong! You haven't proven anything, give me back my book!"

She reached for the Codex, but Caleb pulled it back. "You are only believing what you want to believe," he said harshly. "I didn't want to have to do this."

"What?" She asked nervously.

"Do you know who your father is?"

She took a step back. She'd had fleeting thoughts in the past about her father, but she'd never been courageous enough to ask. She figured he had just run off or something. She had friends in school whose dads weren't around. Shiloh assumed her dad was just not a nice guy and had taken off. Slowly, she shook her head no.

"That's because you don't have one."

She made a perplexed face. "Everyone has a dad," she answered.

"Nope," he said. "Not you. You don't have a dad, and your mom isn't really your mom."

Shiloh laughed. "Okay, now you're really crazy. Of course she is. She has baby pictures of me."

"Any of her pregnant with you?" he asked.

She didn't answer.

"You do know where babies come from, right?"

"Of course I do," she shot back, even though she was a little fuzzy on the details.

"Your mom was never pregnant. That's why there aren't any pictures. You have special powers because you're not a real person. You're not even human. How else would you have them?"

Shiloh swallowed a sour knot in her throat and she felt a little dizzy. This was a more convincing argument. Her resolve was breaking and cracks were forming in what thirty minutes ago was an ironclad case against Caleb. Jude had never mentioned a father, or even a boyfriend that *could've* been Shiloh's father. And she did have special powers. None of her friends could do the things she could do. Jude told her she had to keep them a secret. Why?

"Here. Take a look at this," Caleb spoke up, flipping to the very last written-in page of the Codex, before a few yellowed blank ones.

She'd never seen the last page. She and Jude had only made it about half-way through the book so she never thought anything of it. But now, looking at what appeared to be the handwritten scrawl of some dead language, filled with symbols she'd never seen before, she felt like something big was about to happen. Like she was holding Moses' stone tablets and her entire world was about to be re-ordered.

"What is this?" she asked.

"Read it," said Caleb, pointing to the spaces between the strange symbols, where someone had taken a pencil and translated it into English like the rest of the book.

"And the child will be entrusted to the guardian, one who has been chosen," she paused and swallowed a lump in her throat. Chosen? Light-headed, she went on. "-by blood to protect the child from the forces of darkness, until her eighteenth year when she shall be led as a lamb to the holy place and offer her blood and her life for the Restoration."

Restitutio. Restoration. It had been on the front cover, staring her in the face the whole time.

The light illuminating the darkness, the leveling of the scales. It was all hitting her at once, everything she'd been too blind to see before.

A heavy silence pressed down over the group for a minute, and Shiloh felt Elliott's hand on her shoulder. A tear escaped the corner of her eye and she quickly wiped it away. Honestly, there was some part of her that still didn't believe it, but that part was much smaller now and the majority of her reason couldn't help but believe that Caleb was telling her the truth. She probably could have come up with some explanation, another way to interpret the text, if she tried. But it would've been flimsy, and she couldn't think anyway. Everything in her body seemed to have slowed down, or completely shut off. She was cold and her skin was covered in tiny hard bumps. The back of her neck felt tingly, and so did her fingers. She wasn't crying, but she wanted to be. She took slow, shallow breaths as a cool, sobering sense of betrayal washed over her and she became, maybe for the first time in her life, truly angry.

"Do you believe me now?" Caleb asked, closing the Codex with a harsh snap and staring too aggressively into her liquidy eyes.

She dropped her head to hang heavily at her neck, unable to lift it again into an affirmative nod.

"Okay. Well look, Elliott and I can get you out of here. Someplace safe."

"You want me to leave?"

Caleb threw his arms up, completely frustrated. "Oh my god," he grunted. "Elliott, you take it from here."

Elliott, who Shiloh had come to discover was much, much more tender and compassionate than his all-business older brother, turned to her and pulled her down beside him to sit on a log. "If you stay here, you'll die," he said as gently as he could. "Maybe way before you turn eighteen. Do you understand?"

Shiloh nodded and drug the arm of her coat over her eyes, even though she didn't understand at all.

"Okay," he went on. "Well, we can get you away from here and make sure that doesn't happen. We can protect you."

"How?" she asked.

Elliott looked nervously at Caleb.

Caleb rolled his eyes and joined them on the log. "We have a safe house. Back home where we're from. No one will ever find you there. We can help you reinvent yourself. Change your name and stuff."

"But my mom-"

"She's not your mom, Shiloh. She's your prison guard."

She took a deep breath and tried to steady herself. She was angry, there was no doubt about it. Angry at Jude. Angry at Ezra, who she assumed had to know the truth. Suddenly everyone she trusted was repainted as a liar. She didn't want to leave home. Even knowing what she knew, she still felt in her gut some strange love and devotion to her mother- or whatever she was. But even more than those things, Shiloh didn't want to die.

The thought made her body go numb and frozen. Death? She'd barely even thought about death. Ever. It was such a cold and sterile word. She hated the feel of it. Even though she fought it, her mind played out violent scenes of her own death. She had no idea how it would end, but she imagined being ripped to death by claws and shredded by teeth of some horrid, unearthly creature.

The creatures that Jude fought. The ones Shiloh wasn't supposed to know about. They had been after her all along. Jude was just doing her job.

All of a sudden, Shiloh was overcome with nausea. She could feel the color being sucked from her skin. Her face and palms became clammy. She stood up from the log and took a staggering step back, away from the boys. The shadowy woods and distant house became blurry, moving images and she doubled over, bracing herself on a bristly tree trunk. Her body heaved and she threw up the contents of her stomach, then stood back up, wiping her mouth on her sleeve.

"Are you okay?" Elliott asked.

Shiloh paused, and steeled her resolve. "When do we leave?" she asked finally.

CHAPTER 13

Back at the hotel, Jude and Christopher looked around to make sure no one was watching. It seemed as though the desk attendant had fallen asleep in her chair, and the parking lot was still deserted.

They pulled the two crates out of the back seat of the car and carried them into their room. Jude pulled out another jug and once again, opened it up. She carried it over to the sink and poured a small amount down the drain.

"As far as I can tell, this is just water. It may have nothing to do with whatever is going on here," she said screwing the cap back on.

"Well," Christopher answered, laying back on his bed. "At least we took out a vampire nest. That's something. God knows how many people they hurt."

"That's true," Jude answered. She lifted her hand to rub her eyes and noticed for the first time in the light that her knuckles were, in fact, torn apart. There were bite marks on her shoulder, claw marks on her back and neck. She glanced in the mirror and discovered that she herself looked like the living dead.

"I'm going to go take a shower," she said weakly. She was exhausted and all of her muscles burned.

"Okay," he answered. "So, are we in for the night?"

She looked at him and shrugged. "Honestly I don't know what else we can do. Tomorrow we'll go to the funeral. Maybe someone will talk. Right now, I need to get some sleep. Regain some energy."

"Sure," said Christopher, as he pulled his laptop out of his duffle bag. "Well, you go shower and I'll do a little research. See if I can find anything about these crates of water."

"Good luck," said Jude sarcastically as she turned for the bathroom.

Jude peeled off her sweaty, dust-covered clothes, turned the shower dial to as hot as she could stand it and stepped into the stream. The scolding water pounded against her back and neck and she closed her eyes, leaning against the plastic shower wall for support. When she opened them again, blood-stained water was circling the drain and she watched it disappear down the pipe. She felt like she was always washing away blood; if not her own, than someone else's. She leaned her head back and ran both hands through her hair as the water cascaded over her face, stinging against each little open wound and scrape. After she felt that the water had restored some of her sanity and relaxed her enough to go on, she unwrapped the little bar of hotel soap and finished her shower. Afterwards, she dried off in a crisp white towel that was much too small, and pulled an extra-long t-shirt over her head.

The lights were off and Christopher was laying on top of the covers. His pants and shoes were piled at the foot of the bed. He had changed into sweat pants and a white undershirt which glowed sort of blue in the light from the television. He stared straight ahead at the TV as Jude climbed into her own bed and pulled the covers up to her chest.

"Are you alright?" he asked, rolling over and propping himself up on his side to face her.

She nodded. "Yeah, just sore. The shower helped. Did you find anything?"

"Nothing," he answered, disappointed. He tossed her the remote and made his way to the bathroom to tend his own wounds. Jude flipped through TV channels but nothing good was on. Finally, she turned off the television and the room went dark.

Jude laid on her back with her head on her pillow and her hands resting on her abdomen, looking around at the unfamiliarity. She was tired enough, but she hated hotel rooms and missed Shiloh and her own bed. As the pain in her body subsided, her mind began to race with thoughts of Marco, of the fight, and of what tomorrow might hold.

Christopher came out of the bathroom and tiptoed back to his bed, trying hard not to make any noise. Of course, Jude was wide awake and watched in amusement as he slowly lowered himself onto the squeaky mattress and rolled under the covers. Then, all became quiet.

After laying there for twenty minutes, growing more and more anxious, Jude had enough. She needed to sleep if she was going to have any chance of accomplishing anything tomorrow. She ripped the covers off of herself in defeat and marched the three feet to Christopher's bed.

"Jude," he asked, sitting up from a half-sleep.

"Do you have that book with you? That boring, wordy one?" she asked, crossing her arms over her chest.

"No, I don't," he answered, deeply regretful.

She exhaled sharply and collapsed onto the mattress next to him.

"Well," she began. "Can you just talk then? Recite old stuffy poetry or tell me how to change a tire or something."

She closed her eyes before he even began and he breathed a nervous laugh, pulling the covers from under her and tossing them over her body. She adjusted herself next to him, forming against the hollow shape he left with his hips and his chest. Trying to match her sudden courage, he put his arm around her and placed his hand on her shoulder. A little stunned, he laid silently for a moment, trying to catch his breath.

"Well?" Jude asked.

Without thinking, Christopher dove into

long, rambling stories about anything he could think about; his favorite books, his college professors, his collection of rare coins. He talked forever, or at least he would have. In less than ten minutes, Jude was asleep.

* * *

Shiloh crossed the field again, but this time she didn't run. She zipped up her hoodie and pulled the hood over her wispy blonde hair. The air wasn't cold, but her body was. Her bones were. Caleb and Elliott turned back to wherever they came from and Shiloh didn't watch them go. She stared at the soft ground beneath her feet with every step, moving numbly in the direction of the yellow porch light.

She had forgotten that it was dark, and midnight, and that she was alone. She made no particular effort to avoid being seen through windows, or be especially quiet. Even when she made it back to the house, she opened the back door as if it were mid afternoon and she was just home from school. She walked carelessly through the kitchen and up the stairs, pausing for a moment in Jude's bedroom. On her way past, she caught sight of the picture on Jude's nightstand. Without hesitation, she picked it up and laid it down on its face, so that she didn't have to look at it anymore, then made her way upstairs to her room.

She went to her desk where her school backpack hung over her chair and dumped it out on the desktop, not bothering to arrange the books and papers into a neat stack. The first thing to go into it, without hesitation, was Herschel the Alligator. Then she went to her closet and began pulling clothes off of hangars. She tried to be reasonable. Two pairs of jeans, a few t-shirts, and a pair of pajamas. She pulled an unknown quantity of socks and underwear out of her dresser drawer and stuffed it all into the backpack, then placed her overalls and the jacket she'd been wearing on the floor by her bed, deciding to wear those tomorrow. She slung the open bag over her shoulder and carried it to her bookshelf. There was no way she could take them all, or even half of them. She limited herself to two, and she had to make them count. First, she chose *The Lion, The Witch and the Wardrobe* by CS Lewis. She had all seven books in the series on the shelf, and she was only half-way through the fourth one, but this one was her favorite, and she had gone back to it several times. The second and final book she chose was special. It had been Jude's first, and the dust jacket had fallen off long ago, leaving a faded blue, fabric-stretched cover with the silvery autograph of Shel Silverstein stamped in the lower right corner. Some of the blue dye had been thinned and smeared when she accidentally spilled a glass of water on it three years ago. Among her earliest memories was Jude reading poetry to her from this book almost every night when she was a baby. They'd read the whole thing all the way through several times. It wasn't every night now, but sometimes Jude would still read it to her. On nights when she'd had a tough time at school, or just couldn't fall asleep, Jude would stroll over to the bookshelf and pull the book down, then collapse onto Shiloh's bed and cross her ankles and they would do what they always did when they read the book. Jude held it closed and spine down so that Shiloh could place her finger somewhere over all of the pages. Jude would open to that page and they would start reading. By now, Shiloh could rehearse most of them by heart, but she loved to listen to her mom's measured cadence whispering the rhyming phrases as if for the first time. She knew Jude wasn't looking at the words on the page either. Half of the time, her eyes were closed as she recited the poems she'd long known by heart.

She held the book in her hands and her palms started to sweat and radiate heat. She thought she might be sick again. Absently pulling the book to her chest, Shiloh began to cry. For a minute, she sat down on her floor and rocked back and forth, squeezing Shel Silverstein for whatever ounce of her mother he may have retained in his pages. Her mother as she remembered her, not as she knew her now. As who she really was. She sucked in a hard breath and wiped her eyes. Resisting the urge to tear the pages right out of the book, she shoved it into her backpack and pulled the zipper.

Shiloh climbed into bed and stared at her ceiling. She wouldn't be getting any sleep, but she needed to at least try. Tomorrow after school, she was running away and never coming home.

* * *

Jude reached around behind her back to pull a pillow over her face and shield her eyes from the sun. When she realized what she was doing, she woke up, startled. Sunlight was beaming around the edges of the thick curtains of the hotel window. It had to be late in the morning. She tossed the pillow aside. As she moved to sit up, she discovered that her arm was pinned between Christopher's side and bicep. She was laying against him, the front of her body molded to the back of his, and he was still sound asleep.

For a second, she just laid there wondering what she'd gotten herself into. Once again, she had ignored all of her better judgment and allowed herself to impulsively give in to whatever it was she felt for him. And once again, she'd come down from the high and it all seemed like a really bad idea. She lifted her head and shoulders to look over Christopher's body at the alarm clock by the bed. It was nine thirty. She hadn't slept that late in a long time.

As carefully as possible, she slipped her arm out from under him and rolled over to the other side to get up. As her muscles engaged to pull her body out of bed, they smarted and pulled and she let out an accidental groan.

Christopher started to stir, and realizing Jude was no longer next to him, he opened his eyes.

"Good morning," he said through a cracking

voice. He dropped his lazy hand onto the bedside table and felt around until he found his glasses. When he did, he slid them on to his face and smiled a little at the sight of Jude in full color and form.

"Morning," she answered, rubbing her hand over the back of her neck and turning away. She was in a big hurry to find her pants, and she tossed her backpack onto her bed to look for them.

"Sleep okay?" he asked, sitting up.

"Mhm," she answered, avoiding eye contact.

He laughed, but did his best to conceal it.

As Jude bent down to dig through her backpack, she winced again when her shoulders pinched and she did her best to rotate them.

"Are you hurt?" asked Christopher as he threw his feet onto the floor.

"Oh, no I'm fine." She found a bottle of Tylenol and poured two pills into her hand. He took a few steps toward her and put both of his hands on her shoulders to rub the sore muscles, but before he got any further she slid away toward the bathroom. "I'll be find by noon. There has to be coffee in here, right?"

By the bathroom sink was a very small coffee pot and package of generic ground coffee. Still pantsless, she poured water into the machine and set the pot back under the drip. She unwrapped a small paper cup from the sanitary plastic lining, filled it with water, and threw back the pills. Then, she set it back on the sink and leaned both arms onto the counter to watch the coffee drip into the pot.

Christopher was getting dressed across the room and she stared hard at the coffee maker, but in her peripherals she could see him moving, periodically breaking the light from the window as he lifted his arms to pull on his shirt. She exhaled slowly and pressed her fingers into her eyes in an attempt to stay focused.

"So, the service is at eleven," Christopher said breaking the silence. "What should we do until then?"

Finally, the coffee was done and she poured herself a cup. The hotel creamer was powdered and there were only three sugar packets but it would have to do. "Um," she answered slowly. "Idunno, I guess we could go back to that factory. See if maybe in the daylight there's more to find. Did you want coffee?"

"No thanks. Do you really think there's anything to be found?"

No, she didn't. Really, she was feeling like she was spinning her wheels in this town when she could be at home with Shiloh but she needed to stay a little longer. At least until after the service. Maybe it was just a particularly gnarly gang of vampires that had been causing all this trouble, and they were gone.

"Could be," she answered weakly.

Her phone was on the nightstand and she picked it up and dialed Ezra's number.

"Good morning," said Ezra, picking up the

other line. As always, she sounded alert and chipper. "I expected to hear from you a little earlier. How's Tidewater?"

"Oh it's fine," she answered. "We got into a decent fight last night and are a little slow to start this morning. Did Shiloh get off to school okay?"

"Yeah," answered Ezra. "She seems like she's still kind of in a funk though. She probably just misses you."

"Well, I miss her too. Have her call me later, okay?"

"Of course. So what was this fight? Vampires?"

"Yeah," she answered. She took a sip of her coffee and made a sour face, but took another sip anyway. "Yeah, they were mostly unskilled, but there were several. No survivors though."

"Good. Any leads on what else is going down out there?"

Jude shook her head. "No, not really. Except a bunch of crates full of water jugs. We followed the cops to this old warehouse where some kids were caught breaking in. That's where we found the crates. And the vampires."

"Did the kids know about the vampires?"

"No idea," answered Jude. "But the crates seemed to matter to them."

"And you have no idea what is in the jugs?"

"It tasted a little salty. Like salty dirt."

Ezra paused. Jude could hear her shift the phone. "You drank it?"

"No," answered Jude defensively as Christopher crossed his arms and cocked his head at her. "I just tasted it."

"Well, I'll do some research but it sounds like you don't have much yet."

Jude rocked back on her hips and leaned against the counter. "Yeah, we have nothing."

"You'll find something," Ezra encouraged. "Call me if you need anything."

"You too."

They hung up the phone and Jude went back to her backpack and pulled out her clothes. "I'm gonna go get dressed," she said before disappearing into the bathroom.

* * *

Shiloh was trying to act normal. She had never needed to fake anything before. Not like this. She'd never really lied at all, and she'd been feeling horrible about it since she turned the fake permission slip allowing her to go home with Caleb in to her teacher. She felt horrible as she scrawled Jude's name as neatly as she could on the line. Even before that, when she was riding to school with Ezra, she knew she must've looked like a crazy person. Every time she spoke it felt like her voice was too high and that she was talking too fast. In trying to look normal, she worried that she looked exactly the opposite. And now, she had a huge pit in her stomach every time Mrs. Brooksdale spoke to her because she was certain that she somehow knew. She'd excused herself to the bathroom three times already even though she only actually had to go once. She was doodling in her notebooks instead of paying attention in class. Her whole body was full of nervous energy and she kept tapping on things and bouncing her leg up and down. She'd never felt anything like this before. To calm her nerves, she kept closing her eyes and focusing on her breathing. She told herself that she was just being paranoid; that no one else even noticed that she was acting strange. She just needed to steady herself.

Across the room, Elliott kept shooting her pleading looks and mouthing things like, "relax." Shiloh kept looking at the clock. It was not even lunch time.

At eleven, she had reading group, which was usually her favorite part of the day. Elliott was in her group and they sat next to each other at the round table in the back of the classroom with Mrs. Brooksdale. When Elliott and the other kids all pulled out their copies of *Because of Winn-Dixie*, Shiloh went light-headed. In her anger the night before, she'd forgotten to put her copy of the book back into her backpack. Already this morning, she had to borrow a pen from her neighbor, and look on with another student when reading the text for science.

"Mrs. Brooksdale," she said weakly, pale-skinned and trembling. "I forgot my book."

Mrs. Brooksdale looked more concerned than disappointed. "Shiloh, it isn't like you to be this unprepared. Is everything alright?" she asked as she pulled an extra copy out of the stack and opened it to the appropriate page.

When Shiloh didn't produce an immediate answer, Elliott nudged her under the table and she lifted her head quickly. "Yes ma'am, I'm just a little tired. I'm sorry."

"Well, sometimes things happen," the teacher answered, handing her the book. "Just remember your copy tomorrow. You need it to make notes in the margins."

Shiloh nodded and ducked her head into the heavily used paperback and thought about breathing. In. And out. She just had to make it to three o'clock.

CHAPTER 14

After they were dressed and ready, Jude and Christopher went to the hotel lobby for breakfast. They were the only souls in the place except for the front desk worker - different from the night before - and a middle aged maid who said nothing as she filled napkin holders and plastic spoon containers. The options were less than ideal, but Jude ate a few stale donut holes with a glass of orange juice and they bounded out into the town of Tidewater.

They drove past the factory once more, but it seemed quiet and they decided not to even get out of the car. It was a shot in the dark that Jude suggested it anyway, and was really only because she had no other leads. But by the time they'd made it back into town, they still had an hour to kill before the funeral service.

Since the sun had come up, it did seem that Tidewater was a little more active. Still not what one would expect on a Monday morning, but the shops along Main Street that weren't wrapped in police tape hung "open" signs in their windows and a handful of people walked down the streets, popping in and out of coffee shops.

Christopher pulled the car under the awning of a gas station to fill up.

"Do you want anything from inside?" he asked, ducking his head back into the car after he'd climbed out.

"No thanks," Jude answered, as she typed a text message to Ezra on her phone. Shiloh was on her mind and though she felt like Shiloh's mood had improved, she couldn't stop thinking about the conversation they'd had just before she left. It was a quarter after ten and Shiloh was in school. She'd considered calling St. Mary's and asking to speak with her, but Jude worried that would just make it worse, so she settled for pestering Ezra.

While Christopher was inside, Ezra reassured Jude that everything was fine and that Shiloh would call as soon as school was out, and Jude put her phone back in her pocket. She wasn't satisfied, and she still didn't feel quite right, but she told herself that she just needed to relax. When Christopher returned to the car, he carried two bottles of water and a package of Reese's candy. He tossed them into the driver's seat and went to pump gas, leaving the door open.

While they filled up, another vehicle, an old pick-up truck, pulled in to the pump across from them and an older man stepped out. He was talking loudly on a cell phone and Jude and Christopher couldn't help but overhear his conversation.

"Did you see the news this morning? Another

missing person." Pause. "Yeah, young guy, late twenties. Said he stepped outside his house because he heard a noise and never came back in." Pause. "I know. Don't know what's goin' on in this damn town but I tell ya, I think it's time to move."

Christopher got back in the car and glanced at Jude to make sure she'd been listening. When the old man got back into his truck, Jude pulled her phone back out of her pocket and Googled local news. Several headlines popped up about the missing man.

"Authorities have determined that Thomas Wooldridge, age 28, was taken from his yard against his will," Jude read aloud. "Drag marks in the grass near his home on Atlanta Avenue indicate that there was a struggle. As of this time, there are no leads on who his attacker may be. Residents of Tidewater are strongly urged to remain inside and lock all doors and windows until the suspect is apprehended. The case has been ruled as an abduction and Wooldridge is suspected to be in grave danger."

Christopher leaned his head down to rest on the steering wheel and listened as Jude finished the news story.

"So what is that now, four people missing, including Marco?"

"Something like that," she answered. She rubbed her eyes. "Let's find Atlanta Avenue and see if the cops are still there. Maybe we can talk to someone."

Christopher punched the street name into

his GPS and a green pathway lit up the directions. "It's just a few blocks over," he confirmed, starting the engine.

They arrived at Atlanta Avenue in less than five minutes and began scanning for the house. When they came up to a small brick one-story with a driveway full of cop cars, they figured they'd found the place.

Christopher parked across the street and they both got out and walked up to the edge of the yard. There was police tape encircling the property and officers with German shepherds moved through the grass looking for evidence. A small crowd had gathered around to watch and people with concerned looks and crossed arms stood in tight bunches talking as the investigation continued. They decided to divide and conquer.

Jude stepped up to one cluster of people and listened as they whispered and speculated, but it seemed that no one had information beyond what was offered on the news.

Christopher overheard one man in a plaid button-up mention that one of the officers was his brother. He zeroed in on him and made a point to introduce himself.

"How long have the police been here?" Christopher asked the man in plaid.

The man didn't take his eyes away from the crime scene but answered Chris. "Oh, they've been here since about five this morning."

"Found anything?"

The man shook his head and spat on the pavement. "Nah. Not yet. They're pretty sure there was more than one kidnapper though. On account of the boot prints."

"Boot prints?"

The man spat again and tipped his head. "That's right. My brother said there's multiple sets of prints. Some kind of work or military boot. Thomas was wearing sandals and they found his prints too."

"Interesting," said Christopher. He stood there for a few more seconds, then thanked the man and turned back for Jude who was listening in on another conversation a few yards away. "Hey, do vampires and demons wear shoes?" He whispered into her ear when he reached her.

She turned and furrowed her brow. "What?"

Christopher pulled her away from the crowd. "I was just talking to a guy over there. He said the cops believe that there were multiple attackers all wearing similar boots."

"Huh," answered Jude. "I mean, I guess they could? But why?"

"Maybe it's some kind of uniform," Christopher suggested.

Just then, one of the dogs started to bark as he buried his nose into a brush pile at the edge of the yard. Multiple police officers ran over to the dog and crowded out Jude's line of sight. They were too far to hear so they got as close as they could and waited for the group to break up. Finally, the cops started to step back and move toward their squad cars in the driveway. One of them carried a small plastic bag with something inside of it. It looked like a piece of paper but it was still too far to make out any markings. As the crowd of spectators all merged near the cars and the officers tried to keep them away, Jude and Christopher stayed back, waiting. Christopher kept his eyes on the man with the plaid shirt.

"He's our best bet at getting info I think," he told Jude. "His brother's a cop."

The police continued to keep the crowds at bay, and eventually the swarm became smaller and smaller as people broke off and went in their own direction. The man in the plaid shirt was among the last to leave and when he did, Christopher took off in his direction.

"Hey buddy!" he called like he knew the guy as he was within a few yards.

The man turned around and nodded at Christopher and Jude.

"Hey, so did they find anything to help with the investigation? What was in the bag?"

The guy looked around like he was checking to make sure no one else could hear, but Christopher got the sense that he liked to be the guy that knows things. He crossed his arms over his chest and spoke in a low voice. "Yeah, but you have to keep it to yourself. The police ain't ready to go public with it yet."

They both promised not to share his secret

with anyone and he took a step closer.

"In the brush pile over there near the scene of the struggle, they found an envelope. My brother said it was empty, but there was a wax seal on the back. A real, wax seal. Strange, right?"

"A seal?" Asked Jude. "What did it look like? Was it a symbol?"

He shook his head. "No, he said it was letters. BYH. Seems to me to be meaningless, but they think it could be connected. They'll get to the bottom of it."

Chris nodded. "I'm sure they will."

Jude pulled her phone out of her pocket to check the time. It was 10:45. "We have to go if we're going to make it to the service," she said, nudging Christopher in the side.

"Right," he answered. "Thanks." He stuck his hand out and shook the hand of the man in plaid.

"Stay safe out there," the man said.

Christopher returned the salutation and they parted ways.

The funeral service was held in a small Baptist church near the river. When they pulled up, the parking lot was packed and there was a line out the door. It was no surprise. Jude had seen this before. When children die, everyone mourns. It doesn't matter if you knew them or not. After all, it was the universal truth that brought Jude and Christopher to the service in the first place. Yes, they were hoping for the possibility of getting closer to the killer, but at the heart of it, Jude needed to go. As a mother, as a friend, as a human, she felt that in a way, however small, she was connected to this child and she owed him her respects.

They had stopped by a grocery store on the way in and picked up a small arrangement of white roses. As she carried them into the church, shaking hands with puffy-eyed strangers, Jude wondered where the tradition came from. Why flowers? Like a child, like anything that lives, flowers are beautiful only for a short time. They grow, they bloom, and then, eventually, they die. That is the natural order of things. But it suddenly felt wrong, and even cruel, to pluck them from their roots in their prime. And then to bring them to the funeral of a child...

Opting not to carry them all the way inside, Jude quickly rid herself of the roses. She placed them on a small table near the front of the sanctuary where a photograph of Marco was displayed, along with a worn and well-loved stuffed bear. She thought of Shiloh's Herschel and faltered a little as her breath caught in her throat. She steadied herself against Christopher, wrapping her arm under his as they made their way toward the casket and the family.

Jude was physically incapable of looking at, and especially into, caskets. She'd seen enough of them to know that she didn't have the constitution for it, especially ones that were adorned with golden cherubs and inlaid roses and designed for someone much too small for such a fate. She kept her eyes down, or when safe, straight ahead and did her best to keep her stomach where it belonged. She knew about herself that death was not a thing she handled well. She didn't like the sterility, the finality. She didn't like the associated words and phrases that people mutter in nervous and breaking voices when in the presence of it. *We're sorry for your loss. I can't imagine what you're going through. They're in a better place.* They felt gummy and acidic on her tongue, and sounded cold and meaningless to her ears. Vampires and monsters were different. She could look past the humanity of those things on most occasions, though she still wasn't fond of cemeteries. Death, for her, had always been a dark, lurking figure like a phantom she couldn't shake. It was a frequent visitor to her family as a child, taking her aunt, her mother, her father, and her cousin Jacqueline. It hung about her now, around herself, around Shiloh. It was a fear so intense that on the occasions when it could not be repressed, Jude had to fight the catatonia that tempted her to shut down completely.

Just past the casket stood the boy's parents, crying and holding one another. Weakly, they shook the hands of visitors as they passed and Jude felt deep sorrow for them, having to stand and greet people like you might at a wedding or business conference. Nonetheless, as the line moved she moved with it and she stepped up to the grieving couple.

She opened her mouth to speak but nothing came out. She shook her head and placed and offered a gentle touch on the arm to both of them. She wished that she was Shiloh, who wouldn't have been able to heal them or bring back Marco, but who may have been able to give them some peace. Of course, she wasn't Shiloh, and while they shared many attributes, it was the other part of Shiloh- the part that came from a place of divine sanctity- that allowed her those abilities. So Jude just whispered an apology and walked away.

The mother accepted leaned in slightly to Jude's touch, then stiffened her back and wiped her eyes with an already drenched tissue.

"Thank you for coming," she said cordially.

Jude nodded and Christopher stepped forward, holding the father's hand in his after a long shake. "We're so sorry," he whispered. "Your family is in our prayers."

They both nodded numbly and Christopher took Jude's hand again and moved to leave the sanctuary, but as he did Jude pulled back and leaned into the mother's ear.

"I'm going to find out who is responsible for this," she whispered, taking for a moment Marco's mother's hand. "I promise. And when I do, they will pay."

Marco's mother looked at Jude, a perfect stranger, with both shock and gratitude. Their eyes met for an intense moment, and Christopher pulled Jude away.

"Come on," he mumbled, glancing around at the crowded room.

He held Jude's hand tightly until they were standing in the bright sun on the front porch of the church.

"What the hell was that?" he asked anxiously.

Jude rubbed her hands down her face and dropped them at her side with a slap. "Idunno, I wasn't thinking," she admitted. "I wanted to say something and I was angry. For them."

He nodded, crossing his arms over his chest and looked at her sympathetically. "I understand."

"I don't think anyone heard. And she has no idea who I am."

"Right. Okay." He put his arm over her shoulder, and she didn't protest but rather leaned against him and took a long, slow exhale. "You just have to be careful."

"I know. I will. Can we just get out of here?"

Jude and Christopher got into the car and headed back to the motel to research the initials from the wax seal. Jude texted Ezra that the funeral was a bust for information but that they were still looking.

CHAPTER 15

Never in her life had time passed so slowly. Shiloh must've looked at the clock a hundred times an hour. She looked so much until she swore it broke from all the pressure she'd put it under and time had stopped moving all together.

However, three o'clock finally did come. And when it did, she wasn't so sure she felt any better.

Ezra had to work a shift at the library and would be getting off just in time to come pick her up from school, meaning she would be near the back of the long car-rider line. Caleb was supposed to get there early and be the very first car. As the kids were ushered down the halls and toward the front of the school, Shiloh dug out her wrinkled yellow permission slip.

"Are you alright?" Elliott asked as Shiloh obsessively smoothed out the slip.

"I'm fine," she answered, out of breath for no reason other than that breathing had suddenly become almost impossible.

They stepped outside and sure enough, Caleb's old, rusty car was sitting right in front.

Shiloh scanned for Ezra but she was nowhere to be seen.

She squeezed her backpack straps until her knuckles turned white. Caleb was looking through them at the car window, motioning for them to hurry up, but Shiloh was frozen. She couldn't make words come out of her mouth and she couldn't pull her feet from the sidewalk. Elliott, exasperated, grabbed her by the arm and drug her to Coach K, who was in charge of the car rider line. When Shiloh just stared wide-eyed like a trapped animal at the coach, Elliott took the crumpled, sweaty permission slip and handed it to him.

"Shiloh is coming home with me today," he said smiling.

Coach K glanced over the note and clipped it to his clipboard. "See you tomorrow," he said chipperly. He fist-bumped Elliott, like he did with all of the students. When he offered his fist to Shiloh, she just stood there.

"She's probably still thinking about math class," Elliott joked. "None of us understood any of it. See ya' later Coach K." He waved goodbye to the gym teacher and pulled Shiloh to the car. "Shiloh, snap out of it," he mumbled as he walked past a second grade teacher and a sea of students.

She climbed into the back seat with her heart pounding against the wall of her chest. Elliott sat in the seat next to her and offered words of attempted comfort as Caleb pulled away from the school.

He looked into the rear-view mirror at

Shiloh's pale and shaking reflection. "Lay down in the seat," he said unsympathetically. "If someone sees you it's over."

Shiloh did as she was told, operating on auto-pilot. The car rattled and lurched down the road.

"Do you have everything?" Caleb asked.

"Huh? Yeah," answered Shiloh mechanically. But it hit her at once that in fact, there was one very important thing she'd forgotten. "Jack!" She shrieked, sending Elliott nearly through the roof.

"What?" asked Caleb, visibly irritated.

"My dog! We have to go get him!"

Caleb laughed like it was out of the question. "No way. Absolutely not. If we go all the way back to your house we will never get out of here without being caught. Forget it."

Shiloh sat up straight in the seat and looked out the window of the car so that every passerby could see; an act of defiance that she knew Caleb would take note of. "Ezra is on her way to the school. She won't even know I'm not there for another ten minutes." She reasoned with both him and herself, but spoke with unwavering determination. "I'm not leaving without him," she said blankly, crossing her arms over her chest.

He shifted in his seat and looked back and forth between Shiloh and the road. "Okay," he finally growled. "But no more stops after this until we're way out of town, understood?"

Shiloh nodded in agreement and ducked back down below the window as Caleb pressed the gas pedal and the car sped toward her house.

Back at home, everything was quiet, but it wouldn't be for long. Shiloh pushed from her mind the thoughts and images of Jude tearing down the driveway at a hundred miles an hour, crashing through the back door and ripping the house apart looking for her daughter. Eventually, Gideon would be called, and the police. Miss Doris would sob into her handkerchief and deliver casseroles. The yard would be crawling with people, moving in and out of the house, looking for clues, but there would be none. Shiloh would be long gone.

She knew that Ezra was probably sitting in the car rider line back at school waiting to pick her up and there was no time for sentimentalism. She leapt from the car and ran to the back door while the boys waited with the engine running.

In the kitchen, she stood by the door and called Jacks name. Her feet were planted in the threshold, as if there was something barring her from taking another step inside. After calling for him five times, the lazy copper hound came lolloping into the kitchen with his tail wagging and tongue hanging. Dropping to her knees, she wrapped him in a tight hug around the neck; a hug that she desperately needed to fortify herself for what was to come. Then, she called him outside and into the car.

Jack stretched himself out along the entire back seat and put his head in Shiloh's lap. Elliott was booted to the front seat next to Caleb.

"That's it, right?" asked Caleb.

Shiloh took a deep breath that tightened the bottom of her lungs and let it out slowly. "That's it," she answered. Her voice cracked with a harsh finality and she watched out the window as her home got smaller and smaller, until it was cut from her view by rolling hills and trees.

* * *

Jude's cell phone rang right around three-thirty while she and Christopher sat in the hotel room scrolling through dozens of tabs about crates of water, the initials BYH and the most recent victim, Thomas Wooldridge. Nothing was coming of the now two hours they'd spent conducting Google searches and Jude was getting frustrated. The caller ID read "Ezra" and she slid her thumb over the green answer button, hoping to hear Shiloh's voice on the other line. Instead, what she heard was a frantic Ezra, talking indiscernibly fast.

"Ezra, slow down," Jude said, standing up from her cross-legged position on the bed, already with that sinking feeling in her stomach that something was wrong. "What's going on?"

"Shiloh," Ezra blurted. "She isn't here at school, she left."

"What?" Jude croaked, pressing the phone harder against her ear and hoping she'd just heard wrong.

"She left," Ezra repeated. "The gym teacher said she rode home with her friend Elliott."

Jude took a breath and brought her hand to the back of her neck as Christopher stood and stepped to her side, alarmed. "Okay," she said fighting panic. "Maybe she got mixed up about the plans?"

"I don't know how she could have. I told her I was coming to pick her up."

"Dammit," Jude muttered. "Okay." She switched her phone to speaker and scrolled through her contacts, confirming what she suspected. She had no number saved for Elliott or his uncle. She opened the internet application and punched the name Elliott Todesco into the search bar with shaking fingers. "I have no idea where he lives. No idea how to reach him. What the hell do we do?"

Christopher immediately opened a new tab on his laptop. "She's with Elliott?" He asked. Before Jude could answer, he typed Walter Murdoch into the search bar. "Here," he said, taking his own phone from his pocket and dialing a number. He handed the phone to Jude and as it rang, he read off an address to Ezra. "They live on Lindsay Street. The house number is 47."

The phone rang and rang, but no one answered it. When the voicemail picked up, Jude squeezed the phone in her hand, nearly crushing it. "Go to the house, Ezra," she said urgently. "We'll leave now. Be there as quickly as we can. Call me as soon as you hear anything at all."

She hung up with Ezra while Christopher continued to redial the number he'd found for Walter Murdoch online but over and over it just went to voicemail.

"Maybe it's not the right number," said Jude as she frantically tossed things into her backpack. She ran into the bathroom and gathered everything, including Christopher's toothbrush and deodorant, and stuffed it into the bag. "Or maybe it's been disconnected. God, how could I be so stupid? I knew something was up with Shiloh. And why the hell did I not get more information on Elliott? His phone number, his address?"

"Well, it would've been a little strange if you'd asked him for his address," answered Christopher as he pulled his shoes on.

Jude came back out into the main room and slung her bag over her shoulder. "I need to stop worrying about what may look strange." She ripped the charger for Christopher's laptop out of the wall and began coiling it around the computer. "I never should've left. Why am I here? I can't do anything to help these people. I have my work cut out for me at home."

She was talking fast and moving faster, checking to make sure she'd gotten everything. It wasn't worth the time to load the crates into the car, so Jude pried the lid off of one with way too much force and the wooden boards cracked and split apart. She pulled out one jug of water and decided that would have to be enough.

"Come on, we've got to go." She sprinted to the door and into the parking lot.

Christopher ran out after her slinging his bag over his shoulder. "Jude, wait," he called after her when she threw open the driver side door.

"What?" She yelled, irritated that he was slowing her down.

"Let me drive," he said calmly, standing by the front of the car. "I'll drive and you can keep in contact with Ezra."

"Right, okay," she answered, sliding into the passenger seat without getting out of the car.

Christopher got in, buckled up and started the engine. He looked over at Jude who sat leaning far over with her head in her hands, looking smaller than ever. He put his hand on her back. "We'll find her. She'll be okay."

Jude shook her head without lifting it. "I hope so."

Christopher sped down every road they took but it wasn't fast enough. Not for Jude who hadn't put her phone down since the first time Ezra called. She'd been dialing like a mad woman, chewing on her fingernails in the passenger seat. Already, she'd made contact with Gideon, Mrs. Brooksdale at St. Mary's, and Ezra several times and they'd only been on the road for twenty minutes.

Twenty minutes was what it took for Ezra to get to Walter Murdoch's house on Lindsay street. She was on the phone with Jude when she arrived, and she put it on speaker and stuck it in her pocket. There were no cars in the driveway and the house appeared to be empty. Still, she jogged up to the front door and knocked. When no one answered, she knocked again.

"Well?" asked Jude. "What's going on?"

"No one is coming," answered Ezra, distraught. "I don't know what to do. I don't think anyone is here."

"Should we call the cops?" Christopher asked.

Jude shook her head. "No, not yet. If we call the cops, they'll slow us way down. They'll have me sit and wait someplace and I can't do that. I know her way better than they do."

"You have to get inside," Jude told her. "Try a window."

"Break in?" she asked anxiously.

"Yes, break in!" Jude didn't mean to yell, but she didn't have time to discuss the moral implications of breaking and entering. Times like these called for very simple, Machiavellian philosophies.

Ezra looked around the outside of the cape style house for any open windows. She had to climb behind a few bushes to test them but they all seemed to be locked. "I can't find a way in," she told Jude, who was still in her pocket.

"Can you kick down the door?"

"I'm not you," she answered flatly.

"Is there a basement? Back door? Ezra, you have to find a way into that house."

Ezra had never done anything like this before. She was a by-the-book sort of person, not to mention small in stature and very even tempered. It required a certain level of brashness to do things like break into strangers houses. But Ezra loved Shiloh like she was her own, and she was finding fast that great love can make a person act very out of character.

She scanned the yard until she found a large branch that had fallen from a tree. She picked it up and snapped it in half, and carried it around to the side of the house where she would be out of sight from anyone driving by.

"Ezra, what are you doing?" Jude asked from her pocket. "Did you get in?"

"I'm about to."

"How?"

"I'm going to break a window."

"With what?" Jude asked, surprised.

"A stick." Ezra surveyed the branch and sized it up against the window.

"A stick? Well make sure you-" Jude stopped talking when she heard the shattering of glass.

Once she'd made a hole in the glass, Ezra drug the stick along the edges of the window pane to knock out any shards that might cut her on her way in. She pulled her sleeve down over her palms and hoisted herself up onto the sill.

"I'm in," she said as she swung her legs over the wall and into the kitchen of the unfamiliar house.

"Oh thank god." Jude breathed a sigh of relief. "Is anyone there? Do you see Shiloh?"

Ezra took a few steps into the kitchen and called out. "Hello? Anyone here? Shiloh? Elliott?"

There was no answer and she began to move carefully through the house, still carrying her stick over her shoulder like a bat, ready to swing if there was any trouble. "Shiloh, it's Ezra, are you in here?"

"Where the hell is this uncle?" Jude asked both Ezra and Christopher.

"I'm pretty sure that no one is home," said Ezra regretfully. "All of the lights are off. The place is a mess though. Like no one has been here in a while." She noted the dirty pots on the stove and dishes on the table, clothes strewn out all over the floor.

Jude looked at Christopher. "How well do you know Walter Murdoch?"

He shook his head. "I don't," he answered. "When Elliott came to St. Mary's, I was told that he was living with his uncle who has lived in Bedford for years. Walter had once been a church member but he hasn't been coming for a while."

"Well, he isn't here," said Ezra as she began opening doors in the hallway. The first thing she found was a dirty bathroom. The next door she opened was a bedroom with only a small window and very little natural light. She tried to flip the switch but the light didn't come on. She could see that it was the bedroom of a grown man. There was a queen bed and a dresser and men's clothing dumped onto the bed.

"Power seems to be out," she related to Jude.

Finding nothing in that bedroom, she went

across the hall to open the third and final door. Inside, she found what she assumed was Elliott's bedroom. There was a bunk bed and a few small toys here and there, with papers and socks scattered on the floor. At the foot of the bed, however, something caught Ezra's attention.

"Jude, is Elliott an only child?"

Jude shrugged. "I don't know," she admitted. "I know nothing about him."

"Well, I think there's another boy in the house," she said, holding two pairs of shoes, one small and one larger. She began to notice that there were two different sizes of clothing, and both bunk beds were unmade and appeared to have been slept in. "Maybe an older boy," she added.

On her way out of the room, she tried the light switch just out of curiosity. Again, it didn't work. In the bathroom, she turned on the faucet and no water came out. "Jude, I don't think anyone has been paying these bills," she said, moving back into the kitchen. On the table was a stack of mail and sure enough, buried in the stack were several notices of unpaid electric bills, water bills, mortgages and credit card statements. Nothing had been paid in months.

"I have a bad feeling about this," she told Jude as she sifted through the piles of unopened mail.

They still had hours left in the drive and Jude couldn't stand not being there. Every second that passed was one more that separated her from Shiloh. She knew if she was standing in that kitchen with Ezra, she would find something. A clue that would help her locate her missing daughter.

"Look for car information," she told Ezra. "The school said she was picked up in a car by Elliott's uncle. So uncle or not, she got into a vehicle with someone associated with Elliott. Maybe the registration is around someplace, or inspection notices."

"Good thinking, I'll check," Ezra replied.

Jude could hear her moving through papers and opening drawers.

"I can't find anything," said Ezra growing frustrated. She turned toward the refrigerator and noticed that there were several papers attached to its side. Among photographs and phone numbers, recipes and postcards, there was a bill held on by a magnet shaped like the state of Texas. It was from Crawford Auto Repair Shop in town. "Wait," she said, unfolding it and scanning its contents. "I found a mechanics bill."

"What does it say?"

Ezra read down the paper. "Total Amount Owed: $428 for repair of the alternator." She continued scanning, mumbling through irrelevant information. "Oh, here it is. Customer name, Walter Murdoch. Vehicle: 1994 Gray Oldsmobile Cutlass."

"Gray Oldsmobile. Okay," Jude answered. She inhaled deeply and let herself believe for a moment that they were one step closer to Shiloh. "Can you just go drive around. See if you can find the car?"

"Yeah, of course," said Ezra, already on her

way out the front door. Intentionally, she left it unlocked.

"Check anyplace a kid might go. Parks, ice cream shops, Shiloh loves that circus themed place on Twelfth Street. Check the movie theater. Idunno, there aren't that many places to go in Acadia."

"Sounds like she forged a permission slip to go home with Elliott," said Christopher, trying to diffuse the palpable anxiety. "She's probably just running around town someplace with him."

"I can't believe she would do something like that," said Jude. "Not willingly or without good reason. That's not like Shiloh. She doesn't lie. I don't even think she knows how."

"It may be out of character but you said she's been in a funk for a few days," he answered.

"That's one way to put it," added Ezra through the phone. "I'd say that the word *funk* doesn't quite describe it. She's not acting like herself because she hasn't *been* herself."

Jude tried to convince herself that they were right. Shiloh was caught up in her own head, dealing with some childhood angst, and blew off steam by skipping school with her friend. But it wasn't right. Jude was a regular professional when it came to ditching class, but even her rebellious self hadn't attempted anything so bold at eight years old. Shiloh would never.

CHAPTER 16

They had been driving for a very long time and Shiloh was getting tired. It was only evening, but the stress and anticipation of the day had worn her out. However, she didn't dare close her eyes even for a second, because she had come to realize that Caleb was a very bad driver. He did okay on the streets through town, but once they got onto the highways that ran across the state, he was a disaster.

"How old are you?" she asked him when he swerved slightly into the shoulder as a big truck drove past them in the other lane.

He said that he was sixteen, but he was irritated by the question so she had been quiet ever since. Even Elliott sat silently in the passenger seat and Shiloh had plenty of time to contemplate what exactly she'd gotten herself into. By now there was no question that Jude was on a mad hunt to find her, or anything that might lead to answers. Shiloh really didn't know where she was. Most heavy on her mind now was the fact that she didn't know what was going to happen to her when she got wherever it was they were going. It was getting darker.

The sky was dark gold and orange now and she thought about her front porch at home and how that spot offered the best view of any sunset she'd ever seen. Before long it would be night time and completely dark, and she would be in an unfamiliar place. There would be no talking and laughing at the dinner table with Ezra. No snuggling on the couch watching reruns of old sitcoms, and Jude would not be tucking her in. She felt a sharp pang of remorse as the car rattled down roads that were now mostly deserted, and she wanted to go home.

"Elliott," she said trying to sound strong and clear minded.

The boy turned around to face her and saw that she had her fist wrapped tightly around Jacks collar and the other hand balled up in her lap.

"I think I changed my mind," she muttered.

"What do you mean?"

"I mean, I think I want to see my mom. I want to hear it from her."

Elliott was about to speak, but Caleb interjected. "Forget it," he said darkly. "We've come this far. There's nothing your *mom* can do for you."

Elliott shot him a disapproving look and then turned back to Shiloh. He reached out his skinny arm and put a hand on her knee. "I know you feel sad," he whispered. "And probably scared. But if we take you home you won't be safe, remember? We'll be with you. I promise, we'll make sure you're okay. We'll be your new family. Right Caleb?"

The older brother glanced narrowly in the

rear view mirror. "Yeah. Sure." He took a turn off of the main road and onto a small two-lane. "Here we are," he announced, sounding happier than he had the whole trip.

Elliott looked around through the window. "It looks... different," he said to Caleb as they entered into town. "Why's everything closed? There's police tape."

"Where are we?" asked Shiloh, pressing her face against the glass.

"Tidewater," answered Caleb. "Where me and Elliott are from. You're going to love it here."

It seemed like a nice thing to say, but Shiloh didn't like the way his mouth twisted into a tight grin when he said it.

* * *

Christopher's car tore down the driveway to the Mikhale house just as it was getting dark. Jude didn't even wait for the vehicle to come to a stop before she jumped out of it and ran for the door. She burst into the kitchen and immediately began calling for Shiloh. In truth, she knew she wouldn't answer. Shiloh wasn't home.

Still, she searched everywhere. Every room, every closet, every corner. As she was jogging up the stairs to Shiloh's room, Ezra's headlights spilled into the driveway. She'd been driving around town, periodically checking in back home, looking everywhere, but had found not a trace. Jude didn't pause at the top of the first set of stairs, or in her bedroom.

She continued up to Shiloh's room, and stopped short at the landing.

The string lights were still on, and the room was dim except for where they splashed luminous color on the walls and top of the bed. Jude pulled the chain on the ceiling light and immediately took inventory. Shiloh's school things were laying in a messy pile on and near her desk as if they'd been dumped. She had her backpack with her. She looked around the room for anything else out of place. As she slowly turned her body in the center of the floor, she paused and caught a sharp breath when she came to Shiloh's bed. Laying face down on the comforter was a book that Jude would recognize anywhere with its threadbare leather binding and yellowed, fringing pages. She walked to it slowly, like it was dangerous. When she reached the bed, she lowered herself onto the mattress and picked it up, turning it over in her hands. Christopher and Ezra appeared at the landing.

"Is that the Codex?" Ezra asked gravely, already knowing the answer.

Jude felt her stomach harden into a ball and sink. Her body went cold and she leaned forward, putting her hand over her eyes. Suddenly, the threat level had escalated. Jude could no longer tell herself that she was just out playing hooky with Elliott.

Christopher and Ezra both made their way to Jude. "We'll find her," said Chris, taking the book and fanning through the pages to see if any had been marked.

Jude threw her head toward the ceiling and released a sinister laugh, shaking her head as tears fell from her eyes. "I should've seen this coming," she said, vocalizing a thought that had been beating against the inside of her mind since Shiloh didn't come home from school. She fell back onto the bed and pressed both of her hands into the sides of her head. She had to focus. She couldn't give in to the overwhelming desire that she felt to fold into herself and cry. With her head on the pillow, she noticed two other things. Herschel the Alligator was missing in action, and so was Jack. "I don't think she plans to come home," she said weakly.

After a moment's contemplation, she stuck out her hand and Ezra pulled her up off the bed. Together, they made their way back downstairs.

"So, she read the Codex, found out about the prophecy, got scared, told her friend and they ran away. Right?" asked Ezra, oddly hopeful. "At least she's not in any immediate danger."

"We don't know that that's what happened," Jude reasoned darkly.

"It seems to be the most likely scenario," said Chris. "We can find her. How hard can she be to track? She's eight years old."

"Who the hell is driving that car?" asked Jude, racking her brain. "We have to go back to Elliott's house. That's where we'll find answers." She pulled a long handled axe out of the back of her bedroom closet, and then they were back in the car, speeding toward Walter Murdoch's house.

* * *

Caleb drove a little farther, through town and then beyond it, where the environment became more rural and marshy. Shiloh wondered where they were going but didn't ask. Finally, they turned onto a poorly paved road lined with trees and swamp, and Caleb turned off the headlights.

"What are you doing?" Asked Elliott.

"I don't want anyone to see us," answered the older of the boys as he stared intently down the road.

It seemed logical enough. After all, people were by now looking for them. But when Caleb stopped the car in front of a dark, abandoned factory, Shiloh had to swallow a lump in her throat. "What are we doing here?" she asked carefully.

"This is where we're staying tonight." Caleb opened his door and climbed out of the car.

"What?" asked Elliott. "This is a factory. We can't stay here. I thought we were staying with Aunt Mel."

"Elliott, relax," answered Caleb. "It's just for the night."

Shiloh didn't move from her seat and eventually, Caleb opened her door. "Come on, get out," he told her.

Jack lifted his head skeptically, then dropped it back down on her lap. "I think I'll just sleep in the car," Shiloh answered, steeling herself to the seat.

"You can't sleep in the car," answered Caleb.

"Now get out, let's go."

"Caleb, stop talking to her like that," Elliott demanded, but Caleb laughed at him.

"I saved her life, I'll talk to her however I want." He reached in and grabbed Shiloh by the arm, pulling her out of the car.

When Shiloh let out a shrill scream, Caleb scolded her. His breath was hot against her skin and his heart was racing. She could feel it as he pulled her out against his chest. Jack jumped up in the seat and leapt down from the car to stay with her.

Caleb was holding her arm too tightly and she asked him to let go but he wouldn't. Instead, he drug her into the dark factory.

Caleb finally let go of Shiloh, who held on tight to Jack at her side. He felt around the big, hollow room and located a flashlight. "Let's go up-stairs," he said, already making his way down a damp, littered hallway.

Shiloh and Elliott followed him apprehensively up the concrete stairs. At the top, they could hear quiet chatter.

"Is someone else here?" Shiloh whispered.

Caleb didn't answer. The voices grew louder as they approached the last door on the hall. Caleb knocked the butt of the flashlight against it in a rhythmic pattern and in a few seconds, it opened up.

The room was lit with lanterns and candles and there were several people inside. The man who opened the door was older, maybe around Gideon's age. He had short hair and he looked exhausted.

"Caleb," he said gravely. "We've had a set-back. Did you bring the girl?"

At once, Caleb, Elliott and the strange man at the door all laid eyes on Shiloh. Shiloh herself just stood there, suddenly cold and nauseous. Her mouth was open but she couldn't speak. She gripped Jack even tighter, balling the extra skin around his neck up in her fist.

"What's going on?" asked Elliott, with detectable concern in his voice.

"Just get in," he barked, shoving them both through the doorway and into the room.

There were five or six other people inside, all men. Some of them looked young, around Caleb's age. Others were much older. They all wore the same black coat and boots and were sitting in a rough circle around a few lanterns, with papers scattered around them, speaking quietly in concerned voices. When Shiloh stepped in, they all looked at her wide-eyed. She couldn't read the expression on their faces. It was a strange blend of happiness, fear and malice, and she was certain that she was someplace she never should have been.

One man in particular had not taken his eyes off of her since she walked in. He was dirty and sweaty and had some kind of pirate sword tattooed on his neck just below the right side of his jaw. "You brought her," said the man with the sword tattoo, standing and crossing the room toward her. "Wow, I can't believe you actually did it." He took a step toward Shiloh and released a sort of amazed and vicious laugh. "Hello," he told her, too close to her face. "You know, you are a very special little girl."

Shiloh took a step back. "Thanks," she said dryly.

The man reached out and brushed his clammy hand down the side of her cheek in awe, like he was touching a relic or some valuable, ancient statue. When he moved, a vein in his neck popped out and ran right through his sword tattoo. "Sven, come check it out!" he called behind him, and a shocking, disfigured man came forward. He kept swiping his black tongue across his strangely pointy teeth bent and down to look at her face-to-face. He smelled like rotten meat, and Shiloh was horrified.

"You are going to be a part of something huge," said the man with the sword tattoo. "It's going to change everything." His voice was manic and his breath was sour. His eyes were too wide, and bloodshot. "Doesn't that excite you?"

With his hand on her face, Shiloh became filled with a powerful sense of dread that made her knees weak and the hair on the back of her neck stand up. There was no light in his eyes. No warmth in his hands. There was darkness and evil in his heart. She could see it, like she could see other things; in the back of her mind, shadowy and dim. She could see into this man's soul and what she found there was a cold, black shell. Every alarm inside of her went off at once. She knew she was in danger. Why had she not seen it before? Did she just ignore it in Caleb? Why did she not pay more attention to what her body and her instincts and her supernatural senses had been telling her all along? These were bad people. They were not here to help her. They wanted nothing to do with saving her life. What they wanted, she realized in an instant, was the opposite.

Shiloh turned to Caleb. "No," she answered, looking directly at the older brother. "I want to go home. Now."

She tried to be firm, crossing her arms over her chest and punching out every word precisely and fiercely, but he looked at her with vacant eyes and shrugged. Before he could even respond, the man with the sword tattoo grabbed the back of her neck. "It's too late for that," he told her. She shrieked as his fingers wrapped around and squeezed. "You're very important to us," he sneered. Then, he drug her over to a metal door and pulled it open with a screech.

"No, stop!" Shiloh protested. Elliott stood behind them with his mouth gaping and his eyes filling with tears. But the man didn't stop and Caleb just watched. He pushed her down onto the floor and slammed the door, leaving her alone in a small, dark room.

Shiloh heard Elliott yell at Caleb and moments later, he and Jack were thrown in with her. Shiloh grabbed Jack once again and buried her face into his coat, bawling.

Elliott tried to comfort her. "I'm not sure

what's going on," he said earnestly. "I'm sure Caleb will explain it. Everything's going to be okay."

Shiloh drug her sleeve across her wet eyes and nose. "How can you still trust Caleb?" she asked, her voice too high and loud. "He's the one who is doing this to us! He's going to hurt us, can't you understand that! This was a trap!"

"Okay, you have to be quiet," Elliott pleaded in a whisper. He crawled closer to Shiloh and Jack. "What do you mean it's a trap? Who is the trap for?"

Shiloh shrugged. She could see nothing in the extreme darkness that filled the small closet, and confusion and confliction flooded her mind. This was certainly a trap. There was no doubt that she was in serious danger. But she saw the Codex. Not everything Caleb told her was a lie. He just used the truth to manipulate her into running away and the lies he told were about *his* intentions, not Jude's. Her mother was still not her mother at all, and her destiny was still to die. Now, she was completely alone and there was no one left to trust. "I don't know," she admitted. "But those guys out there are not good people. I can feel it."

"Well what do we do?"

Shiloh leaned back against the cold concrete wall. They were trapped with no way out. "I don't know," she said again, rubbing her head with the palms of her hands. "I'll think of something."

CHAPTER 17

Jude didn't bother checking to make sure they were unseen when she jumped out of the car and walked right in to Elliott's house with Christopher and Ezra behind her, all armed with flashlights. She entered through the living room door which Ezra had left unlocked, and made her way to the kitchen. Stepping around the glass shards from the broken window, she stopped to examine the papers on the table.

"I read everything in that stack," said Ezra. "There's nothing helpful. Just late notices and warnings written out to Walter Murdoch. The electricity has been shut off. Nothing in the house works."

"Someone isn't paying," Jude noted, mostly to herself. "So if this is where Elliott has been staying, who has he been staying with?" She looked at her friends and stood with her arms crossed at her chest. "We should split up. I want to see the boys room. Chris, maybe you look over the kitchen again. You'll be a fresh pair of eyes. Ezra, you can search the other rooms down the hall. Don't ignore anything. If it looks important, it probably is."

They split up and Ezra went back into the darkened bedroom of the boys alleged uncle. She set her flashlight on his dresser, pointing up at the ceiling so that most of the room was dimly illuminated, and began going through his drawers.

Most of what she found was to be expected. Clothes, socks, belts. Under a stack of folded t-shirts, she found a photograph. She held it under the light for a closer look and saw the image of a man in his thirties or forties with his arm wrapped around the waist of a woman around his age. They were both smiling at the camera. She flipped the picture over and on the back, written in pen was the simple note, "For Walt, With love from Catherine."

Ezra tucked the picture in her pocket and continued searching through the room, turning over books and shuffling through piles of laundry and junk.

Christopher searched through the kitchen ignoring the pile of bills on the table which had been searched enough. He opened drawers and found nothing out of the ordinary. He saw the mechanics bill on the fridge, the one that Ezra had found with the car information, but there was nothing else of significance under any of the quirky magnets. He made his way around the room, stopping at two doors. The first one was found to be a closet. Inside there was nothing but a few mostly empty bags of chips, some canned vegetables, and cleaning supplies. The other, however, opened to a set of stairs that led into a basement. As soon as he opened the door, he was hit with a pungent odor, and he swallowed hard. Hesitantly, he began down the stairs allowing the beam of his flashlight to lead.

The smell only got stronger as he moved further into the room. In the weak light, it appeared to be like any other basement. The floor was dirty concrete and the walls were covered in chipping paint and plaster. He bumped into a washing machine and tripped over a few odds and ends that had been tossed down there for storage. The only thing that stood out was the smell.

Although he really didn't want to, he knew he had to find the source. He shined his flashlight all over the floor, looking for anything that could produce such a sour odor but he didn't see anything. As he turned around, he caught sight of the corner or some kind of chest that had been placed under the stairs. A shudder crawled up his spine as he moved toward it. When he was a few feet away, the smell became so strong that he had to cover his face with the sleeve of his sweater. He steadied his beating heart. With his eyes shut tightly, he reached out and flipped open the metal latch that held the lid of the box shut. Still refusing to look, he lifted the wooden lid with the heel of his palm and as it cracked open, the hot, stomach churning scent of rot and decay rushed out toward him. He dropped the lid with a clatter and jumped back. Gagging, he knelt down on the floor and spat into the drain at the center. He coughed and wiped his watering eyes, then moved for the crate again. This time, he held his breath completely and lifted the lid. His heart racing, he shined his flashlight inside.

Christopher opened his eyes just long enough to see what he needed to confirm his suspicion. The curly hair and shoulders of a man, presumably Walter Murdoch, were illuminated in the glow. He slammed the lid shut and sprinted up the stairs.

Jude had been searching the boys room like a crazed detective. Ezra was right about there being two of them. One was certainly Elliott. Jude found a school folder with the St. Mary's logo printed on the front, and Elliott's school work stuffed inside. The other boy was definitely older. The room was littered with clothes and shoes, and a few odds and ends here and there. Some action figures were strewn around on the top bunk, and books and empty water bottles cluttered the desktop.

There was, however, a single drawer under the top of the desk and when Jude went to pull it open, she found that it was locked. The desk itself was made of some cheap wood and it took no effort for her to pop the front of the drawer right off, snapping free from the glue that held it together. Pens and pencils fell out and she tossed the wooden board behind her and shined the light into the hole she'd made.

It was stuffed full of papers and notebooks. She pulled out the first thing she laid her hands on and unfolded what appeared to be a letter addressed to a boy named Caleb.

"*Caleb, I hope everything is coming together on your end. You know how important it is for your brother to befriend the girl.*"

She stopped and read back over the phrase *the girl* and the pit in her stomach grew tenfold.

"*Don't let the us down. I'll be sending someone along to handle the issue of your uncle. I know it isn't easy, but we all have to make sacrifices for the Brotherhood.*"

The letter was signed by Professor D and marked with the post-script, "Praise Yarik." Urgently, Jude pulled out another folded piece of paper. Again, it was addressed to Caleb.

"*So glad to hear that the plan is coming together. With your brother enrolled at St. Mary's it's just a matter of time now. We have been in communication with our contacts in Bulgaria and they will be shipping the consecrated Chornomorsk water within the next week or two. All that's left is your part. Remember, gaining her trust is very important. We don't want her to put up a fight, or be alarmed and tell her mother.*" Again, it was signed Professor D, and under his name, "Praise Yarik."

Enraged, Jude shoved her arm all the way back into the desk and drug out everything inside of it with a furious scream. Out poured more correspondence between Caleb and Professor D and they all led to one very obvious, horrifying conclusion: Shiloh was the target of some sick, demented plot, though Jude still had no idea what that plot was.

When she heard Jude screaming profanities, Ezra came running into the bedroom and found Jude sitting in the pile of papers. "What is it?" She asked, kneeling beside her.

"Shiloh's been taken," Jude relayed. "The other boy's name is Caleb. Elliott's older brother. I don't know." She brought her hands up to her head and thought as hard as she could. "Nothing in here says where they plan to take her or what exactly they plan to do. It's all very carefully orchestrated. No names other than Caleb. No details, no specifics. "She dropped her hands and ran them over the papers, searching for a letter she may have missed, when she uncovered something she hadn't noticed before. It wasn't a letter at all, but an envelope, the only one in the pile. Turning it over, all of the oxygen fled from her lungs when she saw the red wax seal.

"Oh my god," she breathed, in complete shock. "You have got to be kidding me."

"What is it?" asked Ezra, looking at the envelope over her shoulder.

"This seal," Jude said in a low, disembodied voice. "It was in Tidewater. BYH. Those are the same initials found at a crime scene." She grabbed one of the letters and reread it. *Sacrifices for the Brotherhood. Praise Yarik.* She played it over in her mind, rearranging letters. She'd misinterpreted it before. The initials were not meant to be read as BYH. They were meant to be read as BHY, with the Y being the largest in the center, and the smaller B and H on either side. "Brotherhood," she said, standing up and clutching the envelope and letters in her fist. "The Brotherhood of Yarik. That has to be it. That has to be who took Shiloh." The cases of water, the uniformed boot prints. None of it made any sense at the time but it was all right under her nose. The tragedies in Tidewater, the missing jogger, Thomas Wooldridge, Marco Sanchez, they really had been connected to Shiloh all along.

"Oh my god," said Ezra frantically opening up a search tab on her phone. "Okay, I'll start looking. Is there any other useful information in those letters?"

"I don't know," answered Jude. "Not much. Let's just grab them and go."

As she piled everything up, Christopher stumbled into the room, pale and retching.

"Are you okay?" Jude asked him as he held himself up on the desk. "I think I found Walter," he choked out.

Ezra made a disgusted expression and Jude shrugged it off. "Great," she said sarcastically. "Well, that's someone else's problem. We have to go back to Tidewater."

Outside the closet door, Shiloh could hear some of the men arguing. Caleb's voice was among them, and the voice of the man who had touched her, along with one or two voices she didn't recognize.

Elliott was frantically trying to come up

with an escape plan, but Shiloh hushed him and pressed her ear against the door to listen. They were arguing in muted voices, muffled even more by the door between them, but she could make out most of what was said.

"I'm just surprised, that's all!" whisper-screamed an unfamiliar voice. "She's like, a little girl!"

"You knew that!" Caleb argued back. "Everyone knew what we were getting in to! That's why I was sent to Acadia! You can't back out now, Dillard!"

The man with the pirate sword tattoo was next to speak. Shiloh recognized his slippery voice. "No one is backing out," he hissed. "Try to leave and you'll be the next sacrifice."

Elliott grabbed Shiloh's hand.

"I'm not backing out," said the first guy, Dillard, more calmly. "I guess I just didn't expect her to be so young."

"Well, whatever," said a fourth voice. "We have a bigger issue to deal with right now anyway. When the boys got busted by the cops, they confiscated the crates. We don't have enough water to perform the ritual. We sent for more but the shipment is at least a day out, and the guys at the warehouse were completely wiped out What the hell did that? Now we have no guards for the ritual." He paused here, catching his breath. "And before they were dusted, they were sloppy and that little boy's body was found. Then there's the girl. What are we going to do with her? You know her mom's looking for her. From what I hear, she'd lethal. If she gets close to us, it's over."

The man with the sword tattoo spoke again. "Alright, alright, relax, boys! I'll track her down. Take her out. No problem."

There was some discussion and disagreement about how that should be done, but finally it was decided that it was worth a shot. The man with the sword tattoo, who the others were calling Hook, would travel to "take care" of Jude. Sven would go with him while the others stayed back to receive the shipment and continue making offerings of human blood to something called Yarik.

"What's Yarik?" Elliott whispered to Shiloh.

Shiloh didn't answer. It became quiet among the men on the other side of the door.

"Brothers," someone began confidently. "With the girls blood we *will* restore Yarik to his full glory, and when we do, he will bestow upon us the riches and immortality that we are owed. Be joyous, the day of victory is drawing near!"

At that, all of the men cheered and celebrated and Shiloh slumped back against the wall. "Yarik is a demon," she said flatly. "She wasn't sure how she knew it, but she did. "He's a demon, like the ones my mom goes out to fight. They're going to kill my mom, and then they're going to kill me."

CHAPTER 18

After ignoring all objections, Jude climbed into the driver's seat of Christopher's explorer and started the engine while Christopher and Ezra dove in and buckled up.

"I cannot believe this," Jude fumed as she threw the car into reverse and backed down the driveway. "We were just there! How the hell did we miss this?"

"Well, there wasn't much for us to find," Christopher answered from the back seat where he leaned over the center console. "They're keeping this very well hidden. Even the Synedrion didn't know what was going on."

Jude pulled her phone out of her pocket. As she swiped her thumb over the screen, Ezra in the passenger seat took it out of her hands. "Who are you trying to call?" she asked.

"Gideon," Jude replied, and Ezra pulled up her contacts and pressed "send" over Gideon's name.

"Brotherhood of Yarik," Jude blurted before Gideon even got through his *hello*. "Have you heard of them? They have Shiloh."

Gideon thought for a second. "No, I don't think I have," he admitted. "But I can look it up. Where are they from?"

"No idea," answered Jude. "Right now they're in Tidewater. That's all we know."

"Where are you?" he asked.

"Heading *back* to Tidewater."

"Right. Tell me everything you know."

She could hear him shuffling around in his study, moving books and papers as he looked for any material that may mention the Brotherhood.

"We don't know much," she said discouragingly as she pulled the car onto the highway and pressed her foot down on the gas. "The boy that led Shiloh into the trap is Elliott Todesco. He is with another boy, an older brother named Caleb. Caleb has been in contact with the brotherhood for months, maybe longer. They've been waiting for an opportunity to kidnap Shiloh. I think they plan to raise this demon Yarik."

"Wait, the water," Christopher interjected.

"Water?" asked Gideon.

"Yeah, we found a bunch of shipping crates full of jugs of water," he went on. "They were being guarded by a band of vampires that Jude and I neutralized in Tidewater. One of the letters in Caleb's desk mentioned water."

Neutralize? Jude mumbled as Ezra reached under the seat to pull out the letters they'd found in Caleb and Elliott's room."

"Yeah, the letter says that the Chornomorsk

water would be arriving soon."

"Chornomorsk," Gideon repeated a few times. "Chornomorsk Varna. It's a river somewhere in eastern Europe."

"Well does it mean anything?" Jude asked.

"It certainly means something," answered Gideon, in a quieter, calmer voice. He must've been reading.

"What did you find?" asked Jude.

"Well, I found a small excerpt on a demon called Yarik. This entry was written in the fourteen hundreds. As far as I can tell, this was the last time this demon was called upon."

"Well what does it say about him?"

"He was first recorded by Slovak villagers around 900 AD. Says here that he was a demon of the deep, confined to the Black Sea. They believed that he was the source of a damaging curse on their fishing industry and had drug several children into the water where they drowned. They called upon a priest to cast the demon out of the sea."

"How'd that go?" Jude asked sarcastically.

"Well, actually it seems to have been a success," Gideon answered. "Yarik was separated from his physical body and cast into the body of a fish native to the Chornomorsk River. Huh, there's a picture of it here. Looks sort of like a large catfish, barbed ray sort of hybrid."

"Gideon, focus. What else?" Jude urged. They were hours away from Tidewater, and it was well into the evening. The roads would be mostly empty and she intended to cut their travel time in half.

"Yarik was condemned to the body of this fish and not seen or heard from again until the time of this entry in the fourteen hundreds. A group of men fished him out of the Chornomorsk River with intent to raise him. They required water from the Chornomorsk, and the-" he stopped abruptly.

"What is it?" Jude asked.

Ezra placed her hand on Jude's shoulder, assuming the worst.

"They required the breath of the Chosen. After the child was held underwater, the demon was raised back to its full form and the child was given to him as a sacrifice to bring him up to strength."

Ezra squeezed Jude's shoulder and dropped her head into her free hand. Jude took a faltering breath and pushed the car to move even faster down the highway.

"Once raised to full health, Yarik killed all of the men present at his awakening and then proceeded to slaughter a number of villagers before the Synedrion apparently cast him back into the sea."

"They're going to try to raise him again," Jude stated, gripping the wheel with white knuckles.

"Should I fly out there?" Gideon asked.

"No, there's nothing you can do from Tidewater, just keep looking and call with anything you find."

"The nearest Synedrion task force is located in Florida," he added. "Should I alert them? I'm sure they could come and help you."

"There are Synedrion task forces?" Christopher asked in momentary fascination.

Jude exhaled. "No," she answered. "Not yet. The last thing we need is to scare these guys off and have them take Shiloh deeper into hiding."

The Synedrion had its virtues, but tact was not one of them among the militant strong arms of the organization. Jude remembered very well her first encounter with them, when they drugged and kidnapped her right out of her own New York City apartment. These groups were stationed around the globe to contain and control areas of high demonic activity. They would storm into the town of Tidewater paying no mind to the attention they drew to themselves. Generally speaking, it didn't matter. Those ranking higher in the Synedrion had resources and ways of making incidents go away and convincing communities of frightened victims that what they experienced was feral coyotes or natural disasters.

Jude hung up with Gideon and stared vacantly down the dark highway as trees and signs blurred past. Her mind raced a mile a minute. Shiloh had been with Caleb and the Brotherhood for almost nine hours now. That seemed like plenty of time to raise a demon under the right circumstances. But what weighed heaviest on her mind was the fact that it had actually been much longer since she and Shiloh had been together. Shiloh checked out emotionally long before Jude even left for Tidewater for the first time. When did she read the Codex? At what point, and for what reason, did she begin to doubt Jude's love for her? If she'd have dug deeper, all of this could've been avoided but she was too distracted. Now she was hot and dizzy with the growing fear that maybe it was too late.

* * *

She had no idea what time it was, but it felt late and Shiloh's eyes were heavy. Even as her mind raced and body trembled, she struggled to hold her head up. She could no longer hear conversation on the other side of the door and assumed that those who were still there had gone to sleep, and the sword tattoo guy went off to locate her mother. She couldn't sort out her emotions, and she was still furious at her mother, but the fear that something would happen to her made her sick.

She knew she should've been focused on an escape plan, but she couldn't bring herself to concentrate. She leaned up against Elliott and Jack and drifted into a restless sleep; one marked by nightmares and the discomfort that comes from sleeping on a cold hard floor in an unfamiliar place.

The next time she opened her eyes completely felt like a long time after she'd first closed them. Someone had abruptly opened the closet door and was talking at her.

"Get up," the voice said, though she couldn't see the face through the flickering, candle lit darkness and her blurry eyes. The voice wasn't yelling, or even speaking harshly, but it was firm and almost nervous. "Come on, get up, both of you. It's time to move."

She suddenly recognized the voice as Dillard's, the man who earlier had been surprised that she was so young. She rubbed her eyes and nudged Elliott, then pulled Jack up by his collar.

"Are you letting us go?" she asked hopefully as they all emerged from the closet and into the light from the lanterns.

Dillard shook his head quickly. "Now you know I can't do that," he answered regretfully. "No, I'm just here to move you. They're all worried that this place has been compromised."

"Compromised?" Shiloh asked.

"Mhm," answered Dillard. "Someone knows about the factory. If it's your mom, we can't have her showing up here and ruining the whole occasion."

Shiloh, Elliott, and Jack followed closely to Dillard who carried with him a dim flashlight. He was not an especially intimidating man. Kind of short and a little chunky around the midsection. He wore one of those creepy brotherhood robes but it was tight around his belly and swelled around his neck. He had light colored hair cut short, and kept wiping sweat off his forehead. They walked behind him down narrow cement stairs and Shiloh recognized that they were nearing the door where they had come in. But before they reached it, Dillard stopped and pulled out a length of rope from his pocket.

"I have to tie you up," he stated.

"Why?" asked Elliott, who was crying now. "Where is Caleb?"

"He's coming back," Dillard promised as he wrapped the rope around Elliott's wrists. "We're worried you're going to run off."

He turned to Shiloh, who had been scanning the factory through the darkness. She couldn't see a door, but she had to try. As Dillard stretched the rope toward her, she sprung away and darted off into the big empty room, hoping to get lucky and make her escape.

"Dammit," Dillard grumbled as he swung his flashlight in the direction in which she'd run. "Get back here!"

He pushed Elliott down with his arms tied behind his back and ran off toward Shiloh. "Where are you?" he screamed.

She slowed her steps to avoid tripping and falling, since she couldn't even see her own hand in front of her face. She did everything she could to stay out of the flashlight beam, and watched it as it circled the room. Finally, she caught a lucky glimpse when the light slid past a heavy steel door, and she made a break for it, but too fast. Dillard heard her bolt and leapt after her, shoving her to the ground. She cried out as he wrapped her arms in rope, but no one was around to hear.

"Why did you have to do that?" he asked, out of breath. "I wasn't going to hurt you."

"Yes you are," Shiloh countered. "You *are* going to hurt me." She wriggled and fought but he was much stronger and eventually, he had her wrapped so tightly in rope that she could barely take a full breath.

He pulled her up by the rope and pulled up Elliott in the same way. Jack followed closely behind, keeping his head turned toward Shiloh as Dillard led them out of the factory and into the salt air.

Shiloh drug the sleeve of her shirt across her damp, tear-streaked face. "What's going to happen to me?" she asked weakly.

Dillard hesitated.

"Just tell me."

Dillard stammered and sputtered. "You should wait until Dunning and Caleb get back."

Shiloh had had enough. She took a deep breath. "Why can't anyone tell me the damn truth?" she shouted.

Now that they were outside, it was Dillard's aim to move quickly and quietly. He panicked. "Okay, okay," he answered. "They're going to—they're going to s-sacrifice you."

She exhaled. It was worse than she'd expected. "For what?" she asked evenly.

"To raise a demon. Yarik. He's powerful."

"What's in it for you?" Shiloh asked.

Dillard looked ashamed. He rubbed his chin with his palm. "Wealth," he said quietly. "Wealth and immortality."

"You're going to kill me so that you don't

have to die?" Shiloh asked in disgust. "And why me, anyway?"

Dillard looked genuinely confused. "Your life is the binder. Your breath, technically," he answered. "It's the only thing that can raise him. Don't you know the kind of power you have? Your blood can raise all kinds of demons. We personally don't need your blood, we need for your lungs to stop. But your blood, your bones, they're powerful. Your mind is powerful too."

Shiloh kept walking but her questions paused. So that's what her mother was hiding. Shiloh was capable of bringing to life all kinds of terrible evils. She was a danger to society. That's why she had to die. But she didn't feel like a danger. She didn't want to hurt anyone at all.

"What will it be like? The sacrifice?" she asked finally. "Will it hurt?"

Dillard offered a weak, sympathetic smile. "I really don't know. I'll try to make it quick."

CHAPTER 19

It was late, nearing eleven, when they finally arrived in Tidewater. As soon as they came into the deserted town, Jude pointed the car towards the abandoned factory where she and Christopher found the crates of water. They had to be holding Shiloh there.

From the town limits, they didn't tap the breaks until they reached the factory and came squealing into the parking lot. Jude had the car door open and a knife strapped to her forearm, and dove out as it came to a jolting stop. She burst in through the factory door with Christopher and Ezra behind her, doing what they could to keep up.

"Shiloh!" she yelled into the dark. "Caleb! Where are you?" She called several times but there were no answers.

Christopher tried his best to keep the flashlight beam in front of her as she moved erratically through the building. The dust of dead vampires from their last visit still coated the floor. Otherwise the room was empty and her voice echoed off the cracking walls.

He pointed the beam to a stairway. "What's up there?" He asked. "I don't remember seeing these stairs last time."

Jude started off towards them.

"Be careful," Ezra cautioned as they all moved up the stairs.

At the top was a long hallway and Jude crashed through each door along it, finding them to be mostly empty; some old folding chairs, overturned file cabinets, large pieces of equipment, but no Shiloh. No demon. No Brotherhood.

The fourth door on the hall, however, was cracked open and there appeared to be a dim light behind it. She crept towards it and listened in, but heard nothing. She signaled to Christopher and Ezra to move forward quietly, then pushed it open. Stepping inside, she found it to be empty of people, but full of stuff. There were sleeping bags and pizza boxes strewn around the floor, and a battery powered camping lantern sat flickering on a table, but it was enough to light the room.

"Someone has definitely been hiding out here," said Ezra. "Several people."

"Yeah, a bunch of teenage boys from the looks of it," Jude answered, kicking a crushed beer can across the dirty linoleum floor. "There's no one here now. They've moved on," she said, and she slammed the heel of her hand into the wall, causing it to crack and the plaster to crumble.

"We're getting closer," Christopher offered, pulling her toward the door. "They were here. Probably where they were getting organized and receiving the water."

As they were about to step into the hall, there was a crash behind them as a door clattered open and someone rushed at them. Jude was hit in the back with tremendous force and she stumbled forward, trying to suck down oxygen that had been beaten out of her lungs. Christopher caught her as Ezra turned around and took two steps back, reaching for the dagger in her pocket.

The attacker swooped in and struck Christopher in the mouth with a punch. Christopher's head fell back and the man jumped on him, while another one took on Jude. Very quickly, Jude realized that what she was fighting wasn't a man, but a monster. An old one. He was strong and quick, with a bloated belly and stretched, pink skin. His fangs protruded out from his upper jaw and his hair had been gelled into spikes. He was all muscle and didn't bother landing blows but instead went right for Jude's throat. In his grip, she could barely move or breathe. He smashed her into the wall and leaned in for the kill when she lifted a knee and jabbed it into his groin. He loosened his grip for a second, and Jude ducked away from him. Ezra swooped in from behind and buried her dagger into his thick, veiny neck. In the time that the vampire took to react to the sudden pain and get a hold of himself, Jude grabbed him by the head and slammed it against the door frame. Ezra scrambled for something made of wood and ran back with a broom. Jude grabbed the handle and smashed it against the wall, snapping the head off and leaving a sharp, splintering point, which she plunged into the vampire's chest.

Gearing up for the next one, Jude took a deep breath and turned to Christopher who was rolling around on the floor with what definitely appeared to be a man. Christopher was weakening after having taken several punches to the face and chest. Jude pulled the knife from the strap on her arm, grabbed the man by the back of the neck and threw him into the room with the lantern. Being human, he was much weaker than the vampire, but he had come prepared to fight. He seemed pleased that Jude had thrown him, with a demented grin spread across his face. As he fell, he caught himself on a flimsy wooden table. A glint shot through his wild eyes as he noticed a metal chain on the table top and grabbed at it. While he wrapped it around his fists, Jude noticed the old, green shape of a cutlass tattooed on his neck.

He had dark and untrimmed facial hair following his jaw line, patchy under his chin. He was unwashed and unkempt, wearing jeans full of holes and a filthy black t-shirt, and sweat pooled on his upper lip and beaded on his forehead. He looked at Jude like he was a starving hyena and she was a slab of meat. Apparently unable to keep still, he crouched and swooped spastically with darting eyes and panting breath.

Jude waited calmly for him to make the first move, noting the exact position of her feet, and the grip of the knife in her hand. She took slow, measured breaths and kept her body square with his as he paced and circled.

"Where is Shiloh?" she asked him.

He laughed. "I imagine your girl is in the belly of the beast by now."

Jude steeled herself. His goal was to unhinge her and as long as she maintained her composure, he was not a threat. "I know she was here," she answered. "Tell me where they've taken her."

He licked his lips and took a clumsy step toward her. "No can do," he jeered. "I'm here to take care of you."

Jude used the toe of her shoe to kick around the dust under her feet. "Well, there's three of us and now, only one of you."

"I'm enough," he boasted.

"Well then do you think you're ever going to make a move?"

Predictably, the man took the bait and hurled himself at Jude, leading with his left shoulder. For all of his ego and talk, all Jude had to do was step to his side and give him a little shove to send him barreling into a stack of boxes. Really, this wasn't a fair fight. Jude was physically designed and professionally trained to fight monsters, not people. And while sometimes people had an intellectual edge (though not in this particular case) they never stood up to the physical strength of the monsters Jude regularly encountered.

She allowed him to regather himself and he

stood back up laughing and spitting.

"Tell me where my daughter is and we can both walk away."

Without a thought he lunged again, this time throwing a punch aimed at the side of her head. She deflected it with the swipe of her arm and stepped in to access his now wide open chest. She grabbed him with both hands around his collar, sure to grab handfuls of flesh with it, and lifted him off the ground.

He threw his head forward, using his forehead as a bludgeon against her own, and hit her hard. The pain flooded behind her eyes, causing them to water, but she held on long enough to throw his body forcefully to the ground.

He landed on his back coughing and gagging, then scrambled back to his feet.

"You know I'm going really easy on you," she told him, giving him yet another chance at walking away from the fight. Her head was still hurting and the blow had made her nauseous, but she refused to let it show.

"Don't do me any favors," he replied, but she could tell he was shaken. If possible, he was even more spastic than before, out of breath and off balance. But his demeanor had shifted from mania to rage.

"I met that little girl of yours," he said, wiping his arm across his damp, bloodied face.

Jude could sense the closeness of Christopher and Ezra as they moved in behind her.

"She was a pretty thing," he went on. "Looked a lot like you."

"Where is she?" Jude demanded, stepping toward him.

He was bent over slightly, gripping his midsection with his forearm. "Go home, mama bear," he grumbled. "She's done with you. She's going to serve a greater purpose now and you've been exposed."

"You don't know what you're talking about," she hissed.

"Don't I?" he swallowed hard. "We didn't kidnap your girl. She left willingly. To get away from you. Some mother you are."

Jude leapt at him, fueled by the anger that rocked her legs and ricocheted up her spine to her hands. It was exactly what he wanted; to get at her heart. But it was a misstep on his part. The pain didn't throw her off her game, but gave Jude a sharper edge, a stronger will. She grabbed him with her left hand and slashed through his shirt near his collar bone with the knife in her right. The blow was non-lethal, but it hurt. He launched back, gripping his chest with his hand while blood trickled out between his fingers. He looked down at the wound in shock.

Jude stood over him as he leaned back against the wall. "Last chance," she hissed between gritted teeth. "Tell me where I can find my daughter, or I will plunge this knife deep into your belly and give it a good twist. Then I will leave you here to die and go find your friends on my own."

He looked up at her with his bloodshot eyes and a shadow fell over them. His fists were clenched and he showed his teeth like a rabid dog. He was muttering something, fumbling around with his free hand. "You'll never get the chance," he fumed, still shaking as blood continued to stain his shirt red.

Jude moved in closer and got in his face. She slapped the wall behind his head with her hand and raised her knife again. "Where is Shiloh?" she yelled, their eyes inches apart.

Suddenly from behind her, Ezra yelled out a word that Jude had never heard in the context of a fight before.

"Gun!" Ezra shrieked. "He has a gun!"

The word rang in her ears and took a second to register. The metallic click and cold barrel against her ribs finally made it clear. The man with the sword tattoo grinned. "Sorry girly," he whispered. "You're not going to-"

She plunged the knife into his gut as she swept the gun away from her body and out of his hand. It landed with a clatter against the floor and slid a few inches as the man dropped to his knees, choking and spewing. Blood poured from the wound in his stomach and ran warm over Jude's knuckles. It was an unsettling feeling, human blood on her hands. Still, she twisted the knife and he let out one last moan, then slumped over motionless.

Christopher and Ezra stood behind in terror and shock, both mouth-open staring and holding their breath. Finally, Jude stood up, shaking a little but otherwise unaffected. She didn't have time to care or take stock of her injuries. Those things would take away from the brain power she needed to find Shiloh. She stood with her back to her friends and looked down at her bloody hand and the knife, then at the man's body. No dust. Definitely human.

Finally, after taking a few deep breaths to slow the spinning of her head, she turned. "I need to wash my hands," she stated calmly.

"Of course," Ezra answered, much quicker on the uptake than Christopher. "What should we do about him?"

Jude shrugged. "I don't love the idea of traveling with a body in the trunk so we leave him. Call the Synedrion. They'll take care of it."

Though it was definitely frowned upon, the reality that some human beings would die in the performance of Jude's job was inevitable and the Synedrion understood that. This guy pushed Jude's body count up to three. The first, she'd killed when Shiloh was taken to raise Molech at the age of four. The second happened about three years ago, when a deranged mental patient escaped from police custody and somehow made his way to the Mikhale house, looking for Shiloh. That one was the worst. Jude didn't want to kill him but because of his altered state, he was unstoppable and didn't react to punches and pain. She snapped his neck after he broke down her closet door in an effort to get to Shiloh's room. Now this guy. Tattoo guy. It never felt good, but she never regretted it. The Synedrion was equipped to slip in and clean up any evidence that might implicate Jude in the crime of manslaughter. They would just have to do it again.

The trio made their way down the stairs and outside to the car where Jude found a water bottle and did her best to rinse the still warm blood from her hands and knife. The others stood quietly and watched, waiting for her to suggest a new destination. The truth was, she was now at a complete loss. She had no idea where Shiloh could be, and her potential informant was laying in a pool of his own blood upstairs.

* * *

After a short drive in a rickety pickup truck, Dillard pulled up to what Shiloh could barely make out as a dock in the darkness. She knew she was near the water because the air smelled salty and damp and staticky, and because the black silhouettes of trees and grasses had all vanished and in front of her was a big open field of nothingness. Occasionally, a flicker would twinge the surface of that field and she could tell that it was the surface of a river. On the other side there were small lights speckling the shoreline.

"Where are we now? Is Caleb here?" asked Elliott, as Dillard led them out of the truck with their hands still bound up by the rope.

"We're at the old shipping docks on the Rappahannock," he said, as if he were leading a tour group and not dragging two captive children to be held against their will. "Caleb's here."

Elliott exhaled a sigh of relief, but Shiloh had long lost all hope that Caleb was going to help them. She didn't resist Dillard as he led them. It had not worked out last time and resistance would likely be met with punishment, maybe delivered by the other men, who were less gentle. She didn't want to begin to think about what that could look like.

They walked down a short gravel driveway to a wooden shack which hung about ten or fifteen feet over the water. The front half of it sat on the edge of the bank and the back half sat on a long dock which was supported by heavy wooden beams and ran pretty far into the wide river. Inside the shack were the men Shiloh had recognized from before, including Caleb. He stood up from his chair when they came into the small, messy room.

"What are you doing?" he asked Dillard, irritated as he walked over to Elliott and began untying him.

"He tried to run," Dillard argued. "You said to make sure they don't try anything."

Caleb shook his head and pulled the rope away from his brother. Then he patted Elliott on the back. "I meant her," he said, thrusting a dirty finger at Shiloh.

Elliott looked up at Caleb in shock. "They said you're going to sacrifice her," he started. "It's not true, is it Caleb? You wouldn't hurt her. Tell them it's not true."

Elliott looked wide eyed and expectantly at him but Shiloh's eyes were cold where they were trained unflinching on Caleb's. She knew now who Caleb really was.

Caleb shifted and put his hand on Elliott's shoulder, leading him away. "Come here a minute," he told him. "Relax, everything's going to be fine." He walked Elliott out of the room and out of earshot, but Shiloh knew that Caleb was going to try to convince Elliott that what he was doing was the right thing. Elliott was her friend and she cared about him, but he was also weak and trusting, and she wasn't confident that Caleb couldn't sway him over on to his team. Now they were separated and she became, if possible, even more alone.

She couldn't worry about it. Dillard had Jack by the collar and was asking what to do with him.

"Tie his legs and throw him in the river," proposed a dark skinned, muscular man.

"Don't you dare!" Shiloh screamed, flailing her arms.

He stood up from his seat and came toward her. "Don't worry, you'll see him on the other side."

Shiloh waited for him to get close enough and then kicked him hard in the shin. He screamed and lifted his leg like a wounded animal.

"If you hurt him I'll kill you!" she threatened through gritted teeth.

The man laughed between wails. "What are you going to do?"

Without hesitating, Shiloh filled the room

with a high pitched, ear piercing scream. Suddenly, the older man stood up from behind a paper-covered table and yelled, "Enough!" as he slammed his fist down onto the table top.

Shiloh stopped screaming and all of the men straightened up.

"Whatever is going on, that's enough," he said angrily. He was a tall and slender guy with glasses and a balding head. He looked like a teacher or something, not a member of a murdering secret society. "I need to go back over this ritual. Leave the child alone."

The dark skinned man went back to his chair in a huff and Dillard looked at her with guarded eyes. "I'll just tie him up outside," he promised her, gently pulling Jack toward the door with a long length of cord.

Elliott had not come back yet and neither had Caleb. The older man went back to studying the papers on the table while the others went back to quietly discussing strategy.

"Has anyone heard from Hook?" asked one of the younger boys.

"No," answered a couple of the guys who were sitting around him.

"Wonder if he found the mother."

One of them took a sip from a can and crushed it in his fist. "If he did, he's probably dead in a ditch someplace by now."

The young guy shook his head. "No way," he argued. "Hook is a monster. You know he'd rip her apart."

"I've heard this woman is deadly," said a third voice.

"Maybe we should go look for him."

"You go look for him, Cruz," said Caleb, joking as he came back into the room. "You can take the mother, right?"

Cruz rolled his eyes and leaned back in his seat, suddenly silent.

"Where's Elliott?" Shiloh asked, concerned.

"He's asleep," said Caleb. "In the car."

"Did you hurt him?"

"You think I'd hurt my own brother?" Caleb answered defensively. He shook his head and turned to the table where the older man was working. "I'm practically doing this for him," he mumbled as he went.

After a few minutes of discussion, they called the others over to the table and Dillard came back inside, offering Shiloh a weak smile as he passed by her on his way to the table. Discreetly, he nodded toward the door, where he had left it cracked open just a little. In the moonlight, Shiloh could see Jack, circling a patch of grass growing out of the gravel to lay down.

They all gathered around as the older man spoke about the plan, but he kept glancing over at Shiloh and speaking softly so that she couldn't hear. She only made out a few phrases. The water would be delivered in the morning. The pool was ready. Immediate sacrifice to sustain power. None of it made any sense to her at all, but it all sounded like death.

It was very late, and she wondered where her mother was. She was sure she'd come looking for her. Probably Ezra too. Maybe even Christopher. And she was sure that her mother could take Hook in a fight, no problem.

CHAPTER 20

"Okay," said Jude, with one hand on her hip and the other rubbing the back of her neck. She'd spent the last fifteen minutes pacing around the car, trying to come up with a plan, and with every passing moment, Shiloh was slipping away. Finally, she just had to resolve herself to do something. "We're going to split up. It's already late. We can cover more ground this way."

"Where do you want us?" Christopher asked, stepping forward with his arms crossed.

"You are going to stay here," she answered. "If anyone comes back here, you let me know immediately. But stay out of sight. This is a stake out. Don't engage. If you see someone, follow them. They may lead you to Shiloh."

Christopher nodded and Jude turned to Ezra. "You are going to go downtown. Get to know the place on foot. See if you can find a bar, a restaurant, a pick-up game, any place where people may be gathering and talking. Blend in. Keep your knife in your pocket."

"Always," Ezra replied. "What about you?"

Jude shook her head and pressed her fingers over the dull ache above her eyes. "Idunno," she said, exasperated. "I guess I'm going to drive the outskirts. Look for unusual activity." She dropped her arms hard by her side and Ezra took a step closer and put her hand on Jude's shoulder.

Jude wanted to break, even if only for a moment. She felt the heat of Ezra's hand on her arm, the zap of human sympathy. The allure of collapsing into the arms of her friend and slipping away from the present chaos was powerful. Jude took a quick, sharp breath and stiffened her spine.

"Come on, I'll drop you off in town," she stated, pulling away and climbing into the car.

After Jude dropped Ezra off, she continued on through town looking for anything that might lead her to Shiloh. It was late, just after midnight, and she couldn't see far beyond her headlights. She had the windows down and did everything she could to maintain composure as she drove further into the night. Maybe she was getting closer. Maybe she was getting much, much farther. About five miles outside of town, she heard the sound of a distant train and listened as it came closer. Finally, she saw the lights coming out of a thick forest and drove toward them. She followed the tracks on a narrow gravel road for a few miles searching for buildings. Old abandoned rail yards made perfect hideouts for anyone looking to disappear. It wasn't a great idea, but it was something. She was about to give up and turn back when finally, she caught sight of a dilapidated brick structure standing dark against the indigo sky.

Eagerly, she swerved into the pothole ridden gravel lot and jumped out of the car, leaving it running. She pulled her knife once again and charged in, kicking through the plywood covered entryway.

"Shiloh!" she yelled, feeling her way around. She pulled her phone out of her pocket and switched on the light. "Are you in here?" There was a set of stairs to her left and they looked treacherous, but she made her way up them, carefully to place her weight slowly on the spongy wood risers, calling Shiloh's name as she climbed.

Suddenly, there was a crash, like someone kicking a trash can, and she whipped around. "Who's there?" she asked, her energy rising.

She waited for a minute, then took two steps in the direction of the sound. Something launched out from behind an old metal workbench but it moved too fast for her to get a good look. She followed it, running to the other side of the room and frantically swinging her flashlight in every direction. She stopped and nearly hurled her phone against the brick wall when the light fell on a mangy cat, cowering from her rage in the corner.

She took a step back and lowered her arms, trying to take a steadying breath. "Get out of here," she said quietly. When the cat didn't move, she said it again, this time yelling through a breaking voice.

The cat took off and bolted down the stairs.

Jude stepped into the corner where it had been hiding and leaned face-first into the cold wall. She was trying not to lose it. Focusing on her breath. Squeezing her eyes shut. Biting her lower lip so hard she could taste the copper twinge of blood. It was all for nothing. Eventually, she lost the battle against the flood of emotions burning and swelling in her chest. And then it was coming out all too fast for her to keep up. She pounded the wall with her fists and screamed into the now silent and crumbling building.

Once she cried out everything that was inside of her and her head spun and ached, she slid down to the floor and curled up into herself. She was no closer to finding Shiloh and the reality that she may be out of time settled down heavy over top of her. A list began to run inside of her head. She would have to tell the Synedrion. Maybe there was still time for another to be called. They would come out and conduct an investigation. They would probably look for Shiloh. When they didn't find her, they would leave and go back to their all-important mission and what would become of Jude? Her destiny would be null and void. She wouldn't be the Keeper of the Chosen anymore. She would have to move. Maybe to the west coast. Or Europe. Somewhere far away from everything she knew and anything that could possibly remind her of Shiloh. Her baby would be gone. Never to wrap Jude in a hug, or charm her with that girlish smile, or fill the room with her sweet laugh again. No more reading on the porch, movie nights, puzzle pieces all over the house. She'd be gone. Just like that, like a vapor. A haunting memory. A wonderful dream. Maybe Jude would just go away too. The tears and choking breath returned and Jude pulled her knees to her chest and rested her head between them.

She was beginning to think that she may as well start the vanishing process right then and there. She could slip easily into a deep depression, catatonic in this abandoned building, never to be seen or heard from again. Eventually she'd waste away. There were ways she could make it go faster. If it became necessary. Then her phone rang.

The bright light in the heavy darkness burned her eyes. After some blinking, she read Christopher's name on the cracked display. She took a deep breath and answered the call.

"Yeah?" she asked, emotionless.

"Jude, I've got something." His voice was quickened with hope.

She sat up straight and clutched the phone with both hands. "What is it?"

"A GPS. From that dead guy's car. It was parked around back."

"Really?" she asked, already standing and moving for the stairs. "What was the last destination?"

"Well, there's a bunch of stuff on here, but there's this one place that he's been to several times in the last few days."

"Where?" she climbed into the car and pulled

the seatbelt across her chest.

"On the water. Looks like a dock or something."

Just like that, she was yanked up from darkness. With renewed spirits, she spun the tires on the loose gravel and sped in the direction of Christopher. "I'm on my way to get you," she told him, and hung up the phone.

Jude grabbed Ezra from town and then raced back to the factory, completely abandoning the speed limit. When she pulled up in front of the building, Christopher was waiting outside with the GPS in his hand. She barely stopped the car while he jumped into the backseat and started directing Jude where to go.

"You're going to take State Road 642 for about twenty miles until it hits the river. The dock looks like it's on a little side road. It's big, like an old shipping dock or something."

"Was there anything else in the car? asked Ezra.

Chris shook his head. "Nothing much. About twelve empty cigarette boxes and some greasy fast food bags. A creepy Brotherhood robe."

"The GPS is enough," said Jude, pushing the little car to its limit on the all but abandoned back road.

Every few minutes, they passed by a house or a trailer, mostly run down with old cars in the driveways and flickering yellow porch lights. One small gas station was mostly dark except for the lights above the pumps, but no one was fueling up and Jude flew right past. Christopher and Ezra were theorizing and strategizing about what they might do when they arrived at the dock. They asked for Jude's input, but she didn't offer much more than quiet acknowledgement and generic agreement. She was thinking about Shiloh. It couldn't be too late. If Shiloh had been killed, she would know. She would feel it in her bones and in her blood. Her daughter was out there. She was on this dock and there was simply no other option.

* * *

Shiloh had been sitting on the floor with her hands tied up for a long time. She was sore and itchy and, though she was relieved that the men were not paying her any attention, she had no way to escape and Elliott had still not returned. Finally after the older man, whom they were calling Professor Dunning, finished speaking and everyone reached some kind of understanding, they started to disburse and gather things throughout the room.

"I'll take this stuff downstairs," said Cruz. "Dillard, get the girl."

"I'll get her," spoke up the dark skinned man.

"Don't think I can handle it, Andrew?" Asked Dillard, defensively.

Andrew rolled his eyes and grabbed Shiloh by the back of her shirt. "Well, you nearly blew it last time, Dill."

Shiloh squirmed, but Andrew pulled her like

a sack of garbage toward what appeared to be a hatch in the floor.

"Hey!" the old man yelled. "There's no need to jerk her around!" He took a deep breath. "Have some respect, she's about to change your life."

Andrew immediately loosened his grip on Shiloh's shirt and instead guided her toward the hatch with a hand on her back. "Sorry, Professor," he mumbled.

In the hatch, there was a ladder that appeared to lead down to the dock. "You first," said Andrew, releasing Shiloh's shirt and nudging her toward the hatch.

Shiloh glanced around the room, considering her options once more, and once more determining that she didn't have any. The room was full of big, excited men and she did not stand the slightest chance of escape. She knew that whatever was at the bottom of those stairs was not going to be good for her. Somehow, she felt certain that her time was running out. *No crying,* she told herself. Stoically, she lowered her foot onto the first rung, and made her way down into the darkness below.

* * *

It took Jude about ten minutes to reach the dock, and as soon as got within a half-mile, she slowed down, and made her way by light from the moon down the long stretch of road.

As they came closer, they could see a slumping shack hanging over the edge of the river bank under a tall, moth-swarmed street light. A pier stretched out behind it high above the river. "Wait, stop," Ezra said suddenly, pointing towards the shack from the passenger seat as Jude silently brought the car to a pause, straddling the road and the dirt to stay out of sight. "There's someone over there."

Standing on the edge of the light were the shadows of what appeared to be about five people. They moved in and out of the darkness and seemed to be talking to one another as they unloaded something from the back of a box truck.

"What is that?" Jude asked, leaning forward toward the windshield.

"More of those crates," answered Christopher.

"She's here," Jude stated confidently, Jude unbuckling her seatbelt and moving for the door handle. Suddenly, Ezra's arm appeared out of nowhere, sweeping Jude across the chest and pushing her forcefully back against her seat. Jude was a little stunned and looked at Ezra with sharp eyes, trying to withhold her frustration.

Ezra immediately felt the palpable presence of Jude's rage and realized that she'd acted very out-of-character. "Sorry," she said quickly. "But we need to think this through. You can't just rush them." Ezra looked away from the activity in front of them and locking her eyes on Jude's. "If we aren't careful we could blow it. We haven't seen Shiloh yet. Let's wait."

Waiting was not at all what Jude wanted to do, but Ezra was right. It could be disastrous to rush in, not knowing where Shiloh was or who she was with. So they waited. Jude's muscles twitched and tensed as they watched the five men unload crate after crate, and carry them inside of the shack. Finally, after fifteen crates, they pulled down the metal door of the box truck and stood under the light talking for a minute. Then, three of them broke off from the pack and went into the building.

They waited another five minutes to see if anyone else was coming out. "I think those two are on watch," said Christopher. "I don't think they're going in."

"I think you're right," Jude answered. "We're going to have to get around them. We can't wait anymore." She looked at Ezra who nodded in agreement and they all grabbed their gear. Jude carefully slid her long axe out from the back seat and over the heads of her companions, and slipped out of the car.

There wasn't much vegetation to hide in, just some neck-high brush that grew along the shoulder, but it would have to do. Jude slung the axe over her shoulder as they crept as quietly as possible toward the dock, keeping a close eye on the two guards who paced casually around in the parking lot, pausing periodically to exchange words. As far as Jude could tell, they did not expect any interruptions.

The sound of a barking dog startled her and one of the guys turned toward the corner of the building. As the dog continued to bark, the bark became more of a sealy wail and Jude recognized the cry. "That's Jack," she whispered. Jack's presence was proof that Shiloh was somewhere nearby. Her heart rate began to rise and she struggled to ground herself, focusing on her breathing, making note of the warmth of her muscled limbs, connecting her body with her mind. For the last few hours, they'd both been spinning fairly out of control, with no regard for one another as she became increasingly panicked. But now, with the knowledge that Shiloh was just around the corner, waiting somewhere for her, the warrior inside of her was coming together, preparing to do what it was always meant to do. She reached her hand around her back and gripped the handle of the battle axe, becoming intensely aware of her surroundings as she inched toward her targets.

They made it to about twenty feet away when a tinny sound broke through the dense quiet very near to Jude's ear. She paused and whipped her head around to where it had come from. Christopher was scolding himself, cursing under his breath at the tin can that he'd stepped on.

Of course, the two men standing outside of the shack had heard as well, and began swinging flashlight beams frantically across the gravel lot. The trio stood still, pressed into the prickly brush, but both men were walking straight toward them and it was inevitable.

As they got closer, Jude realized that they weren't men at all, but boys. One of them looked familiar. Maybe one of the boys from the factory being questioned by the police before Jude and Christopher found the crates.

Jude waited until they were two or three feet away and then reached out from her hiding place and grabbed the closest of the two. She put him in a headlock and pulled him back into the shadows with her arm around his neck, and ripped the short hunting knife from his hand as he squirmed and struggled. The other stood open-mouthed and trembling, with his hand shaking around the handle of an impressive looking dagger.

Ezra and Christopher stepped out from the brush and moved in on the other guy. Christopher jumped him and clapped his hand over his mouth and he and Ezra dragged him into the trees.

"Don't say a word," Jude demanded, as the boy in her grasp choked and gagged against the dull end of the blade of his own knife. "I know who you are, and I think you know who I am so let's not play games with each other. Where's Shiloh? What's going on in there?"

"Don't tell them anything," said the other boy weakly, darting his glance between Christopher and Ezra after briefly yanking Christopher's hand away from his mouth. Christopher sprung at him and pinned his back against a scrubby tree.

With both boys bound, Jude exhaled. "You're going to want to listen very carefully," she stated. "Because if you do anything to draw attention to yourself, I'll slit your throats in a heartbeat."

"We're human," the boy in her arms choked out as if that simple fact came with inherent protection.

Jude laughed darkly. "Yeah, well that makes you even more deplorable than the things I usually deal with. I already took out your friend back at the warehouse."

The two hostages exchanged nervous glances with each other and the boy under Jude's arm gagged. "I can't breathe," he pleaded desperately. "Please."

Jude loosened her grip slightly to let him speak. "Is Shiloh in there?" she asked, pressing the side of her face against his.

"Shut up!" the other urged, muffled under Christopher's hand, but the kid in Jude's control was shaking.

"Y-yeah, she's in there," he answered. "Please."

He looked like he was about to cry and couldn't have been more than eighteen years old. Jude backed off a few inches, keeping her hands on his shoulders. "What's your name?"

"Charles," he answered quickly.

"Charles, listen." Jude exhaled sharply. "I don't think you realize what you've gotten yourself into. Do you really want to die for this?"

"No!" He shook his head rapidly. "No, I swear. I don't. Please let me go."

She nodded and took a deep breath. "We may be able to work that out. But you'll need to tell me what I'm going to find inside."

The other guy with tried to lurch forward toward but couldn't wriggle out of Christopher and Ezra's grip.

Defenseless in the clutches of Christopher and Ezra, he lost most of his courage and began to beg for his own release.

"You don't want to die either, do you?" Jude asked him.

He shook his head.

"Good," said Jude. "Then we each have something to gain from the other. How many guys do you have down there?"

They hesitated to answer, but finally, Charles spoke up. "There's seven, not counting us."

"That's good," said Jude. "And what about Yarik?"

"He's not been raised yet," said Charles. "They're working on it now. But he's no joke. If they pull it off," he shook his head, coming to the realization of what he'd become mixed up in. "He's a monster. Huge. And dangerous."

"We'll be careful," answered Jude with a snark. "Now, where is Shiloh?"

Charles looked at the other guy who made muffled whimpering sounds through Christopher's palm.

"Where is she, Charles?" Jude asked again, moving in closer to his trembling face.

"I don't know," he answered finally. "I really don't. I've been unloading the truck. I haven't seen her since we got here."

"So she's here?" Jude asked, glancing briefly at Ezra and Christopher.

"Yes, with the others."

Jude turned the blade of the knife over so that the sharpened side was now pressing into the skin of his neck. "I swear to god, if you're lying-"

"No, no, I'm not!" he squealed, breathing heavily. "She's still alive. I swear. They wouldn't hurt her. Not until they raise Yarik. They can't do it without her. She's in there somewhere."

She couldn't waste much more time on these two idiots. Jude patted Charles down until she found his cell phone in his pocket. She pulled it out, released him from the headlock and threw him onto the gravel road. Standing over him, she raised her axe above his head. He cowered under the blade, eyes closed tightly as he begged her to spare him.

"If I ever see you again, I'll kill you without a second thought," she promised.

He opened his eyes, and scrambled to his feet, stumbling on his unsteady legs.

Jude moved toward Christopher and searched his captive for a phone. "It isn't on me, I swear," he told her. It's in my jacket pocket right over there by the truck."

"Let him go," she told Christopher, who took his arms out from around the other guard and wiped his slobbery hand on his pants.

Both boys stood on shuffling feet, unsure of what to do. "Go!" Jude yelled through gritted teeth, and they both took off down the road, away from the shack and the Brotherhood.

Jude watched until they were almost out of sight and then turned in the opposite direction, running for the shack and for Shiloh.

"What's the plan?" asked Ezra, catching her breath as they came to the door of the shack.

Jude jiggled the handle and found it locked. She rested her axe over her right shoulder and held it there with her right hand, then stepped back two feet from the door. Without much pause, she lifted her knee to her chest and thrust her leg through the wood, just below the knob. It splintered and knocked the door right off the hinges, and Jude charged inside.

"So, the usual plan," answered Ezra anxiously as she and Christopher filed in behind Jude.

They found themselves standing inside of a square room, maybe thirty by thirty feet in size, and mostly empty. There were a few shelves containing what appeared to be fishing supplies left over from when the building was a tackle shop. There was a counter running along the back wall piled high with papers and garbage, and Jude threw herself over it, landing on the other side with her axe raised. But there was no one behind it. There was no one anywhere.

"Where the hell is everyone?" Jude yelled, kicking through the glass display below the counter.

"They have to be in here somewhere," Ezra

answered, stepping toward her. "Two men went in and didn't come out."

Jude nodded and caught her breath. "Right. Okay, so where did they go? Is there another door?"

They all began combing the room, looking for a second exit or an attic.

Christopher noticed a small partition wall and moved around it, looking for a door. He took a few steps forward and heard the floor moan under his weight. When he looked down, he discovered that he was standing on top of a hatch.

"Jude, over here!" he called, and Jude and Ezra both came running.

"Thank God," said Jude, when she saw the square, plywood covered hole in the floor. "Okay, when I open it, we're only going to be able to come down one at a time. I'll go first and give you the all clear as soon as I know you can move in."

They both nodded and Jude placed the butt of the axe handle on the floor for support as she knelt down to lift the wooden door. It opened on rusty hinges and she looked down. There were no steps or ladder, but there was a dim yellow light below. It was too dark to tell how far the drop was, or even if she would be dropping onto something solid or plunging into the river. She had no choice but to risk it. She gave one last glance to her friends and dropped down into the dark.

When her feet landed on a solid foundation, she exhaled and looked around, finding herself on a lower dock maybe a foot above the water. But she wasn't given much time to assess her surroundings as three men marched rapidly toward her from the far end of the dock, which extended maybe forty yards out over the Rappahannock.

As they came, she tried to look behind them, where lanterns provided spotty light over the wooden boards, but she didn't see Shiloh.

She glanced quickly up at the hatch where Ezra and Christopher stood looking down at her. "Okay, they've seen me. Hurry," she said, bending at the knees and gripping the axe handle with both hands.

The three men reached her as Christopher and Ezra dropped down from the hatch and landed at her sides. They were startled by the size and ferocity of these men. The first one, with dark skin and dark eyes, was well over six feet tall. He had broad shoulders and big hands, curled up in fists. The second guy to reach them was smaller in height, but fit and squirrely, with long arms and legs and an enraged expression on his face. The third was the biggest, maybe around 300 lbs, with light blond hair and a plump face. All in their twenties and all obviously strong. This was the heart of the Brotherhood, dressed in long, black cloaks with red trim and the 'bYh' symbol stitched into the sleeves. They wore high, black boots and were each armed with large, fixed-blade knives with the symbol on the handle.

They spread out on the somewhat narrow dock and surrounded the trio.

"One for each of us," said the dark skinned man.

The others seemed less confident, but Jude knew that they weren't going to be as easy to sway as the two guards. Jude, Christopher and Ezra formed a tight triangle, each with weapons raised and pointed, but everyone seemed to be in a sort of holding pattern. Jude took the opportunity to get a better look at what was going on beyond the dock. Two of the four other men were pouring jugs of water from the crates into a large tub or pool of some kind. One guy, who appeared older and possibly in charge, stood behind a small, poorly constructed table where he read over several pieces of paper. He didn't pay her any mind as he concentrated intensely on whatever he was reading.

She kept scanning, getting more and more frantic for a glimpse. A wisp of blonde hair, a blur of denim and paisley. Anything to reassure her that she was in the presence of her daughter. Finally, after what felt like an eternity confined to the space of forty seconds, she laid eyes on what she'd been praying for. Off to the side, just barely in the light with her arms and legs tied, was Shiloh. She was leaning against a dock pillar, guarded by a much younger boy who unlike the guy behind the table, was intensely focused on Jude. He looked furious; out for blood. But Shiloh appeared unharmed. Even though she was tied to a dock over the water four hours from the bed she should've been sleeping in, and even though she was surrounded by men who in a matter of minutes intended to feed her to a demon they would raise, Jude allowed herself a breath of relief. Shiloh was within sight.

Jude bolted for Shiloh, hoping to press through the barricade formed by the three men between them, but they closed in tightly and cut off her path. She was ready to simply plough through them but Christopher urged her to pause.

She was flared up, her blood was pumping hot and her fingers twitched. She was ready to rip these guys apart one limb at a time to get to Shiloh.

She looked the dark skinned man in the eye and tried to reason with him. "Don't make me do this," she said rationally, with her axe pointed at his gut.

He rolled his eyes. "We're not letting you anywhere near the girl," he said flatly. "You may as well forget it."

"You don't understand," she told him. "I'm stronger than you are, I'm more cunning than you are, and I have far more training and experience than you do. I *will* get to her. I'll go right through you if I have to."

"What happened to Rick and Charles?" asked the chubby, blonde one.

"They're gone," Jude said honestly. "They made the smart choice. You can too. Get out of here."

"And Hook?"

Jude exhaled. "Your hit man?"

She took their silence as a yes. "He's dead.

And it was easy"

The blonde swallowed a hard lump in his throat.

"Get out of here," Jude tried one more time. But this time she wasn't feeling very generous. Shiloh was just barely out of reach, and Jude intended to close the distance quickly.

As if by some silent agreement, the three men charged all at once, the dark skinned one taking on Jude, the blonde going for Ezra, and the third moving for Christopher.

As far as Jude was concerned, they had declared war, and she had no plans to show an ounce of mercy.

Her attacker was too close for the long-handled axe to be very effective, but she did what she could, using the handle more than the head. She shoved the heavy steel against the man's chest and opened up the space between them slightly, but he held on to her by her collar. With her elbow, she jabbed him in the neck, then in the jaw in rapid succession. The blow to his jaw weakened him and he recoiled as blood began to pool in his mouth. He spat it at her and lifted his knee into her stomach. She folded into the strike and coughed as it felt like her lungs had been popped for a second, but she quickly caught her breath. With both of his hands locked on her collar, she swung the handle of her axe out to her side and over to lay on the tops of his arms. She pulled down hard and rolled the bar down the thinly covered bone, a move she distinctly remembered learning because it was one of the few that Gideon had performed on her that actually caused her pain.

He released her collar and as soon as he did, she punched him in the face and kicked out his knees. He hit the dock hard, his head spinning, and she bent down to land another blow to his nose, leaving him badly beaten but alive and no longer a threat.

She turned to find that Christopher was managing to hold his own. He'd wrestled his attacker to the ground and was pinning him to the dock. Ezra, however, was struggling with her assailant. He was much larger than she was and, though it appeared that he hadn't laid a hand on her, he had backed her to the edge of the dock and she was centimeters away from being pushed over the edge. Jude elected to leave her assailant writhing on the dock and closed the distance between her and Ezra's attacker with two wide steps, grabbing him by the back of his cloak. He hadn't seen her coming and turned toward her, startled.

He had big eyes and a round face. When he got a good look at Jude, she could tell something registered in his brain and he knew exactly who she was.

"You're her mom, aren't you?" he asked, almost mystified.

"Of course I am," Jude replied. "Who are you?"

"She said you'd come. I'm Dillard," he answered, surprisingly calmly. He stood there in front of her unsure of where to go. He was looking for an out, but Jude was blocking him, keeping him at the pointed tip of her axe.

"You can still leave," she said. "If you go right now."

The man wrestling with Christopher was struggling and could be heard gasping and moaning just a few feet away.

"What's it going to be?" asked Jude, taking small, tentative steps toward him.

"Dillard, do something!" yelled Christopher's attacker.

Jude looked briefly at Christopher, then back to Dillard.

As his friend screamed again, Dillard leapt to the side of the axe and made a break for Christopher, landing on top of him and rolling him off of the beaten body of the third man. He wrapped his thick arms around Christopher's throat whose face immediately began to turn dark red as he tried unsuccessfully to suck in a breath.

Jude bolted toward him, jabbed Dillard in the ribs with the blunt end of the axe, spun it around, and plunged the pointed end into his chest.

He moaned for just a second, spitting up a mouth full of blood. As his eyes began to drift, he managed to croak out the word *sorry*, and went still.

Jude watched him die and a strange, horrible feeling overcame her. But only for a second. She was pulled back by the sound of Christopher's man screaming.

"Okay, wait!" he shouted, raising his arms in protection in front of his chest. He sat up and was about to speak, but Jude cut him off. "Leave," she demanded, already sprinting down the dock to Shiloh.

She didn't bother to glance behind her as he pulled himself up and slumped away. Her axe was heavy and burdensome and she couldn't run very well with it in hand. Electing to rely on the knife clipped to her belt, she dropped the axe and called back for Christopher and Ezra to grab it. It was a miscalculation she'd regret moments later.

CHAPTER 21

There were four men left; three who appeared to be older, and one young teen-aged boy, presumed Caleb, guarding Shiloh. It of course occurred to Jude as she ran toward her daughter that Caleb was a child. Not young enough, however, to fail to understand the consequences of his actions. Not so young that he didn't know what it meant to take a life. He saw her coming down the dock and took a few steps forward, drawing the attention of the others toward Jude. Two of the three started toward her, forming an obstacle between her and Shiloh. A dangerous place to be. The oldest was busy praying and chanting and preparing for the ritual, and didn't seem to be aware of Jude's presence at all. This, she guessed, was Professor D, the leader of the Brotherhood whose signature was on all of Caleb's letters.

Without pause, Jude used the force she'd picked up from running to charge right into the closest of the two men bracing for her arrival. She knocked him back several feet, and he took a few staggering steps before losing his balance and falling backwards onto the dock with Jude standing over him. She'd hoped to make it a quick fight and raised her knife above his chest. Just before she brought it down, she sensed a presence behind her and turned her head to find the other man holding her axe and poised to swing. She caught on just in time and as he swept the axe horizontally through the air, aimed at splitting her in two at the mid-section. She dropped her body to lay flat on top of the man on the dock and felt the wind from the weapon glide across her back. When the blade was past her, she leapt off of the squirming man beneath her and attacked the other, wrestling the axe from his hands. It was a large and unwieldy weapon, and he was obviously untrained so it had taken him a second to regain control after the wide swing he'd just completed. She had the opportunity to grab the cool steel pole on either side of his hands and was trying to get it back, but he was remarkably strong. Both were large, muscled men – the final measure of protection installed to ensure that the ritual went smoothly.

When Christopher and Ezra arrived behind her, Jude didn't look up. "I'm fine here!" she grunted, grappling with the man holding her axe. "Go get Shiloh! Get her off the dock!"

Ezra immediately made her way around the fighting and toward Shiloh, who was calling her name. Christopher, noticing that the first man was regaining his footing and moving in to attack Jude from behind, stayed back. Just as he was standing, Christopher pushed him back down, drawing his knife. But Christopher wouldn't kill. If asked, he would say that wasn't true. He would say that he could do it. If he had to. If Jude needed him to. But she knew he would never be able to deliver the final blow. It seemed that his opponent could see right through him. He grabbed Christopher by the wrist and twisted it until his grip was broken and the knife fell from his hand. The man grabbed it and turned it over onto Christopher. Seeing this, Jude gave up on the axe handle and turned to kick the knife out of the man's hand. It went skidding down the dock and dropped into the river. Behind them, Ezra was squaring off with Caleb who was looking at her like fresh meat.

"Christopher, go!" Jude demanded, pointing at Ezra while she evaded strikes from Christopher's attacker.

Finally, Christopher gave her a resolved nod and ran to help Ezra.

Jude couldn't help but feel relieved, even in the midst of the fight. With Christopher and Ezra both working to detain Caleb, she was left to take on these two attackers alone. The help of her friends was always appreciated, and sometimes invaluable, but she was a better fighter when all she had to worry about was herself.

The man with the axe lifted it above his head and dropped it in a fluid slice. Jude dodged it and the blade landed deep into the wooden boards of the dock. While he struggled to pull it out, she turned for a second to the other robed attacker. She let him lead, and he threw a punch with his whole body behind it. Stepping just to the side of him as she was trained, Jude used his own weight and directional energy to push him forward so that he kept falling to the floor. She positioned the knife under his belly and drew up on it as he tumbled, landing unavoidably on the blade. She cut him deep, probably fatally, and he screamed, landing face first on the dock. Then she shifted back to the other guy. He had decided to abandon the axe, unable to pry it from the dock. He saw his friend bleeding on his belly and his eyes narrowed in rage. He stomped toward her with his fists formed into hard balls at his side. He swung at her and landed the strike right on the side of her head. For a second, her vision blurred as she staggered back. She forced herself to refocus as he was still coming, and swung a strike back at him. He knocked her arm out of the air and lifted his leg to kick. She grabbed him around the calf and lifted, sending him off balance and falling backwards. As he hopped, thrusting his leg to regain it from Jude's grasp, she sunk the wet, bloody knife into the hard muscle of his calf and he dropped hard, howling. She was about to finish him off when the man on the dock grabbed her around the ankle. She turned and saw that he was bleeding badly but still alive. He had barely any strength and she easily shook off his grasp. With her leg freed, she kicked him hard in the ribs, and as he curled to absorb the blow, she bent to plunge the knife through his back. With that, he was finished.

The other man was limping, with dark blood oozing from the back of his leg where he'd been stabbed, but he was still determined to destroy Jude. They moved toward each other. Jude was in the zone, intensely focused on nothing other than his bloodshot eyes, his sweat soaked chest, the gait of his steps and the one leg dragging. The short distance between them was rapidly closing. She saw nothing but his face, thought of nothing but his destruction. Until she heard the shrill scream of Shiloh just on the other side of her attacker.

Professor D was pulling her toward the tank, her arms and legs still bound. He was grinning and whispering, completely unconcerned as Shiloh squirmed and screamed. Jude looked for Christopher and Ezra and found that Caleb was putting up a good fight. Christopher was wrestling him on the dock and Ezra, also responding to Shiloh's scream, started toward her as quickly as her injured body would allow.

"Shiloh!" Jude yelled, as Ezra reached the child. Professor D shoved her back as he forced Shiloh to stand over the tank. He said something. Laughed. Shouted some kind of twisted praise toward the sky. Then, he grabbed Shiloh by the back of the neck and plunged her head into the water.

Jude launched forward, aiming to simply go right through the body that stood between them, but it didn't work. He threw an upper cut and sank it into her gut, pulling up toward her rib cage. She coughed and gagged, but retained her balance. Stepping back, she held her left hand to her burning abdomen and lifted her right toward the man. Behind him, Shiloh kicked and struggled, her head still submerged. It had been at least ten seconds. Ezra was behind him, doing everything she could to pull him away but he was completely unaware, wild eyed and foaming at the mouth.

Jude was running out of time. She took a deep breath and focused all of her strength against this last, final obstacle. As he stepped forward to swing again, she side-swiped him and drew her knife across his neck. She was pleasantly surprised to find that the knife had landed where she'd hoped and pulled like butter through the flesh against his throat. He was just as shocked. His eyes widened and he grabbed at the slice with his hands. He choked and spat blood as he tried to form words. She didn't wait around to hear what he had to say. She placed both of her hands on his chest and forced him backwards, until he took a few steps and fell into the river.

The path was clear. Christopher seemed to have Caleb under control and Ezra was relentlessly going after the leader, Professor D. Jude made a break for them and as soon as she reached the pool, she grabbed him by the back of his cloak and hurled him to the ground with relative ease. Shiloh, still conscious, pulled her head out of the water and gasped for air, leaning against the walls of the tank. Inside, a large, vicious looking fish swam laps, churning up waves along the inside edges. Jude grabbed Shiloh and carried her away, rubbing her back and squeezing her into hugs as she coughed up water.

"You're okay," she promised, unable to pull her hands away from the child. "Everything's okay."

The leader sat with his knees to his chest on the dock, staring at the tank in despair. Christopher had Caleb in a chest lock, clamping his arms down by his sides. As soon as Jude pulled Shiloh out of the water, Ezra was there helping to comfort and check over her.

Jude took a long, deep breath and let it out slowly. It was late, after three in the morning. Her body was exhausted, and her mind even more. She couldn't imagine how tired and worn out Shiloh was, and she wanted to get her in the car and go home.

Once Shiloh caught her breath, Jude swept sopping wet hair from her eyes and gave her a soft smile. "Are you alright?" she asked gently. She had been furious when she found out that Shiloh willingly ran off with Caleb and got herself into this mess, but now, holding her and having her back, she couldn't find that anger.

But when Shiloh looked back at Jude, her expression was startling. Shiloh was distant, cold, even angry herself. She was scared, hurt and confused, and all of those emotions translated to anger that fluttered and sparked in her blue eyes. Jude went to wrap her in a hug again but Shiloh pulled back. Instead, she slid off of Jude's lap and into Ezra's arms. Ezra gave Jude a look of concern and surprise as Shiloh buried her face in Ezra's neck and did her best not to cry.

Jude pressed her fingers into the achy spot between her eyes and closed them tight. She didn't have the energy to fight Shiloh just then, so instead, she stood to her feet and helped Ezra get up with Shiloh sitting on her hip, refusing to let go. They were all about to head back to the other end of the dock to regroup when the sound of rushing water caught their attention. They turned and saw that the water in the tank was churning, cresting and splashing over the sidewalls. The leader scrambled to his feet with his mouth gaped open and ran toward it. Caleb stopped resisting Christopher and became still, his eyes trained on the tank.

The reactions of those standing on the dock were dramatically varied as a horrific creature rose up out of the water and released a long, spine curling screech. It was huge, roughly 8 feet tall, with a wet, slime-coated body that looked bloated and water-logged. It's coloration was a greenish-gray and it had long arms and legs with webbed hands and pointed claws. It's face was angular and had a shredded, rough appearance with narrow, deep-set eyes and long, catfish-like whiskers at the corners of its mouth. For the first few seconds, it seemed to stagger, remembering how to use its legs. It was an utterly absurd creature, and for a moment or so, Jude had to convince herself that what she was seeing was real. When it gained its balance and let out a second ear-piercing screech, she accepted it and prepared for one more fight, knowing that this one was going to be different.

The leader jumped to his feet and hurried toward the beast. Jude was already standing and going for her axe, still stuck in the dock boards, when the leader stopped right in front of the monster and bowed his head. He dropped to his knees and started babbling, praising the creature and begging for its blessing. Ezra pulled Shiloh back.

The demon looked down at the small, prattling man at his feet and, without a moment's pause, he reached down and grabbed the man by the neck. He lifted him off the dock with one hand, leaving his feet dangling. Even as this was happening, the old man continued to praise the beast and did not resist, even as it began to shake him and tighten its grasp around his throat. Ezra covered Shiloh's eyes and turned her away. The demon looked the man in the eye with a cold, inhuman gaze and tightened its fist, knuckles bulging from the strength of its grip. The man's face turned redder and redder as he slipped further from life. He began to squirm, realizing that the demon had no intentions of showering him with immortality and riches, but it was too late. Finally, the man's spine snapped and the demon sank its teeth into his still warm flesh.

Caleb could be heard gasping and panicking as Jude arrived at her axe. With little effort, she popped it out of the splintering boards and marched back toward the demon.

When it saw her coming, it finished slashing through the throat of its sire, now still and lifeless. It dropped him like garbage onto the dock and turned for her.

It was moving towards her with narrow, vacant eyes and for a second, she shuddered, unable to erase the image of the man who was just ripped to shreds in front of her. She gripped her axe and prepared to swing. But as it got close enough to move in for the kill, it stopped suddenly, as if it had caught the scent of something better on the air. Slowly, it lifted its head to look beyond Jude, over her shoulder. She turned to see that it had locked its eyes on Shiloh.

"Hey!" Jude yelled, waving her arms and the axe in the air and trying to regain its attention. But in one quick and ferocious motion, it swiped Jude with its scaley arm and threw her with tremendous force to land on her back about three feet away from where she had been standing. With her out of the way, it made a dash for Shiloh, where Ezra was holding and rocking her across the dock.

Jude scrambled to her feet to find that her lower back grabbed at her when she stood up. She disregarded the pain and ran for Shiloh, but Yarik was already ripping her away from Ezra. Jude watched, praying for her legs to carry her faster as the demon dropped to its haunches over her daughter, hungry. Ezra, who had been tossed aside like an old rag doll, stood up and leapt on top of it, thrusting her knife into its back.

Jude arrived as the beast reacted to Ezra's blade and released another high-pitched scream. It reached behind with both arms and grabbed a hold of Ezra, sinking its claws into the flesh of her back. Jude tried to wrestle Yarik and force it to release its grasp, but he peeled her off of him with ease and gave her a ferocious growl. Ezra was unable to stand for herself or support her own weight as the demon swung her around in the way that a dog rips up a stuffed toy, locking and shaking. Then, it drew her back and flung her forward. She flew several yards down the dock and into a pillar, against which she crumbled and collapsed.

"Ezra!" Jude yelled and started toward her motionless friend, but she only made it a few steps and turned back, knowing Shiloh was once again his target.

She glanced around for Christopher, but he was still holding on to Caleb who was fighting him again, eager to get to Yarik and claim his reward. As Yarik moved to pick up Shiloh, Jude got between them and shoved him back. He staggered a little, evidently surprised by her strength. As he regained his balance, Jude raised her axe once more. It was her strategy to keep him at an axe's length and use his uncoordinated, gangly girth against him. She wouldn't be able to out-muscle him, but he moved like a monumentous toddler, taking short-ened steps and planting them too hard. He seemed to lead with his head which kept him generally unbalanced and, having had nothing but fins for centuries, his limbs appeared foreign and new to him. He swung and clawed unpredictably, but his erratic movements added to his lack of balance. All of these things, Jude catalogued quickly as she weighed her best chances of victory.

Yarik lunged at her and she stepped back, keeping her axe pointed at his chest and maintaining that critical distance. He was thrown off by the weapon, shifting this way and that trying to figure out how to get to her. As he grew increasingly frustrated, he began to stomp and snort, snatching at the air and crouching down only to stand suddenly back up again. He went to scrape the claws of his feet against the soft, spongy dock boards and Jude lurched forward, stabbing the point of her axe into his bloated belly. She pulled it out quickly before he could grab it and lunged for him again, plunging the point into his thick, slimy skin just above the first puncture. Yarik hurled and swatted at the axe but Jude held it tight with both hands gripped around the handle. Behind her, she knew Shiloh still sat alone, unguarded, trembling and exhausted.

Out of the corner of her eye, Jude saw Ezra move and she breathed a quick sigh of relief as the demon shifted to her right. Jude followed, swinging the axe around to meet him. She swirled her body to track him, lifted the axe and sliced it through the air at a sharp diagonal angle toward the ground.

She landed the tip of the blade right at the demon's midsection and carved a deep slice through its abdomen. While it was grabbing at its wound, Jude lifted the axe to deliver the final strike. As she was about to drop the axe down and split the demon in two, he unexpectedly dove to her side, and instead, the blade landed with a crack on the dock. When Jude lifted the axe, she discovered that a large break had formed in the handle just below the blade. If she used it for another strike, it would simply snap in two against him. There was no time to assess the situation, and in seconds, the injured demon was back on top of Shiloh, who had tried to make a mad dash for the barely conscious Ezra. Jude dropped the axe to the dock and sprinted for Yarik, once again left with nothing but a knife. Shiloh lay beneath him, dwarfed by his size but by no means resigned to her fate. She threw up her knees and did all she could to throw him off. Jude could see her little fists going at him but he was only mildly inconvenienced by her efforts and was crushing her under his weight. His claws were buried into her bony shoulders and she gritted her teeth, refusing to cry.

When she came to within three feet of the creature, Jude sprung from the dock and cascaded through the air, landing on his back and burying her knife into his neck. The blade sank to the hilt, but still the beast continued to fight. Yarik tried to buck Jude off but she held on with her arms locked around his neck. Finally, he did as she'd hoped and pulled his talons out of Shiloh's neck, turning them, instead, on her. Jude clung to his back as he stood to his feet and dug into Jude's arms, trying to rip her off of him. Blood, or something like it, gushed from his multiple contusions. He was weakened, but fueled by an intense, unstoppable rage; a trait with which Jude felt she was relatively familiar. Before it was able to pull her arms apart, she plunged her knife into its back just to the side of its bony, protruding spine. It fell to the dock and Jude landed still clinging to its back. He was ripping long, deep gashes through her shirt and into her skin and she felt like she was in some fight-to-the-death style rodeo. She could feel her own blood soaking through her tank top and gluing it to her shoulder blades.

Yarik reached for Shiloh, even under the unrelenting punches and jabs that Jude was delivering. He grabbed her by the ankle and drug her toward him, already snapping his jaws. Shiloh was yelling for help and fighting with everything she had. Yarik moved in for the kill, squeezing her as she squirmed against him.

Jude was practically face to face with Shiloh, with only a demon between them. She wrapped her arms once again around Yariks throat, and squeezed with every ounce of strength she could muster. When the opportunity presented itself, she gripped the knife in her sweating palm and punched it through the rough, slime-coated skin at the left side of his neck. She knew she'd done some real damage this time, because when the knife sunk in, the demon reeled back, howling as it shook Shiloh in its claws. Quickly, Jude drew the blade across his throat. Cold blood spilled from the fatal gash and from his twisted mouth as he choked. In his final moments of life, Yarik looked at the helpless child in his clutches, and shoved her reeling backwards into the river.

Knowing Shiloh couldn't swim, Jude gave the knife a final twist as she kept her eyes trained on Shiloh struggling in the water. She was leaning on her toes in her direction, ready to spring into the river but waiting to be certain that Yarik was dead. "Hang on, I'm coming!" she yelled. Yarik dropped to his knees, wobbled and finally fell forward, landing like a collapsed tower on the dock.

As soon as he hit, Jude threw down her knife and dove heedlessly into the black water, aiming for the splashing and gasping girl.

Shiloh was fighting to keep her head above the water and growing weaker with every attempt. She kept slipping below and Jude had to search for disruption on the water's surface in the dark. Shiloh wasn't reemerging, so Jude dove heedlessly into the black river, feeling around in the space where Shiloh had disappeared. Finally, she located her squirming and kicking for her life. She wrapped her arms around Shiloh's waist and paddled upward, calling to her as they broke the surface.

"Breathe, baby," she said, out of breath herself as she pulled Shiloh to the dock coughing and gasping. She hoisted her above her head to place her on the platform.

Ezra had managed to stand up and make her way to the commotion, and she weakly helped pull

Shiloh up. As soon as she was out of the water, Shiloh sprang into her arms refusing to look at Jude.

Jude hoisted herself up and collapsed onto the dock as Caleb could be heard screaming and running in their direction with Christopher in tow. The boy threw himself over Yariks lifeless body and begged him to rise and pay him the debt he was owed.

CHAPTER 22

Jude rubbed her hand over the shooting pain in her collarbone and caught her breath, laying flat on the dock and sopping wet. The gashes on her back and arms stung and burned, but she was alive, and so was Shiloh. Behind her, she could hear Ezra comforting Shiloh, and Christopher lecturing Caleb who was furious that Yarik was gone. Stars were poking out from the deep purple sky and for a second, Jude mused about the persistence of nature, amazed by its unaffected behavior. Gasping to recover the oxygen she'd lost, with her back flat on the hard wooden dock, she realized that was just a little bitter. It never seemed to recognize when her life was teetering on the edge of disaster.

Finally, reluctantly, she peeled herself off of the splintering wood and made her way toward her friends, who were gathered around her dripping daughter by Christopher's car. She walked with intention, sifting through the well of emotions that bubbled inside of her as she went, arms crossed over her chest. Ezra and Christopher saw her coming and noticed the electricity in the air that seemed to be emanating from Jude.

She stopped with a jolt right in front of Shiloh, and looked down at her, arms still crossed in a position that indicated that she was not interested in explanations or apologies. Ezra put her hands on Shiloh's shoulders, already bracing for Jude's rage.

"I cannot even begin to tell you," Jude started, with a measured voice that dripped with anger, "how disappointed with you I am right now."

Shiloh looked up at her mother, her expression mingled fear and defiance.

"You snuck out of the house. You ran off with complete strangers. You could've gotten yourself killed, Shiloh, and you damn near did! Twice! And Ezra, and Christopher, and me along with you!" Her volume rose with as hear heart and lungs seemed to rise up in her chest and she threw her hands up in loss and frustration. The bigger half of her wanted to grab Shiloh and squeeze her and kiss her and thank God that she was safe. And it hurt to fight that instinct, but the other half of her was furious, and that fury rose up from a place of fierce devotion that simply would not accept such carelessness, even in an eight year old child. "You lied to me! You lied to Ezra! What were you thinking?"

"*You* lied!" Shiloh stepped forward pulling away from Ezra's arms, and Jude knocked back, aghast. Shiloh furrowed her brow and crossed her arms over her chest in a posture that was so startlingly familiar to Jude that she almost believed she'd slipped through some kind of portal and was looking at the child version of herself.

"What?" the grown version stammered, suddenly on the defensive.

"You lied to *me*! You told me that I was special! That I had a gift! You didn't tell me I was going to die! So what if I'd gotten myself killed, you wouldn't care anyway!"

Shiloh locked her eyes on Jude's and wouldn't relent, a tiny ball of rage and betrayal, and Jude went cold. Her mind was waterlogged and fuzzy, and alarmingly quiet. Anger was the last emotion she'd been able to remember, so she fell back on it. "Don't you ever talk like that!" she yelled finally.

Shiloh shook her head at Jude. "You can't tell me what to do!" she shot back. "You're a liar! You don't even care about me!" Shiloh knew what she was doing. She was hurt, so she was throwing daggers, hoping to land them deep under Jude's skin; a defense mechanism Jude herself had mastered. "You're not even really my mom!"

Jude was stunned. Standing mouth-open but silent, as the bullet Shiloh had just fired pierced its way through her chest wall and into the dark meaty flesh of her heart.

"Ezra, get her in the car," said Jude sharply as she turned to the river and walked away, with Shiloh's words still ricocheting around inside of her. On the way to the dock, she sucked down sobs that caught in her throat, and knelt down to search her jacket for her phone. Shaking, she pulled it out of her pocket, pounded the buttons that took her to her contacts screen, and clicked the green "call" button under Gideon's name.

She held the phone to her face and almost gave in against the warm panel on her cheek, but she steeled herself. The phone rang three times before Gideon's voice could be heard on the other end.

"Jude, did you find Shiloh?"

"Yeah, we have her. She's fine. I need the Synedrion to send someone down here."

Gideon cleared his throat. "Okay," he said slowly. "Why, what's going on?"

"I need them to come take away the boys that just tried to sell my kid to some demon." She spoke more quickly than her lung capacity allowed and every sentence ended on the fumes of oxygen.

"Jude, calm down, I'm not sure I understand-"

"Two boys convinced Shiloh to read the Codex without me. They fed her some twisted version of the truth and she ran away with them, and it was all part of a plan to sacrifice her to a demon. The boys know who she is. I don't know how, or where they came from, but they know, and they're kids. You can either send the Synedrion or I'll kill them myself, it's your call."

"Okay, okay Jude, I'll send someone," Gideon said calmly. "I'll send someone. Take a few deep breaths. Is everyone okay?"

She tried to follow his advice but she could only take in air in short, stifled spurts, like her lungs were riddled with holes. "Yes, everyone's fine," she said, then hung up the phone.

At the edge of the dock, she collapsed into one of the posts that held it up over the water, throwing all of her body into it and digging her nails into the porous wood. Her chest heaved and tightened and she felt the walls of her throat become dry as it seemed that all of the liquid in her body rushed up to her face. She coughed and gagged and completely lost control, still holding white-knuckled to the pylon, sobbing and hyperventilating until she felt dizzy.

After about two minutes of hard and fast breakdown, she opened her eyes and pressed the back of her hands into them, leaving them blurry and bloodshot. She inhaled sharply and finally got enough of a breath to recenter herself. The dark night sky was washed in a thick blue-black acrylic. It had to be nearing morning. Maybe the sun would come up soon. Maybe it would never come up again. The river rippled in the slight breeze and it could be heard lapping the posts and bank below. Jude brought her hand to her head and drug it through her wet and tangled hair. How could she have been so negligent? Why didn't she hide the book better? Why wasn't she just upfront with Shiloh? How had she fallen so quickly from Supermom, to Traitor and Deserter?

She stood there for a moment longer, racking her brain for answers, second guessing every move she'd ever made that led her to this point, wondering how she would get Shiloh back and horrified that it was too late, when she felt a hand fall against her back.

Startled, she quickly turned around to see Christopher, holding onto a rope with Jack tied to the other end. She glanced behind him to look for the others.

"Ezra got everyone into the car," he said, answering her yet-to-be-spoken question. "There's a lot of tension," he chuckled, "but everyone will be fine."

She turned back toward the lake, hoping to hide her tear-streaked face in the shadows. "Thanks," she whispered.

"Of course." He lowered his eyes and his voice, looking at the broken woman in front of him. "You know, she's okay. She's going to be alright."

He moved in and tried to pull her into a hug, but for whatever reason, she brought her arms to her chest and pushed him away, hard. She wasn't even sure why, maybe because she was angry at herself and didn't think she was deserving of such a gesture. Maybe because she felt that any distraction from thoughts of Shiloh was unacceptable. Maybe because her emotions were all over the place and she didn't have the energy to sort one from another. But she pushed him away and he took a step back, arms still extended toward her.

"Jude, are *you* okay?" he asked gently.

She shook her head. "No, far from it," she answered. She placed her hands on her hips and looked down at the warped deck boards.

"Well, whatever I can do to help, I-"

"You can't," she interrupted, her voice cold and short. "Christopher, I should have seen this coming! Do you know why I didn't? I was running around with you, distracted by some unrealistic fantasy of what my life might have been like had I not been handed this responsibility. My eight year old daughter snuck out of the house, ran off with strange boys and nearly got herself killed. This would be bad for any parent, then add Shiloh's destiny on top of it, and things get even more complicated."

By this point, she was speaking without thinking and words spilled from her lips beyond her control. Christopher was taking small steps back, hands buried in his pockets, trying to shrink away from her.

"I tried to make all this clear to you, but you didn't get it, and now it's messy, which is exactly what I wanted to avoid. I'm sorry, I just can't do it. Not right now. Maybe not ever. I don't know who I thought I was fooling."

She looked at him and he looked away, and she crossed her arms over her chest. "I'm sorry," she said again, softer. Then she turned and made her way to the car, and toward Caleb.

By the time she reached the car, she'd shoved Christopher to the back of her mind. Now, coming into intense focus, was the real object of her rage: the moppy-haired teenage boy who'd promised her daughter to a hell-raising cult. "Where's your brother?" she asked, looking down coldly at the boy bound and sitting against Christopher's car.

"He's asleep," Caleb answered, avoiding eye contact by staring in the direction of his shoes.

"Where?" Jude snapped back, pounding the metal car body just above his head. He jumped, then lifted his head and nodded in the direction of his car; the missing Oldsmobile. Jude had completely failed to notice it between the dark and the chaos.

She wanted to punch him in the face, but held herself back. She was already going to be in deep with the Synedrion when they found her by following the trail of bodies in her wake. She didn't need to beat up a teenager, no matter how deserving he may have been. She turned away from him with deafening silence , and made her way to his car.

She opened the back passenger side of the Oldsmobile and, in the ceiling light, found Elliott laying curled up on the seat, sound asleep. Below him on the floorboards was Shiloh's school backpack, with Herschel the Alligator's head sticking out of the top. Looking at it made her heart ache and Jude grabbed the bag and tossed it over her shoulder.

The sight of Caleb filled her with violent rage, but Elliott she felt some sympathy for. He was just a little boy, smaller even than Shiloh. She had no idea what he knew or if his friendship with Shiloh was genuine, but she had to believe it was. And laying alone in the back seat of a stolen car, with his long hair falling over his face and his light-up sneakers covered in dried dirt, she wanted to help him. For a fraction of a second, she entertained the thought of bringing him home. Caleb was hardened. A thief, a liar, a kidnapper, maybe a murderer. But there was still a chance for his little brother. If he was set on the straight and narrow. But realistically it wasn't an option. She didn't have time to watch over another child. Her lifestyle wouldn't allow it. The Synedrion had the tools to care for him and give him a chance.

She patted his back and roused him from sleep. He rolled his head to look at her, blinking hard and red faced. It looked like he'd fallen asleep crying. When he saw Jude, he sat up startled and backed toward the side of the car like a trapped animal.

"Elliott, it's okay," she said gently, holding her arms out to him.

He was looking at her wide-eyed. "I didn't know," he said quickly. "I swear, I didn't know. Is Shiloh okay?"

Jude nodded. "She's going to be okay. Come here."

After a brief hesitation, Elliott crawled over the seat toward her and wrapped his arms around her neck, letting her lift him out of the car. He rested his head on her shoulder like he'd known her his whole life and she couldn't help but give in to the feeling of holding a child. It's all she'd needed for twenty four hours and though he wasn't Shiloh, she found some small comfort in the warmth of his breath and the softness of his skin. A simple moment of relief after a long, horrible nightmare.

She carried him back to Christopher's car. When Caleb saw him, he tried to stand up fighting the ropes at his ankles, but Jude pushed him back down.

"Elliott," Caleb croaked, craning his neck to look at his brother. But Elliott pressed harder into Jude's shoulder, unwilling to look. Caleb slammed back against the vehicle in frustration and closed his eyes tightly.

"You know, I did all this for you Ell," Caleb began to plead. "I wanted to be able to protect you. Who else was going to care for you, Elliott? Who else except me?"

Jude placed Elliott in the back seat of the car next to Ezra and Shiloh. She hoped to catch Shiloh's eye, but, like Caleb, she was slighted when Shiloh looked quickly away, arms still crossed and eyes still angry.

She closed the door, and glanced down at Caleb. "If you cared for your brother, you wouldn't have brought him to an abandoned dock with dangerous men and a viscous demon. You wouldn't hurt people to –" she paused and it hit her. She wasn't really all that different from Caleb. She untied her flannel shirt from around her waist and pulled it on, rubbing her arms from the sudden chill.

CHAPTER 23

After an hour of awkward silence and avoided glances, a black escalade pulled up to the scene and two large men stepped out. Jude knew them instantly by their black suits and confident, focused approach. The strong arm of the Synedrion, running the nitty gritty operations while the heart of the organization hid out in their cloisters praying and studying.

They both flashed badges but Jude waved them away. "Over there," she gestured to where Caleb was leaning against the car with his head bowed to his knees. "The younger one is in the car."

They nodded and she followed them to Caleb.

"Caleb Todesco, you are officially in the custody of the Synedrion." One of the men lifted him to his feet, untied the ropes and replaced them with proper handcuffs. The other opened the car door and briskly ushered out Elliott, who had fallen back to sleep waiting. "You will be transported to a secure location where you will be brought before a tribunal who will assess your status and determine how to proceed."

Neither boy protested as they were led to the car

and swept quickly inside.

"What will happen to them?" Jude asked the man on standby as the other secured the boys inside the Escalade.

He looked down at her with his face unflinching, completely detached in the military fashion of the Synedrions ground forces. "They will be transported to a secure location where a tri-"

"Right, I heard all of that," Jude interrupted, throwing the man off. He stiffened his back. "What will *happen* to them?"

He nodded slightly and cleared his throat. "They will be monitored. If rehabilitation is an option, they'll be given the opportunity. If not, they are looking at permanent incarceration at a Synedrion facility."

"You know, the younger one is just along for the ride," Jude said, feeling obligated to intervene on Elliott's behalf. "He's not to blame."

The man slid his left hand into his pocket. "I'm sure that will be taken into account before any decisions are made."

Both Synedrion officials climbed back into the vehicle and pulled away. Jude watched them until they were out of sight, then she turned back toward her own ride home, unable to ignore the exhaustion stiffening her sore and depleted muscles and causing her eyes to drift. As she approached the driver side door, she was stopped by Christopher who fidgeted on the pavement.

He wasn't looking her directly in the eye, and

had his hands buried so deeply in his pockets that his belt had to work overtime to keep his pants on his hips. "You shouldn't drive," he said quietly.

She rubbed her hand across the back of her neck and exhaled slowly. He wasn't wrong. Actually, she was relieved that he'd intercepted her because she felt like she could barely hold her head up, let alone safely operate a vehicle. Since she'd yelled at him on the dock, she had time to come down a little. She was still angry, confused, and far too tired to deal with any of it, but she felt a little remorseful. What she said may have been fundamentally correct, but she wished it had gone down differently. What was happening was exactly what she feared since the moment their relationship began to take a turn toward the romantic, and she didn't want to think about what she would lose if he wasn't a part of her life.

She pulled the keys out of her pocket and held them out to him. "Thanks," she said quietly as he took them from her. He nodded, allowing his glance to collide with hers for just a second, and then hurried into the car.

She waited for him to get in and close the door, then walked around numbly to the passenger side. She slid into the seat, not even bothering to glance back to Shiloh, and rested her head against the window. Christopher started the car and they pulled away just as the sky was turning a morning shade of pale, barely interrupting the heavy darkness that had been hanging over them through the whole ordeal. She watched as the dock got smaller and smaller behind them. She noticed, for the first time since it was all over, her thumping heart, still elevated but slowing now as her mind cleared of the anxieties of losing Shiloh, and of the battle that had been fought and won in the past several hours. She allowed it to settle over her thoughts that Shiloh was safe, the bad guy had been eliminated, and everything was going to be okay. Still, there was a heaviness in her chest; an aching emptiness in the pit of her stomach that would not subside, because while Shiloh was right behind her, close enough to touch, she still felt unreachable. She still felt lost.

With Christopher driving and the urgency gone, the drive home took much longer than the drive to Tidewater the day before. And the whole thing was permeated by intense, uncomfortable silence. Everyone except for Christopher drifted in and out of sleep, but it was short lived and unsatisfying. Injuries and anxious minds made sleep hard to come by. They finally pulled into the driveway of the Mikhale house at around nine thirty in the morning.

Shiloh had the door open before the car came to a complete stop. She jumped out and took off toward the house, calling Jack, who had been crammed up against the door in the back seat, to follow behind her. Ezra gave Jude a sympathetic look, then collected the weapons from the trunk and limped toward the house behind Shiloh, leaving Jude alone in the driveway with Christopher.

Jude slung her backpack over one shoulder and

Shiloh's over the other, closed the trunk and turned to him. They both stood a few feet apart, dodging glances and wishing to be anywhere else.

Finally, Jude spoke up. "Thanks for everything, Chris," she said weakly, lifting her head to look at him.

He glanced up at her and gave her a tight lipped smile. "Of course," he answered. "Anything you guys need?"

She shook her head. "No, thanks."

He nodded and held her gaze for just an extra second. She wanted to say something. Maybe an apology, either for the fact that she couldn't be who he wanted her to be, or at least for the way she'd broken it to him. But words didn't come and she couldn't find enough clarity in her thoughts to come up with something to say. He nodded again in her direction, then climbed back into the driver's seat, and disappeared down the road.

Jude staggered down the walkway and into the house. When she stepped into the kitchen, she found Ezra at the counter making an unusually large pot of coffee.

Are you alright?" Jude asked, surprised to find that her voice cracked from disuse. She stepped in close to Ezra and inspected the gashes on her shoulders. "Let me look at you, I'm worried you have a concussion."

"I think we'd know by now, Jude," said Ezra, but she turned anyway and allowed Jude to get a good look into her eyes.

"You seem to be okay," Jude confirmed. "Just don't do anything crazy for a few hours."

Ezra laughed. "I promise," she answered, as Jude lowered herself into a kitchen chair. She tried hard not to, but she couldn't help wincing just a little when her muscles finally gave out and she collapsed into the seat.

"Are *you* okay?" Ezra asked, handing her a big cup of coffee.

Jude nodded as she took a sip. "Emotionally or physically?"

Ezra sat down across from her at the table. "Both."

Jude shrugged. "I'll be fine. I'll be good as new in a few days. But Shiloh may never speak to me again."

"She will. She'll come around. I've never seen a kid as close to her mother as Shiloh is to you."

Jude rested her head in her hands. "I don't know," she admitted. "I really messed up."

"She just needs a little time," Ezra replied.

Jude shook her head and took another big gulp. Nine times out of ten, you could take Ezra's word to the bank. But this time, she was off. She couldn't delay any longer. Time was exactly what Shiloh didn't need; time to sift through the events of the past 48 hours and become even more confused. Jude set her cup down resolutely on the table. The idea of movement sounded unbearable. Then, the thought of deep conversation even more so. But she had to do it. "No," she said, pulling herself up. "I need to talk to her."

"Good luck," Ezra offered as Jude grabbed her coffee cup and Shiloh's backpack, and left the kitchen headed for the stairs.

Jude paused for a moment at the top of the stairs, set the backpack down and looked in on Shiloh. Jack was lying stretched out on her rug with his tail wagging and thwacking against the floor. She was sitting at her desk, absentmindedly spinning her globe.

Jude tapped on the wall to get her attention. Shiloh turned her head quickly toward her, then back away again when she saw who it was.

"Can I come in?" Jude asked.

Shiloh shrugged. "It's your house."

"It's your room."

She waited for a response, and when Shiloh said nothing, Jude took it as an invitation.

She sat down on the edge of Shiloh's bed, and took a slow, deep breath. "We really need to talk," she stated finally, to the back of Shiloh's head.

"Fine," Shiloh answered in a low, irritated grumble.

"I should never have lied to you," Jude began. "I should've told you everything and I know that now, but I need you to understand why I did it."

Shiloh still didn't turn around, but she became very still, with her small hand resting motionlessly over Canada.

"There are a few reasons," Jude continued. "One was that I wanted to protect you. I didn't want you to be afraid or to have to live in the shadow of this horrible thing. You're just a little girl and I wanted you to feel safe and be happy and enjoy being a little girl." She swallowed a lump in her throat. Words were floating across the room, but she wasn't sure if any of them were registering. "The other reason was a little selfish. But-" She paused, dropping her hands onto her lap. "Shiloh, would you please just come here?"

She needed Shiloh in her arms to get through this next part, even if Shiloh still hated her guts and wanted to be anywhere else. She needed the calm in Shiloh's dark ocean eyes, the strength in her touch.

"Please," she said again.

She watched as Shiloh peeled herself away from the desk and turned toward Jude, tight-fisted and staring at the floor. When she stopped about a foot away from where Jude sat on her bed, Jude reach forward and grabbed both of Shiloh skinny wrists, pulling her gently toward her. Shiloh didn't resist and came to stand leaning against Jude's legs.

Jude ran a hand through Shiloh's tangled, dirty hair and down her narrow shoulder and she breathed deeply. "The other reason is that if I told you the truth about who you are and what your future holds I would have to say it out loud, and I was not – am not – ready for that. I don't think I'll ever be ready for that because I'll never, ever be okay with it. And I'm going to do everything I can to keep you safe because I never, ever want to be in a world without you."

She had been fighting a well emotions quaking in her chest in an attempt to be strong, but when she saw a tear spring from the corner of Shiloh's eye and slide down her cheek, she couldn't fight it anymore. She grabbed Shiloh around the waist and swept her into herself, pulling her onto her lap. Shiloh sank willingly into her, leaning hard against her chest and sobbing into her neck. And even through the tears and pain and weight of it all, Jude wanted nothing more than to push Pause and live forever in that moment. Her eyelids were like heavy curtains over her damp and burning eyes and she closed them. Shiloh was warm and clingy against her, and she could feel Shiloh's fists clenching handfuls of the back of her shirt. She heaved and gasped as a weeks' worth of trauma came spilling out of her little body and Jude held her tight, folding Shiloh into herself and breathing deep the healing scent of Shiloh's tangled, honeysuckle hair, relieved by her familiar sounds, even if they were the sounds of a broken heart.

"I'm sorry I ran away," Shiloh blubbered into Jude's shoulder between sharp, quick breaths.

"I know you are," Jude answered, squeezing her tighter and surrendering whatever was left of her anger. "I understand." Then, though part of her didn't want to, she pulled Shiloh back just enough to see her face. She placed both hands on the sides of her head just below her ears and used her thumbs to brush away the big round tears from her cheeks. Then, she pressed a kiss into her forehead.

"I know you have questions about what you

read in the Codex," she began, with Shiloh's head still in her hands. "And we are going to talk about all of those things and I'm going to be completely honest with you, but right now we're both tired and our thoughts are fuzzy and all over the place."

Shiloh nodded in agreement, blinking hard as the last round of tears pooled at the bottoms of her eyes.

"But there is one thing I really, *really* need you to know right now and it can't wait."

"What?" Asked Shiloh with a sniffle.

Jude put her forehead against Shiloh's so that their identical eyes were only centimeters apart and looking back at one another. "I *am* your mother," she said with finality. She paused for a moment and let the gravity of the statement settle around them. "I am now, I always have been, and I always will be your *real* mother. There's no one else. And you're not adopted, or here with me by chance, or some kind of parentless alien baby."

Shiloh tried hard but couldn't keep from grinning.

"You are more related to me than most kids are related to their parents."

"But I wasn't born yours," said Shiloh, unsure of how to phrase her question.

"Yes you were," Jude corrected. "Just like any other little girl or boy, you were mine before we ever even met. You weren't born *to* me," she explained. "I didn't physically bring you into the world. A surrogate did that; someone who has a baby for someone else."

"Who?" Shiloh asked.

Jude shrugged. "I don't know. I probably never will. But that person is not your mom. Your DNA, the stuff in your blood that makes you *you*, is just like mine. I'm your mom, and I don't take care of you because I have to, or because you have a big special destiny. I take care of you because you *are* mine, and I love you more than I ever thought I could love anything in my whole life."

Shiloh was studying Jude, her eyes, her voice, her hands. She locked her gaze and got lost in what she had always known to be the safest place in the world.

"Do you understand?" asked Jude.

Shiloh smiled and nodded her head.

Jude squeezed her hands, afraid of the next question. "Do you believe me?" She waited for an answer, praying for it to be yes.

Shiloh threw her arms back around her mother's neck and held on, and Jude knew that Shiloh believed her. She leaned her head back, and then her whole body, pulling Shiloh up onto the bed with her as her back hit the mattress and she exhaled a long awaited sigh of relief.

Together, they laid there for a minute, breathing against each other, until Shiloh rolled off of Jude's chest and onto her back beside her. She looked at Jude, who had turned her head to look at Shiloh, and Jude laughed as Shiloh began to imitate her. Left arm resting palm up above her head, right hand laying over the rise and fall of her stomach. Left leg bent and pointed upward at the knee. If Jude raised an arm, Shiloh raised the same one, and both went on that way for a few minutes, smiling silently as the smaller of two near clones mirrored the larger. At last, Jude lifted both arms and dropped them onto the bed at her sides and Shiloh sat up.

"What's wrong?" Jude asked.

"I lost Herschel," Shiloh said, having just realized that her bag was left in Caleb's car.

Jude took a deep breath and let it out slowly. She didn't want to move. The bed was incredibly comfortable and had taken the edge off of the pain that she was in. Nonetheless, she sat up, pulled herself off the bed on weak and sore legs, and grabbed the backpack from the top of the stairs. She unzipped it, pulled out Herschel the Alligator, and walked back to Shiloh, who jumped up from the bed and ran to meet her in the center of the room. She thanked Jude over and over as she hugged Herschel to her chest and carried him back to her bed where she restored him to his thrown at the top of the pillows. They both collapsed back onto the mattress, ready for a long nap.

CHAPTER 24

Jude woke up several hours later and lifted her heavy arm to shield her eyes from the June sun spilling golden through the open window. It had to be around four or five and they had slept away the entire afternoon. Shiloh was passed out with her head in the crook of Jude's arm and Jude didn't want to wake her so she very carefully slid out from under her and, feeling groggy and a little unsteady, crept downstairs.

She found Ezra sitting on the couch with a bowl of cereal and wrapped in a blanket.

"Did you get any sleep?" Jude asked, as she sat down next to her on the couch and pulled the blanket over her lap.

"I've been dozing," answered Ezra. "I'm trying not to. I'd like to be able to sleep tonight."

"Hmm," answered Jude, rubbing her eyes. "I'm going to be on a funky sleep schedule all week."

"You're always on a funky sleep schedule," Ezra replied. "How'd it go with Shiloh?"

Jude took a deep breath. "I think it's going

to be okay. She doesn't hate me anymore. I don't think."

"She never hated you. She was just confused."

Jude gave a deep, hard nod. "Yeah well, I'm sure she still is. We didn't get into everything. I can't imagine the questions that are coming. Or how the hell I'm going to answer them."

"You will figure it out as they come."

"I hope so," Jude replied. "For now though I think we're in an okay place."

"That's great," answered Ezra, refocusing her attention on her cereal bowl.

"Yeah…" Jude's voice trailed off.

"What's wrong?"

"Now that I've won back the favor of Shiloh, I might have really screwed things up with Christopher," she answered, leaning back hard against the couch and drawing her fingers through her hair. "If you're pissed at me for some reason, that would be three for three."

Ezra laughed. "I'm not. What happened with Christopher?"

"We had a fight. On the dock. Well, *we* didn't have a fight. I just… flipped out. He was trying to be nice."

"Jude, you were under a ridiculous amount of stress," Ezra reasoned. "He will understand."

"Should he? Or, more to the point, should it matter?"

"What are you talking about?" Ezra asked, her eyes narrowing. She could sense Jude's panic;

feel her pulling away.

"Like I said before, I don't know that I can be in a relationship. Not a real one."

"Oh, come on," Ezra groaned.

"Ezra, think about it. He would never be my number one. I could never dedicate myself to him the way he'd dedicate himself to me. That's not fair. Not to mention that he'll be in constant danger."

"I think he can hold his own," Ezra replied.

"But he can't," she shot back. "Not all the time. And I can't divide my attention. I need to be one hundred percent focused on Shiloh."

Ezra leaned forward and put her elbows on her knees, glaring up at Jude. "Okay, I know the past few days have been hell and you're freaking out, but the truth is that you can't be one hundred percent focused on Shiloh all the time. You would both go nuts. What happened this week doesn't happen every day."

"She's at risk every day."

"I know," Ezra said, softer. "But you are doing an incredible job–"

Jude interrupted with a sharp, pointed laugh.

"You are," Ezra repeated. "And you have got to take care of yourself too or you won't be able to take care of her."

Jude rolled her eyes.

"Besides," continued Ezra. "I'm pretty sure he already knows that he'll never be your number one. And I'm pretty sure he doesn't care. He's going to put himself in danger for you whether you date him or not so you may as well throw him a bone."

Jude laughed again and glanced out the living room window. The sky was starting to glow an iridescent orange and it would be night soon. She wasn't sure if she wanted to go to sleep without resolution.

Unexpectedly, she stood up from the couch.

"Where ya going?" Ezra asked, watching her head up the stairs.

"I'll be right back," she said, jogging upstairs to Shiloh's room.

Shiloh was still passed out and had rolled over onto her stomach, laying at an angle across the whole bed. Jude bent over her and poked her gently in the ribs. Shiloh reacted and curled up, but didn't open her eyes. She tried again, scratching Shiloh's back and whispering her name until she blinked her eyes open.

"Hey," Jude whispered as Shiloh came to her senses.

"Hi," Shiloh breathed.

"Listen, are you going to be okay if I run out for a little bit?"

Shiloh sat up slowly, rubbing her eyes. "Where are you going?"

"I just have to take care of a few things. I won't be gone long. But if you don't want me to, I'll just stay here with you."

Shiloh shook her head. "That's okay," she answered. "I'm a little hungry."

Jude laughed and lifted Shiloh's hand from her lap. "I'll bet you're starving. Come downstairs, I'll make you some dinner before I go, okay?"

Shiloh lazily slid off the bed and leaned into Jude, wrapping her arms around her hips, waiting to be lifted. Shiloh had been on an independent streak since she was six or seven. Not a rebellious one, just an *I can do it myself* one, and Jude did what she could to respect it, even though in many ways she hated it. It had been ages since Shiloh asked to be carried. The only time Jude ever carried her anywhere anymore was when she was dead asleep, or being whisked away from some kind of inconceivable danger. Without hesitation, for fear that the moment would pass, Jude swept Shiloh up and hugged her tightly. Despite her independence, Shiloh was still small, maybe fifty-five pounds soaking wet, and still felt little in Jude's arms. She carried the unusually clingy Shiloh downstairs. When she saw Ezra's bowl of cereal she decided that's what she wanted so Jude poured her a big bowl and got her situated on the couch.

"You're sure you're okay if I go out?" Jude asked again once Shiloh was comfortable and watching Scooby Doo with Ezra.

She barely even looked up from her cereal bowl as she nodded her head. "Yeah, I'll be fine," she answered, mouth full and humming the cartoon theme song.

Ezra already had Shiloh under the blanket and looked suspiciously at Jude.

"Where ya goin?" she asked.

Jude refused to answer, turning to pull on her shoes.

Ezra chuckled and Jude shot her a nasty look.

Shiloh swallowed another bite of Fruit Loops and rolled her eyes. "Tell Christopher I said hi and thanks for coming to help me," she stated, without looking away from the TV screen.

Jude threw up her arms and let them fall with a slap down by her side. "What makes you think that I'm going to see Christopher?"

"I'm not blind," Shiloh retorted.

Even still she didn't seem the least bit interested in the details. She was far more involved in whatever mischief the Scooby gang had gotten into and for that Jude was grateful. She looked at Ezra.

"Don't let her out of your sight," she insisted.

"Good luck," said Ezra with a grin.

Jude ignored her and stepped out the door.

Jude threw the Jeep in park and jumped down before she had time to talk herself out of it. She marched toward the row of apartments and to Christopher's door on the ground floor. Raising her arm to knock, she had second thoughts. She should've called. They could've done this over the phone. It would've been less awkward. This could be interpreted as a trap.

She was about to turn around to go home when his door swung open. "Jude," he asked to her back.

She turned slowly.

"What are you doing here? Are you okay?"

"Yeah," she answered, brushing her hair away from her eyes. "Yeah, I'm fine. I'm sorry. This was stupid. I can come back later, or call or something."

She turned again to go but he stepped out onto the patio and reached for her wrist. Gently, he pulled her back around to face him.

"What's going on?" he asked again.

They held eyes for a moment until finally she spilled.

"Well, I just wanted to come by to say I'm sorry," she started abruptly. "I was way out of line, yelling at you like that. Of course what happened wasn't your fault, I just wasn't thinking clearly. I was upset. I lost it a little."

"I know," he answered calmly, as her voice rose.

"I just don't want you to think that I meant any of that because you've done so much to help us and you've risked your life for us and I'm so grateful and–"

"Jude," he interrupted, putting both hands on her shoulders to steady her. "We're okay."

"Okay," she said, exhaling slowly and re-focusing her spinning mind. "I just never want to lose you."

Again they stood there, still and quiet in the doorway, considering each other. There was something between them and it felt as though they were being reeled in closer and closer to one another until finally, Christopher stepped forward to fill the gap.

He leaned into her, dropping one hand to the small of her back and lifting the other to the back of her head. He paused momentarily, gauging her reaction before pressing a deep, hard kiss against her lips. It lasted for only a few seconds when she pulled her head back a little to look at him.

A quiet moment of understanding passed as her lips buzzed where his had been.

He wrapped his arms around her waist, this time sweeping her into his body. He lifted her off of the sidewalk and turned to go inside with her legs wrapped around his, barely coming up for air as they stumbled through the doorway.

CHAPTER 25

Jude rolled over and noticed the unfamiliar sensation of an arm draped over her body. She opened her eyes to Christopher's dark bedroom and the quiet murmur of his breath as he slept. It was very late. Or early? She must've fallen asleep, though she'd planned not to. Nothing so far had really gone according to plan.

For a time, she just laid there, unwilling to end the moment. She took a slow, measured breath and allowed the events of the evening to settle around her. Somewhat absently, she ran her index finger down the rigid muscle that traced his forearm, following the veins that led over her stomach, to the back of his hand. He twitched and blinked his eyes open.

They both smiled, faces inches away from one another. He pushed a stray strand of hair away from her eyes and leaned in for a sleepy kiss.

"Hi," he finally whispered.

She answered with a nervous laugh, then closed her eyes to let out a long, hard exhale. "I gotta go," she whispered regretfully.

He nodded. "I know."

"I wish I didn't."

"Me too."

She kissed him again, then sat up and slipped out from under the covers. "Stay here. Go back to sleep. I'll talk to you tomorrow."

He nodded again, already dozing, and she slid out of bed to gather her things. She collected her items one by one following backwards the trail that led from the front door to the bedroom. The last article on her way happened to be her shirt. It was balled up on the floor a few inches from Christophers, so she picked up his instead and pulled her arms into it, buttoning it up and breathing deep the oaky scent of his cologne as she slipped out the door to her car.

When she arrived back at home, she crept as quietly as she could into the house. It was dark and still when she climbed the stairs to her room, avoiding the floorboards that she knew to creak, like a teenager.

When she reached the top, she glanced for a second into Ezra's open door, but paused when she didn't see Ezra inside. She assumed they must both be upstairs in Shiloh's room.

Knowing she'd get no sleep until she checked, she tossed her purse onto her bed and tip-toed through the closet door to Shiloh's much creakier stairs, taking them slowly and gingerly to the top.

She didn't go all the way up, but stopped three steps short, where she could see into the room just above floor-level. There in Shiloh's twin bed were Shiloh, Ezra, Jack, and Herschel, awash in dim, colored lights strung along the headboard. Somehow, they looked comfortable enough, so she just let them be and turned to go back down.

Just as she was about to take a step, she heard movement.

She looked back up and saw Ezra pulling herself out from under Shiloh and her hound, and making her way out of bed.

"It's about time you came home," she whispered.

Jude cringed, wishing she'd just gone right to bed.

"I guess you had a good night. Nice shirt."

"Shhh!" Jude replied, nodding at Shiloh who was still passed out under the covers.

Ezra followed Jude quietly down the stairs to her room and closed the closet door.

"So?" she asked, crossing her arms over her chest and smiling wide.

"Ezra, it's like three o'clock in the morning."

"Exactly!" she answered. "That's a good thing right?"

Jude rolled her eyes.

"C'mon," Ezra pleaded like a child. "You have to give me something."

Jude laughed and looked down at the floor. "Yeah, it's a good thing." She couldn't hide her grin, so she stopped trying as Ezra silently celebrated.

"I knew this would happen. I told you everything would be fine. So?"

"So?" Jude answered.

Ezra lowered her voice. "How was it?"

"Oh my god," answered Jude as she pushed her friend by the shoulders through her bedroom door. "Good night," she said laughing as she closed it behind her.

Jude crashed into her own bed, wrapped herself tightly in Christopher's shirt, and fell into a deep, full sleep.

Sleep was broken some time later, after the sun had come up, when her phone buzzed from her night-stand. She rolled over and pulled a pillow over her ears. Eventually it stopped buzzing and as she was about to drift off again, the buzzing came back. With a loud grumble and a toss of the pillow, she dropped her lazy arm over the night-stand and picked it up.

Her blurry eyes tried to make out the number on the caller ID screen, but sleep had been too recent.

"Hello?" she asked in a cracking voice. She cleared her throat and tried again.

"Is this Jude Mikhale?" asked an unfamiliar voice.

"Uh, yeah," she answered, still laying on her back. "Who is this?"

"This is Tyrone Braeton, Synedrion."

Jude let out an audible sigh of frustration and sat up, rubbing her eyes.

"Are you just waking up?"

Now that voice she recognized.

"Gideon?"

"It's ten in the morning," he lectured.

"Yeah, how many people are in here?" she asked

"Three," said another voice.

"Jude, this is Leeland Mose. We're calling to go over the details of the past few days."

She threw her legs over the side of her bed, fished around for her sweatpants, pulled them on and headed downstairs.

"Is now a good time?"

"Mhm," she answered grudgingly.

"Let's begin by walking through the events that led up to Shiloh's disappearance on the 28th. Why did you travel to Tidewater, Virginia on the 27th?"

As Jude came through the living room, Ezra stood from the couch and followed her into the kitchen.

"Is everything okay?" she whispered, sensing Jude's irritation.

Jude responded by putting her phone on speaker and setting it down on the kitchen table.

"Jude? Why did you travel to –"

"Because you told me to," she stated.

Ezra nodded when she realized what was happening and sat down at the table while Jude moved to the counter.

There was some quiet chatter on the other end

of the phone and Jude smacked the lid of the coffee maker shut and flicked the on switch.

"You were advised by the Synedrion via Gideon to assess the situation in Tidewater," continued Tyrone. "Were you aware that the situation was in any way connected to Shiloh?"

Jude was growing angrier. "No, of course not. The whole reason I went was to make sure that it didn't get to Shiloh."

"And is it correct that Shiloh willingly left home with a—" there was a pause. "Caleb Todesco?"

She exhaled loudly. "Yes, that's correct."

"Did you know Mr. Todesco prior to this incident?"

"No."

"What would motivate the child to leave home in such a manner?"

"Okay, what is this?" Jude asked, placing both hands on the kitchen table and leaning toward the phone. "Gideon, what's going on here?"

"It's just a debriefing, Jude," Gideon said quietly. "The Synedrion needs documentation and clarity regarding what happened. A lot of people were killed."

She took a deep breath and rubbed her forehead. "She left because Caleb tricked her into reading the Codex and led her to believe that she wasn't safe at home. Really, he was manipulating her so that she would leave with him so that he could feed her to the fish thing."

"The *fish thing* is Yarik," clarified Leland.

"Yes, that's correct," answered Tyrone.

Jude looked at Ezra shaking her head. Ezra laughed quietly and gave her a look of sympathy.

"At what point did you discover that the child had gone missing?" Leland asked.

"I guess around three in the afternoon."

"The afternoon of the 28th?"

"Yes, she left with Caleb after school."

The coffee finished brewing and Jude poured two mugs, handed one to Ezra and sat down across from her at the table.

"Can you please explain in detail the next action you took? You left Tidewater, is that correct?"

Jude painstakingly explained the back and forth from Tidewater, to Acadia, then back to Tidewater again. She explained how they were led back to Tidewater based on trash they'd found in Caleb's bedroom. She explained the attacks, first at the factory, then at the dock. Everything right up until the Synedrions arrival and collection of Caleb and Elliott.

"So you broke into the home of Walter Murdoch?" asked Tyrone.

"Did you have a better suggestion?"

Again there was disgruntled chatter on the other end.

"How many humans were killed in the course of the proceeding violence?"

"By me?" Jude asked. "All together, I guess it was –" she counted on her fingers. "Six."

The chatter on the other line became louder

and more alarmed. There was discussion about whether or not they had located all of the bodies that Jude had left in her wake. Finally, it was determined that all except for the uncle had been accounted for.

"Oh, we found him. I had nothing to do with that one. He's in a box in his basement." Jude thought they'd be happy about the news, but of course, they were mad that they were only just finding out about it. They discussed, for a few minutes, what to do about him, then came back to Jude.

"Jude, were all of these kills absolutely necessary?" Gideon finally asked.

Jude threw up her arms. "Of course they were," she said forcefully. "I don't just go around killing people. Anyone that died that day was someone who didn't take the opportunity to walk away when I gave it to them."

"So others did walk away?"

"Yeah, another 4 or 5 lived to tell the tale."

More chatter. More rising concern.

"We'll have to get their names," said Leland anxiously. "They'll need to guarantee their silence."

"This is a mess," replied Tyrone.

"So let me get this straight, you don't want me to kill anyone, but you don't want me to let anyone live either?"

Ezra was just listening to the back and forth with her head in her hands.

"Anyone who lives is a security threat," said Gideon. "Any deaths we have to explain or cover up.

It's just complicated, that's all."

"You'll need to participate in an evaluative session. To prove that you are of sound mind."

"Excuse me?" Jude said, rising from her seat. Even Ezra sat back suddenly and looked at Jude, knowing full well that she was about to go off like an atom bomb.

"It's protocol," Gideon stated quickly. "When the body count is this high, we can't ensure your protection against law enforcement or government agencies without it."

"This is ridiculous. You've given me a job and you complain when I do it."

"The evaluation is as much for you as it is for the Synedrion as a whole," Gideon continued, while others whispered and deliberated behind him. "Even when in the right, the taking of human life can have an impact on the conscience. It can get inside of your head and cause emotional turmoil that might lead to depression or anxiety or feelings of guilt. Those things could affect your ability to protect Shiloh."

Jude was shaking her head before he finished speaking. "Look, that may be the case for some people but it's not for me. Seriously. It's not like this is the first time. I do what I have to do."

"The evaluation is necessary as a matter of Synedrion policy," said Leland firmly. "The fact that this isn't the first time you've taken human life makes it even more necessary."

"Yeah, you know what, eight years ago when

you kidnapped me and I was pulled into all of this, I never anticipated killing humans, either. Turns out, they're even shittier than the demons."

"No Jude, you'd find it wise to control your anger. The results of the evaluation may not come out in your favor if you spout off in some burst of rage."

Jude stood quietly in the kitchen with her arms over her chest, trying to bite her tongue even though she fumed at the thought of being scolded by these oblivious, bureaucratic pencil pushers.

"It won't be a big deal," Gideon said finally.

"We will take care of it when we come to debrief the child," said Leland.

The evaluation flew from Jude's focus and she set her coffee cup down with a clatter and a splash. "Debrief the child?" she repeated dropping back into her seat.

"The child is getting older, said Leland. "She will soon be asking questions. It is time that the Synedrion come to guide her into the light of her destiny."

"The *Child* is Shiloh," Jude answered defensively. "And she's already being guided. By me. Remember, the woman you chose to guide her? She's *my* child. So I don't think that will be necessary."

"Well, technically we didn't *choose* you, you were more of a first alternate, so to speak, and – "

Gideon cut Tyrone off before he dug himself any deeper. "It's protocol, Jude."

"What do you mean she's already being

guided?" asked Leland. "What exactly does the child know?"

"*Shiloh*," she repeated. Then she hesitated, and lowered her voice. "And she knows everything."

There were sighs and silence.

"How is she handling it?" Gideon finally asked.

Jude shrugged, even though they couldn't see her. "She's going to be okay." Her answer was weak but it was the best she could do.

"Then it's time to begin her training," said Leland. "Gideon, you will of course be overseeing the training process, along with another, yet-to-be-appointed official. There are a few names on the list, and your input will be considered as we make out decision this afternoon. Can you fly out on Tuesday?"

Jude looked at Ezra in defeat and amazement as these men collaborated and made plans to invade her life at their leisure. They jabbered on for several minutes about logistics and tradition and finally, informed Jude that they would be arriving in two days to begin Shiloh's Synedrion education.

Jude had a fairly strong disdain for the Synedrion. To her, they represented the cold, corporate side of Shiloh's existence. The side that valued her as a technical means to an end, to be formed and molded into the poster-child for human sacrifice and the 'greater good'. But she knew how to pick her battles. She would need to present the air of cooperation when they arrived so that she could influence the process when they started in on Shiloh. Best not to fight the relentless tide of the Synedrion. They'd come either way. She would need leverage with them soon enough.

They made their decisions and finally said good-bye as Shiloh padded down the stairs in her pajamas.

"Is there breakfast?" she asked through a yawn.

"Pancakes?" Ezra asked, already on her way to the pantry. She started humming and buzzing around the kitchen, pulling out pans and gathering ingredients.

Shiloh sat down in the chair next to Jude and rested her head on the table. "I want to do something today," she mumbled into her arm. "Something fun to make up for the last few days."

Jude patted Shiloh on the back and agreed. Her mind was overridden with thoughts, not all of them pleasant, and she was desperate to quiet the noise, even if just for a short time.

It was already a beautiful day, and shaping up to be a hot one as the sun continued to rise higher and higher in the cloudless sky. Jude began thinking of ideas for a fun Sunday afternoon. There wasn't a whole lot to do in Acadia. There was a discount movie theater with three showings a day, and numerous stuffy, dark museums full of the same exhibits that had been there since before they moved to town. But she didn't want to be stuck inside anyway, and she knew Shiloh would get antsy if she didn't get the opportunity to exert a little energy. Then, finally, it came to her.

"I know," she said, tapping the table with resolve. "Swimming."

"Mom," Shiloh answered, lifting her head solemnly from the table. "I almost drowned twice yesterday. Swimming?"

Since the moment Shiloh was launched into the Rappahannock, Jude had been regretting never teaching her how to swim.

"We'll go up to the mountains and find a great swimming hole. We can pack lunch and spend the day up there. You can catch crayfish and turtles and I promise, no fish demons will be invited."

Shiloh loved being outside, splashing through creeks and running along mountain trails. It didn't take that much convincing. Finally, Jude watched her get up from her chair with a refreshing bounce. "I'm going to go get my swimsuit," she declared as she vanished from the room. "Ezra, you have one right?" she yelled on her way up the stairs.

"Of course I do," Ezra called back, as she poured pancake batter into the hot frying pan. She turned to Jude with a smile. "See?" she stated joyfully. "She's going to be just fine."

Moments later, Shiloh returned wearing a flowered cotton dress over her swimsuit and carrying a towel over her shoulder. "Go get ready," she urged as she sat down in front of a plate of pancakes.

"Breakfast first," answered Jude. The three of them sat together at the table and enjoyed hot, syrupy pancakes as Shiloh rambled on about her plans to hunt for salamanders in the creek.

In the middle of a big bite, Shiloh looked over at Jude and casually said, "you should call and invite Christopher."

Ezra lifted her head and glanced cautiously at Jude, who was paused, fork in mid-air.

"Jude," said Ezra quietly, after the pause had become too long to ignore.

Jude blinked. "Why would I do that?" she asked, turning back to her plate.

"Well, weren't you hanging out with him last night?" she asked, not even interested enough to look up from her breakfast. "It would give you an excuse to call him. If you're looking for one." She got up from the table and dropped her dish off at the sink before jogging back upstairs to get ready for the day, leaving Jude wide eyed and still frozen at the table.

Ezra leaned back and watched until Shiloh was all the way at the top of the stairs. As soon as she heard her footsteps lead into Jude's room, she leaned forward hard and erupted into laughter.

"Shut up," Jude insisted, but it came out weak as she felt heat rise to her neck and she tried to disguise her own laughter.

"You can get nothing past her," said Ezra, struggling to breathe. "You think you're slick, slipping out of here at night, telling her you have important things to do."

Jude put her elbows on the table and her head in

her hands as Ezra went on.

"She can read you like a book." She was bracing herself on the side of the table laughing so hard. "Even in the middle of life altering trauma and thwarting attacks from ridiculous sea demons, she can see through you."

Finally Jude stood up. "Alright," she said, shaking her head. "I'm glad this is funny to you."

"Oh, you have no idea," said Ezra, catching her breath.

She was still laughing as Jude made her way upstairs.

CHAPTER 26

Christopher of course didn't hesitate to accept the invitation. Shiloh was buzzing around the living room with a bag full of toys and swimming necessities slung over her back when he pulled down the driveway. When he got out of his car, he was already wearing swim shorts and flip-flops; a radical shift from his usual attire. He came to the door and Shiloh had it open before he got the chance to knock. Immediately, she started talking at him.

Can you swim? Have you ever caught a salamander? Would you like a cold pancake? And so on and so forth. He answered them as they came, just happy to be tagging along, but every time Jude walked by or made a comment, he smiled and reddened like a schoolboy. The first interactions were awkward. And the audience of Shiloh and Ezra didn't help. Finally, Shiloh and Ezra went into the kitchen to pack a cooler full of hotdogs and water bottles, leaving Jude and Christopher alone in the living room.

Even with his swim shorts on, he buried his hands deep into his pockets as he took a few nervous steps in her direction.

"How are you?" he asked timidly.

She laughed, foregoing an actual response as she stepped toward him, filling the small space that was between them.

"Thanks for inviting me."

"It was Shiloh's idea," Jude admitted. She noticed that she was avoiding eye contact and forced herself to stop.

"Well, still," he stammered. "I'm glad. I was hoping I'd get to see you. You kind of left in a hurry."

In a moment of unadulterated courage, he pulled both of his hands from his pockets and reached for hers at her sides. Shocked by the sudden display, she pulled her hands away and glanced back into the kitchen. Shiloh and Ezra sounded pretty busy. She hesitantly brought her hands back down to his and let him pull her into a brief and awkward kiss. Breaking away, they both laughed and squirmed a bit. They tried again, this time more successfully, but when Jude heard Ezra say that it was time to load the cooler into the car and go, she took several steps back and immediately engaged herself in the important task of pulling back her hair. There would be time to work through the new strangeness later.

"You ready?" she asked as Shiloh came through the living room with a bag of hotdog buns.

"Yes!" she answered, and they all followed her out the door to the car.

As someone who paid close attention to town news and talk, Jude knew of a few places people went swimming. They drove up to the mountains just outside of town and down a winding dirt road until they came to a parking lot just where she expected it to be.

They walked a ways down a dirt path until they came to a place along the river where the water was channeled through a narrow gap between two big rocks, creating a small rapid until it spilled out into a deep pool at the bottom. A rope swing hung from the branch of a Sycamore tree over the pool, and the sunlight warmed the rock face to create the perfect place to spread out a towel and lounge around in the heat of the afternoon.

The day passed by in a slow, leisurely way with splashy swimming lessons and buckets full of creek water and crayfish - *mudbugs* as Ezra called them. For Jude and Christopher, unexpected and electrifying touches, and poorly hidden glances. For Jude and Shiloh, belly rides down the tumbling cascade and carefree laughter. It was difficult to believe that the trauma and tragedy of the past few days had happened at all. Harder still to accept that very soon, the Synedrion would invade their home and launch a highly coordinated routine with their marching orders and their precious protocol, and shortly thereafter everything would change. Shiloh would be bogged down by the weight of her destiny and then made to believe that it was an honor; a concept Jude never did buy into. She'd be charmed by their willingness to help her harness her unique energy and eager to absorb all of their knowledge as more and more details came to light. But would she understand it all?

All of this and more begged for Jude's obsessive attention as she moved back and forth between the rock and the river. Everyone was so excessively happy, and safe and alive, and the day was just too good and pure to tarnish it with worry. In these hours, in this clearing in the woods where the river rambled and fell like liquid glass over polished gray stones, joy was endless. Innocence was endless. Shiloh was endless.

Two days later, the Synedrion arrived exactly as planned. Jude opened the door reluctantly to Gideon and one other, younger man who introduced himself as Alizair Rykov and spoke with a heavy and unfamiliar accent. When he first met Shiloh, he stiffened his back and stuck his hand out for a firm, proper handshake. She furrowed her brow at him and finally laughed. Then began peppering him with questions in true Shiloh fashion.

"What's in your briefcase?"

"Books, mostly."

"What kind of books?"

"History books."

"Where are you from?"

"Estonia."

"Do you have super powers?"

"No."

"Do you like dogs?"

"Who doesn't like dogs?"

She led him into the house collecting all of this critical information and Jude noticed a smile creeping onto Alizairs face as he relaxed and came down to earth. Jude began to have hope that this experience wouldn't be an altogether horrible one after all.

Over the next few weeks, Gideon and Alizair spent nearly every day with Shiloh. They introduced her to a hundred different books and told her a hundred different stories of everyone who came before. They explained how energy was powerful but most people didn't know how to harness it, and that she had a special gift to tap into her energy and use it to do good things. They taught her how to focus her senses to enhance and expand beyond the normal range of human awareness. And of course, in time they told her the end of the story. The balance, the prophecy, the sacrifice. Where it all came from and why it's important.

Jude never left their side, monitoring every word they chose and adding her own thoughts whenever necessary, silently gauging Shiloh's reactions. At night, when it was just the two of them, she would rehash the enlightenments of the day with Shiloh before their bedtime reading to offer clarification and reassurance.

Propped up in Shiloh's bed after a long, heavy day of discussion, *The Wind in the Willows* laid closed and waiting on Jude's lap. Shiloh was distracted and tired of talking. Her time had not been her own for the better part of a month, and it was summer. She was desperate for a little destiny-free fun so Jude arranged for her to have the next day off and she was busy thinking of things to do. But Jude was wrestling with other concerns.

"Shiloh, we still need to talk about one really important thing," she said finally, trying to recapture the little girl's attention.

Truthfully, Jude would've loved not to talk about it. She couldn't handle it, not inside of herself when she was alone in the evenings and left to the raw truth of her thoughts. But she had learned that not talking about it was much too dangerous. Not talking could leave Shiloh free to imagine all sorts of atrocities scenarios. To silently obsess about it until her out of control mind destroyed her from the inside out, as Jude's would've done, and had done many times before. She needed Shiloh to know that she was prepared to move heaven and hell to keep her from her fate.

"You mean the dying thing, don't you?" Shiloh asked, like she was saying nothing of any consequence.

Though she shouldn't have been, Jude was blown away by Shiloh's breezy response. "Uh, yeah" she said after a moment's pause to regroup. She looked deeply into Shiloh's face trying to detect anything at all, but Shiloh gave nothing. She just sat and fidgeted with the felt teeth inside of Herschel's big pink mouth. "Shiloh?" Jude spoke again, gently pulling the alligator away.

Shiloh looked up at Jude light-eyed and rosy-cheeked. "It's okay," she answered with a slight shrug of her narrow shoulders.

Jude sat up. "Shiloh, you know I'm never going to let that happen, don't you? I will stop at nothing, I swear to God, if it's the last thing I do I'll-"

Shiloh moved suddenly and put her warm, soft hand over Jude's beating heart. She held it there for a second, eyes closed, listening. Observing. Understanding. Finally, she pulled it away.

"I know, mom," she said. "I know you'll try. But it's okay. I'm not afraid. It's what I'm meant to do."

Jude was officially, and at last, speechless. She sat back on her ankles open-mouthed and out of breath. She had two big fears. #2, her own death. #1, Shiloh's death. Her casual acceptance of such an egregious and absurd 'fact-of-life', as she saw it, was beyond startling. But she just lifted the book off of Jude's lap and began fanning through the pages, looking at the small pencil illustrations that began each chapter. Grace upon grace upon grace. Deep down, the older of the two women knew that this was how it was supposed to be. Shiloh was unafraid. She was accepting of the fact that she was to serve a purpose greater than herself. That she was to answer a call. But Jude wasn't able to dig deep just then, and in that moment she felt angry. Maybe even betrayed. How could Shiloh be so resigned? It was in these moments of being that their differences were thrown into the light. That they differed was a matter of necessity. Shiloh's clarity, her compassion, her tenderness, made her the thing worthy of the destiny she carried. Made her someone capable of such a lofty goal as restoring humanity to righteousness. But she could never fight her own monsters, and so existed Jude. Someone to be reactive, defensive, even possessive of what was hers, fueled by passion and rage. Someone who could fight the monsters. And everyone knows, to fight monsters, you have to have a little monster inside of yourself.

And Jude was filled with monstrous fury that something as pure and good as Shiloh should ever be sacrificed to save something as vile and worthless as humanity.

"Mom?" Shiloh asked, and Jude was startled. She snapped out of her reverie and looked at her daughter, who was holding the book out toward her. "Can we read now?"

Jude didn't answer. She meant to, but she didn't.

"Mom?" Shiloh said again with a smile. "It's not going to happen for a long time, right?"

Shiloh waited for an answer while Jude dug for the words.

"No," she said, but her voice cracked. "No," she repeated. "Not for a long time."

Shiloh gave a deep, resolved nod. "Then why are you so worried about it now?" she asked. "I'm only eight. It's like a million years away."

It was ten years away.

Ten years is nothing. It's instantaneous. It's barely a blip on the radar. But Jude could never bring herself to explain that to the unshakable girl placing the velvet wrapped book in her hand, already opened to their dog-eared page.

Shiloh pressed heavy against her side and Jude closed her eyes, noticing for the first time that they were damp. She took a deep breath. Steadied herself. Put one arm around Shiloh, and began to read, shaky at first, fighting to keep her heart from bubbling up through her throat.

"But Mole stood still a moment, held in thought. As one wakened suddenly from a beautiful dream, who struggles to recall it, but can recapture nothing but a dim sense of the beauty in it, the beauty! Till that, too, fades away in its turn..."

YOU'RE AWESOME.

I hope you loved Book 2 of the Keeping Shiloh series! For Book 3 updates (or just to say hi), you can find me at:

www.ashmeyer.wixsite.com/author
amazon.com/author/ashleighmeyer
and other corners of the internet.

If you're enjoying the series, it would be amazing if you left me a little love (in the form of a review) on Amazon and Goodreads.

Thank you SO much for reading!

Always,

A Meyer